Close Up on Murder

A Spirit Lake Mystery

Linda Townsdin

Dedication

To my husband, Gary Delsohn

Chapter 1

I'd stayed away from Little's Café for two days. Tourists with cabin fever cramming the tables and booths were not my scene. I'd spent the time shooting wildlife photos around the lake—the rain made it more interesting and I was happiest stalking something.

But this morning my brother's blueberry wild rice pancakes called to me. I glanced in the window at the crowd of whining kids, complaining parents and ornery fishermen. A familiar old dog waited next to the entrance. I patted Knute's big shaggy head; he and my dog, Rock, bumped noses and I went in.

Little and his partner Lars were chatting with someone seated at a booth.

"Britt." Little, in his apron, waved me over. My diminutive younger brother's real name was Jan Jr. after our dad, but that's all they'd had in common. Our father had been six feet four inches of meanness; now he was six feet under and no one felt too bad about that. I inherited some of his height and bad temper and while I liked being tall, I was working on the bad temper.

I wove through the tables. Little tilted his head toward the old man in the booth. "Charley's been waiting to talk to the two of us about something."

"Hi Charley." I slid in across from him. "I figured you were here when I saw Knute out front." I lifted my chin toward the counter. "And the gorgeous rhododendron gave you away."

He smiled at the compliment. "I didn't think I'd have any luck with the garden this summer. The weather's a big disappointment for everyone."

I nodded, but the weather really didn't affect me. The bigger disappointment was that I'd been back in Spirit Lake for two weeks and had yet to see the man I loved. I wanted Ben Winter, rain or shine.

Lars interrupted my thoughts. "I'd better make the rounds with coffee. I'll leave you three to have that talk."

Lars was my age, thirty-four, and mostly bald. A thin fringe of reddish-brown curls stuck out from his baseball cap. Skinny-legged and barrel-chested, he wore suspenders over flannel shirts in the winter and over t-shirts in the summer. In L.A. lingo—circus clown meets Paul Bunyan.

Little's gaze darted toward the kitchen, no doubt worried about orders stacking up. "What's on your mind, Charley?"

The old man swallowed, licked his lips, but didn't get a chance to speak. Brown ponytail swishing, Chloe dashed up and handed Little a food order. "Sorry, hungry customers."

Little put a hand on Charley's shoulder. "It's really busy today. Okay if we talk another time?"

"Sure, another time."

Little hustled off to the kitchen. Charley lifted his coffee to his lips with a slight tremor. "Little was just telling me you've been away. I don't get into town much anymore."

"The *L.A. Times* hired me back as a contract photographer." I'd been shooting war and weather disasters across the globe for the past months. Floods, hurricanes, earthquakes, you name it. Mother Nature was at war with the planet and its people were at war with one another.

"How long are you in Minnesota?" His voice wavered as if it didn't get much use.

"I head to South Sudan at the end of summer."

He shook his head. "Terrible what's going on there."

"It is." My entire career had prepared me for the upcoming assignment. My intention was to spend the next month recharging so I'd be ready, but the truth was that I was always ready.

Chloe slid a plate of blueberry wild rice pancakes in front of me. "I went ahead and put in your order."

I smiled my thanks. Most pancakes made me want to curl up and sleep, but my brother's pancakes had an energizing effect—a part of his cooking mystique. I ate them nearly every day.

The rain let up after breakfast, and I walked Charley and Knute home. He lived a mile farther than my cabin, a long way for a ninety-year-old, even with the help of his cane. The old retriever had his own arthritis issues, so we took our time. Rock, a black and white blur, chased squirrels.

We crossed the Paul Bunyan Trail, strangely empty. Most summers it was like a freeway with packs of bike riders like bumblebees with their neon outfits and helmeted heads whizzing by. Bike up! On your left!

At one of our frequent rest stops, I asked, "What did you want to talk about, Charley? I'll be sure to let Little know."

His brow furrowed. "I don't know if your dad ever told you, but I knew him before the drinking got so bad."

"That must have been a long, long time ago." Sarcasm was another character flaw I was working on. My dad had been a heavy drinker since I could remember. Charley was an old bachelor who lived on the south side of the lake. Dad would take him the Sunday papers and spend the afternoon visiting. He also took his thermos of coffee laced with blackberry brandy and loaded with sugar. He'd come home wired and drunk, carrying a rhododendron bouquet from Charley's garden.

"Where did you and Dad meet?"

Charley's kind eyes surveyed me. "You take after him."

Did he mean that as a compliment? I'd stretched to five-ten by junior high and even had my dad's eyes, my best feature when I was healthy and happy, but they broadcast every lost hour of sleep, every anxious thought and every drink too many before I got sober.

He hadn't answered my question. "You were friends with my dad before he left the service, before Vietnam?"

A dark cloud crossed his face. "War can make men do terrible things." He stopped to rest.

I studied him out of the corner of my eye. Was he talking about my dad or himself?

Knute hitched along, favoring one leg, and finally stopped altogether. Charley said, "You go on ahead; we'll take our time."

It would be noon before they got home at this rate. "I'll get the SUV. We're almost at my turnoff."

He squinted at the sky. "Looks like we're in for another shower so I'll take that ride, and thank you for offering."

I sprinted to my cabin, liking the opportunity to get some exercise, and pulled the SUV up next to Charley and Knute within a few minutes. Charley needed a boost getting in, Rock jumped in back and I hoisted the old dog in next to him.

We followed the Spirit Lake south loop to his house. I asked, "Do you have any family?" A nosy question, but someone should be looking out for him.

His milky blue eyes watered. "Just the nice people of Spirit Lake and Knute."

I pulled off the two-lane road and into his driveway and helped him down from the high seat, but getting the eighty-pound Knute to the ground was a bigger chore, even for me.

Charley leaned on his cane. "Would you like to come in for coffee? We can talk about what I wanted to tell you and Little, in case..."

"Coffee sounds good." I searched his face for clues. In case what?

He straightened and pointed toward the west side of his house. "Let me get my shears and cut some flowers for you. Would you like that?"

His house blocked the flower garden, but I remembered the riot of color from years past. "I'd love it. My cabin could use some cheering up in this gloom."

I waited in the yard while he made his way to the house for his shears, wondering what he was having such a hard time telling me. Knute circled and Rock sniffed the air. Both dogs got busy checking the perimeter. They must have smelled something interesting.

Charley's place backed up to the lake and was surrounded by woods much like mine, but his was more isolated. Even the lake took on a deeper blue in this secluded inlet.

Before opening his door, he stooped, picked up a white piece of paper from the porch, frowned at it and shook his head. "Britt, I'm afraid I'll have to offer you that coffee another time." He held up the small rectangle; I assumed a business card. "Something I need to attend to."

"No problem. Is everything okay?" He must not have heard me because he stepped inside and closed the door without answering. I shrugged, not my business. "Rock, let's go buddy."

Back at my cabin, I pushed my yellow kayak into the water and dug in with the paddle, heading straight out from shore, working up a sweat. I'd check with Little later. He'd know more about the old guy's situation, and maybe what Charley needed to tell us.

Chapter 2

The next day, the sun popped out after a brief morning shower and Rock and I headed to town for lunch.

I'd hoped Little's would be less crowded so I could eat in peace, but cars jammed the parking lot. Another option would be to cook my own meals, a radical choice and one I avoided whenever possible.

Knute paced in front of the door, whining and circling. Charley must have had cabin fever too. Rock ran to Knute, but instead of the usual sniffing and bumping noses, Rock mirrored his agitation.

I scratched behind the old dog's ears. Seeing Knute reminded me Little and I hadn't found out what the old guy wanted to talk to us about. Now would be a good time.

Charley wasn't in any of the booths. Little zipped around the kitchen, a whirling dervish with ten arms going at once, stirring, prepping, grabbing items from the refrigerator and barking orders at his helpers. "Hey, baby brother, have you seen Charley? Knute's outside looking for him."

Little didn't look up. "Ask Lars or one of the kids working the tables. I haven't been out of this kitchen all morning. When the weather's bad, everyone comes to town."

"I noticed."

He grinned. "I love it!"

When he wasn't scowling at me, Little had the face of an angel. Creamy skin, eyes the color of Norwegian fjords, silvery blond hair. He took after our mother, now living far away from Minnesota winters in sunny Palm Desert, California.

He frowned at my hair. "I don't like you being in the kitchen with that flying loose, but since you're here can you reach that for me?" He pointed to a giant jar of pickles on a shelf above his workstation.

Inwardly rolling my eyes, I grabbed it and set it on the counter, then left him to his stove. Every trip to the grocery store involved helping a customer snag something out of reach. Early on, I'd envied the petite girls but now I embraced my impressive wingspan.

I spied Lars filling coffees at the big round table in the corner and asked about Charley. He hadn't seen him either. He said, "I figured Ben came to town when you didn't show up for dinner last night."

"Ben's still working on his project." I left thinking about Ben and the events that had brought us together. I'd worked for the *L.A. Times* right out of college for twelve years until they'd fired me for drunk and disorderly behavior a year and a half ago. I also divorced my philandering husband. My boss at the *Times* helped me get a job at the *Minneapolis StarTribune* northern bureau, so I'd moved home to Spirit Lake, stopped drinking and fallen in love with Ben Winter. Last year I'd finally gotten the dark-haired forest ranger with the hawk nose and squinty eyes to admit he loved me. It turned out to be bad timing, because I'd been rehired at the *Times* and had to leave for L.A. two days later. I'd been longing to be with him ever since.

I walked through town asking about Charley. It took all of fifteen minutes to make the circuit. There were only two business streets. One faced the lake and the other was on the highway one street over. My last stop was Robertson's grocery.

No Charley. Maybe Knute was confused. Dogs suffer from dementia just like elderly people. I circled back to Little's.

Knute hadn't moved from his post. Rock paced around him. I ran in and told Lars I was taking the dog home. "If Charley comes in let him know I have Knute and call me if he needs a ride, too."

He nodded, hustling to seat a family of six.

Knute walked much faster than yesterday, but started limping about half way. Once again, I stopped at my cabin for the SUV, lifted Knute into the back seat and drove to Charley's. The old dog moaned when we turned into Charley's drive. If Charley was home, I'd ask about taking Knute to the vet.

I opened the driver's side door for Rock, but Knute bounded over the seat and leaped out, falling in a heap. He gathered his legs under him and limped to the west side of the house. I followed, calling Charley's name. A blood-curdling sound came from the garden and I started running.

Knute stood in the middle of the garden howling at something high above him. I moved closer and the hair rose at the back of my neck.

Charley's severed head was on a stake, his sightless eyes staring down at crushed yellow, pink, and purple blossoms, the green stalks flattened and all of it mashed into the earth like a muddy stew. His head, the massacred rhododendrons, their scent overpowering in the summer humidity and Knute howling up at him was too much. My knees buckled.

Rock's nose in my armpit startled me back into action. I fumbled for my phone and tapped in the sheriff's number.

When I told him where I was and what I was looking at, his response was typical Wilcox. "Don't touch anything and do not call the media. You don't work here anymore, Johansson."

Next, I called Cynthia, my old editor at the *StarTribune* bureau in Branson, and then reached into my jacket pocket for my camera. I photographed Charley, his house with the lake in the background, the destroyed garden, the keening Knute. I turned in a circle taking in the house and woods. We'd have to find the rest of his body.

I had seen worse—carcasses of starved babies in Somalia, bodies dismembered by automatic fire that ripped through entire towns and left carnage everywhere, the horrible aftermath of natural disasters, and deaths of people close to me. My reaction was always the same: hands shaking, stomach gripped by nausea, tears springing to my eyes, a need to sit down and look away, but I didn't look away until the job of documenting was finished. I swallowed my rage and sadness and pity, willed my hands to stop trembling and kept shooting until I had it all.

Still howling, Knute wouldn't move when I tried to coax him away from the garden. I walked to the front of the house. The door was ajar and I peeked inside. The sight stopped me cold.

Destroyed furniture was strewn around the room and a scrawl in black spray paint spread across one wall. "You Will All Die." Did this devastation have something to do with Charley's urgency to get me out of there when I dropped him off yesterday?

Pretty sure whoever did this hadn't hung around, I leaned forward and took as many photos as possible without fully stepping inside.

The sheriff's office was in Branson, thirty miles north of Spirit Lake. Wilcox made it to Charley's house in twenty minutes. It takes me thirty even if I speed on the winding two-lane highway.

In his fifties, wiry and smart, Wilcox started yelling at me even before he got out of his car. "Nothing happened in the three months you've been gone. Nothing! You're back two weeks and we get this?"

I pointed to the garden and explained how I happened to be bringing Knute home. Wilcox pushed his cowboy hat back from his forehead. "Get that poor dog away from here. I can't think with that howling."

I took Knute by the collar. "C'mon boy, we have to go." He kept turning back, but eventually let me lead him to the porch. I filled his water bowl, found a bin with his food and filled the other bowl, but he wouldn't eat it. I got down on the ground and put my arm around him. "You're an amazing dog and a great friend to Charley, Knute. You got us here."

With an almost human cry, he collapsed into a heap. Rock licked Knute's muzzle and then took off into the woods.

Wilcox walked up to the house barking orders into his phone. He finished the call and pulled on plastic booties. "You'd better not have been in there tampering with evidence, Johansson."

"I shot from the doorway. It was open." He checked it out while I waited on the porch. The sheriff thought of the media as adversaries and was civil only when he wanted something from us. He and his wife moved to Branson from Colorado six years ago so she could be near family during their retirement years. Not quite ready to retire, he got himself elected sheriff.

He came back to the porch. "Who hated him enough to do this?"

I wondered the same thing. "Charley was the gentlest old man around. There are a few cranky old guys in Spirit Lake, who like to rant and rave about politics and sports and the juvenile delinquents ruining the town, but Charley wasn't one of them."

Wilcox made a quick circuit around the house. I'd already checked for Charley's body. The hard rain last night had washed away any prints the killer might have left.

He returned. "How well did you know him?"

"Not well. Little kept an eye on him when he and Lars moved back here. I think the church ladies checked on him too. He and my dad were friends years ago."

Rock's bark echoed through the forest. He had as many descriptive barks as Wilcox had cowboy hat positions—over his forehead, watch out, pushed back, you can relax. Rock's bark said he'd treed something, only worse.

We started to follow Rock's barking when Thor, aka Natalie Thorson, the young forensic tech, arrived at the same time as my former colleague Jason, the *StarTrib* reporter. I nodded hello.

An old guy in a pea-green hatchback pulled up behind them. A camera hung from a strap on his neck. He pulled a tripod out of the trunk, already wheezing from the effort.

Jason introduced the photographer as Glenn Hanson.

"You took my place at the bureau?" I asked.

"I'm one of the contract photographers Cynthia uses. Between the college interns and old geezers like me who don't want the full-time grind, she manages to cover the county."

We walked toward the side yard. Wilcox frowned at Thor and tilted his chin toward Jason and Glenn. "What the hell are they doing here?" Thor's face and scalp turned pink under her spiky blond hair.

I stepped forward. "I called Cynthia."

Cynthia was editor of the *StarTrib* northern bureau and my former boss until three months ago when the *Times* hired me back.

The sheriff's eyes narrowed at me. "Did it ever occur to you that we need to keep this quiet until we figure out what's going on?"

I raised my chin. "I work in news, not criminal justice, but I contacted you first, Sheriff."

Thor hustled over to Wilcox, her bag of forensic tools bumping against her legs. He pointed to the garden. Thor stopped short and gasped. Wilcox didn't give her a chance to get queasy. "Britt's dog has found something in the woods. Let's check it out in case it's the rest of him." He nodded toward Charley's head, his voice low. "He's not going anywhere."

Glenn grabbed his tripod and hurried back to his car. "I didn't sign on for this. Hockey games are more my speed." He stomped on the gas and peeled out, his face as green as his hatchback.

Jason shook his head. "Britt, I don't suppose you got some pictures we could use?"

"I did, yes."

"And you'll get photos of whatever is out there?" He waved a hand toward the woods. I nodded.

Wilcox called over his shoulder. "Stay behind me." We followed the sheriff and Thor into the woods. The rain had stopped, but wet drops fell from branches high above, stinging my skin on impact.

Rock stopped barking when he saw me. I patted his head. "Good boy. Go on back to Knute." He melted into the woods.

We all stared down at Charley's remains. The rain and wild creatures had already destroyed many of the identifying marks, but it was a man and he didn't have a head. Jason tore away and threw up in the bushes. Poor kid, no one should have to see this.

Jason came back and with shaking hands, reached in the pocket of his button-down shirt for a notebook and pen. "I've never seen anything this gross, except in the movies."

I shot the scene, knowing the photos were too gruesome for the newspaper, and stayed out of Thor's way as she took her own photos and did her job. Charley's body would be taken to Minneapolis for the detailed forensic work to be done, but Thor did the basics.

Thor's helper, a giant Swede named Erik with massive arms and lots of facial hair crashed through the woods with a stretcher.

Panting, he said, "Sorry it took me so long. I was oot fishing." People up here sounded a lot like Canadians.

Thor said, "Sorry we had to make you come in off the lake."

"Nah, nothing was biting anyway."

Thor squatted next to the body. "We were just trying to figure out what the killer used to cut off his head. An axe?"

Erik studied it. "Chain saw did that." Erik had been a logger. He would know.

Wilcox stuck a finger in Jason's face. "Not a word about this to anyone until I talk to Cynthia." White-faced and not in any shape to stand up to the formidable sheriff, Jason looked down at his notebook.

Several more deputies rolled in and Wilcox sent them to look for evidence. He said I could go. "Come into the office tomorrow morning. We'll need a statement."

He motioned to one of his guys. "Get the pound to pick up Mr. Patterson's dog."

I stepped up. "I'll look after him, Sheriff." A sad, arthritic old dog would not be a good candidate for adoption.

Wilcox looked at Rock, his expression softening. "Johansson's bereavement center for canines?"

"Something like that." I'd had some experience with a grieving dog. I'd inherited Rock when my old friend Gert died a year and a half ago. She'd been murdered in the middle of the winter, three steps from her cabin. Rock had shredded the door and his paws trying to get to her from inside the house as she lay dying in the driveway. Sometimes when I looked at Rock, Gert's eyes seemed to be gazing at me.

Erik lifted Knute into my SUV as if the dog was a feather. I gathered up his bed, bowl and food. The sheriff had a parting shot. "Just so we're clear, Johansson. You are no longer working for the *StarTribune*, correct?"

"That's right."

"So you have no business getting involved with this crime, correct?"

"He was a nice old man and what happened to him is horrible, but you're right, I don't work for the bureau anymore."

Wilcox didn't look convinced but I meant it. In two months I'd be back working long, difficult hours in uncomfortable and dangerous conditions. And I had to be ready for it—rested, clear-headed and strong. I needed to get my body back in shape, eat well, sleep a lot and spend time with normal people doing normal things. And this was not normal.

At home, I coaxed Knute inside, settled him on his bed and called Little. After his initial shock, he said, "I should have kept a better eye on Charley this summer but we've been so busy."

"Now we'll never know what he wanted to discuss with us," I said.

He shook his head. "We always talked about flowers."

"He hinted that he and dad knew each other before he moved here."

"That's news too. I can't believe this happened. Who did Charley ever hurt?"

I heard a clamor in the background. Little said, "Sorry, but I have to go. It's still really busy. Come by later."

Sitting cross-legged on the floor with Knute's head on my knee, I reviewed my photos. Hate emanated from the destroyed flowers and trashed house. Charley's head on display like something out of a medieval war scene spoke of intense anger. The scrawled threat on the living room wall—You Will All Die—chilled me. It meant the killer wasn't finished yet.

Chapter 3

That evening, Knute paced from room to room in the two-bedroom log cabin I'd inherited from Gert, Ben's aunt. During my adolescence, she'd helped me cope with a bullying alcoholic father. He'd focused his anger on Little most of the time because Little was gay, and obvious early on. I did my best to protect my brother from him, and when it wasn't possible to do that anymore, I helped my father leave this earth, a dark spot on my soul.

Knute stopped pacing, then waited by the door and groaned. I stooped to pat his head. With Rock, time helped his grief. I hoped the same would be true for Knute.

I straightened one of my photographs that lined the walls. Framed in black, they illustrated a career full of war and natural disasters, and what I hoped was insight into the people affected—mostly women and children—the dignified way they'd handled their pain. The need to document and communicate is what kept me in the business. I hated bullies and wanted the world to see the faces of lives ruined by their greed and lust for power.

The photos were an odd contrast to Gert's hand-loomed rugs and knitted throws, but her things meant home to me. Right now, I needed that stability, before heading to South Sudan at the end of August. I'd asked to go—Civil War and genocide, famine, underfunded humanitarian agencies, the situation was beyond dire. I photographed and brought to light how war affected the most vulnerable of the world and it was happening there on massive levels.

Today I'd witnessed brutality on a much smaller scale, more personal, and yet the desire to do something about it gathered strength, almost against my will. I left a message about Charley on Ben's cell and went to bed, attempting to shove the images of the day to the back of my mind and concentrate on my joy that Ben and I had reconnected after our rocky beginning.

He called when I was in the middle of a nightmare taken directly from the afternoon's horror. "I'm sorry I've missed your calls, but we've been in the BW for days."

That explained it. No cell phone coverage in the Boundary Waters. "I figured. I wish you could come home. What's happened here is like something ISIS would do. I mean, what the hell, this isn't Syria."

"I'd like to be there. Wilcox wants me to come down too. He says the interior of the house looks like it's a hate crime, but what they did to Charley is seriously twisted."

He and Wilcox often worked cases together. Ben was the expert on anything related to the national forests and plenty of dirty deeds happened in the vast wilderness along the U.S. and Canadian borders. That's where he was now, working on exposing an elusive human trafficking ring.

I sat up, my back against the headboard. "You must have known the old guy, right? What kind of hate crime are you thinking of?"

Ben said, "He kept to himself. There were rumors he was gay and kids used to tease him when he came to town with his flowers."

"A man grows flowers so that means he's gay?"

"None of the town widows could get him interested. Taking bets on which of the old gals would land him was what passed for entertainment in Spirit Lake for years, until they all just gave up and said he must be homosexual. That's the only reason those lovely ladies could come up with to explain their failure; after all, their pies were all top-notch."

I'd missed Ben's dry humor, the twitch at the right side of his mouth.

"And when Little and Lars moved back here, Charley started taking flowers to them at the restaurant. There was more talk."

"That's ridiculous, Ben."

"Yes, it is." His next question didn't surprise me. "You aren't going to get involved in this, right?"

"You, too? I already promised the sheriff."

"It was a vicious crime, Britt."

I could picture his hazel eyes darkened with worry. "I'm going to Branson tomorrow to talk to Cynthia and then give my statement to Wilcox. After that, I promise I'm staying completely out of it."

We murmured about how much we missed each other and how we couldn't wait for the week to pass so we could spend the weekend together. After we said goodbye, I felt more alone than when we were continents away from each other. This was supposed to be our time.

Back in bed, I wrestled with my pillow, wondering why the attack on Charley had happened now. He'd been living in Spirit Lake for forty years. If it was a gay hate crime, why not attack Little and Lars? They were more visible. I clenched my pillow, willing my mind not to go there.

They'd had the restaurant for four years and it hadn't been easy. At first the locals shunned it, but Ben's persistence got the townspeople inside and once they tasted the food, Little's sexual persuasion was the last thing on their minds—bring on the cinnamon rolls.

Sleep didn't come easily. I eventually dropped off but a sound awakened me and I bolted up. Peeking out the window, I saw Knute in the middle of the yard, his white muzzle pointed at the sky. His mournful howl sent shivers through my body. I called to him from the deck, but he didn't want to come in.

I sat on the step and let him howl until he was hoarse, and then we went back inside.

***

My morning at the sheriff's office in Branson left me feeling down. Wilcox didn't have any idea who had killed Charley. As

I'd expected, heavy overnight rain washed away any footprints. No locks were broken, but most people didn't lock their houses. Charley's television and a cache of $6,000 stuffed in a flour canister hadn't been taken. The sheriff wasn't willing to label the writing on the wall a hate crime yet, gay or otherwise. He had his deputies working on it and maybe even the Minnesota Bureau of Criminal Apprehension (BCA) would be involved.

I stopped in at the *StarTrib's* tiny bureau office, a few blocks from the sheriff's. Cynthia didn't look much better than she had before I left for L.A. Her husband died two months ago, and now the bureau might close. She and Jason were both working part-time. Things were tough in the newspaper business.

"How are you doing, Cynthia?" She ignored my question and, running a hand through her graying hair, said, "Thanks for the photos, but we can't use them. Too graphic. They'll run a short piece in the regional section because of the horrific nature of the murder."

That wasn't surprising. The paper might do a story once they found the killer.

***

Back home in Spirit Lake, I pulled on my faded black Speedo one-piece and dived off the dock. The cold shocked my system. A lake 200-feet-deep in places never really warms up, even in July.

Dark sky meant another storm was coming, but I could beat it. My usual route to the city dock and back was a two-mile trek by water. The wind whipped up half way, and I welcomed the challenge of powering through the waves, allowing the steady rhythm of my strokes to calm my mind.

I pulled myself up onto the dock to rest a moment before heading home. Cold sluiced down my back from my wet ponytail and I drew my knees to my chest to conserve body heat.

As I rested for a few minutes, I noticed a few children on the swing sets at the playground across from the lake, and two others splashing in shallow water. I suspected their pale bodies were covered with goose bumps. Too bad the sun had taken the day off.

Next to the playground, the one-room log cabin Chamber of Commerce hadn't changed since I worked there as a teenager handing out maps to tourists. Vending machines were lined up outside the building with sodas, candies and chips to stave off starvation until the families could get across the street to Little's or one of the fast food stands on the highway.

A boat putt-putted up to the dock and a fisherman got out and secured it. The fisherman almost looked like a local with his well-worn multi-pocketed khaki vest and facial stubble. I'd seen him a few times in Little's and at the dock. He probably rented a cabin or stayed at one of the resorts. Many people from the cottages and resorts dotted along the lakeshore used the lake as a water highway, and the city dock was a major hub.

A few raindrops hit my head and shoulders. Time to head back. I started to dive in when the fisherman spoke behind me. "You look like a mermaid with that long hair."

Not sure how to respond to that comment, I nodded toward his boat. "Catch anything?" I'd report to Lars. A former city boy, he'd become a fishing fanatic, the framed photos on the restaurant walls a testament to his prowess.

The fisherman said, "Nope, too choppy out there today. I'm headed to Olafson's for a beer. He leered. "Want to join me?"

The leer made me want to toss him in the lake but I dove into the water for my homeward swim as he clomped down the dock and made his way across the street. The bar parking lot was already full on this weekday afternoon.

How could this be a place where a fisherman could walk away from an expensive boat and fishing equipment, unconcerned about anyone stealing it and yet, two miles south, a sweet old man had been killed in a manner that defied all known rules of small-town life?

The waves were even bigger now and the wind had switched direction. Rain slanted into my eyes and pelted my head. On shore, mothers threw striped towels around shivering shoulders, hurrying the kids to their cars.

I lowered my head and concentrated on churning through the waves, some now two feet high. Thunder boomed. The lake was not a good place to be if lightning struck. A blue and white speedboat appeared on my right. Not wanting to be run over, I stuck up my arm and waved. He waved back. Assured that he saw me, I kept going. The boat throttled down and came up alongside. I treaded water, wondering what he wanted.

The man wore a black rain slicker with the hood tightened to keep it from blowing off. Only his nose and mouth were visible. He hollered over the wind. "Do you need a lift to shore?"

I pointed to the land jutting out ahead. "I'm almost home. Thanks, though." I put my head down and continued on. He pulled away, his boat quickly disappearing around a point.

My arms and legs were heavy as boulders by the time I reached home—a good workout. I scrambled up the muddy incline to the cabin. Rock greeted me inside the door as the house shuddered with a thunder clap, startling Knute from his sleep. He lifted his head, then let it drop back on his paws.

***

I stopped by Little's for an early dinner. My brother took a break from the kitchen and joined me at my usual spot at the counter. Lars dropped off a tray full of dirty dishes in the kitchen, came back out and took the stool next to me. "We had to go in to Branson this morning and give Wilcox any information we had about Charley, which wasn't much."

"Me, too. He wanted every detail from the day I saw Charley here and then yesterday."

Little said, "Charley brought flowers to the restaurant every summer since we opened. One of us took meals out to his house but he never talked about his past." Little's face was even more pale than usual. "He'd talk your ears off about his garden, though."

I told them I'd asked Charley about his family the day I took him home. "He said he had no one."

Lars wiped the counter. "It's even more tragic we didn't know that."

Little hesitated for a minute, then must have made the decision to spit it out. "You aren't going to get mixed up in this are you, Britt? I feel terrible about Charley, but you need to chill and have some solid meals before Marta sends you back out."

I had now officially heard from my trio of watchdogs, Little, Ben and Wilcox. "Don't worry, the sheriff has this covered." I set my napkin on my empty plate. "Thanks for another delicious meal, guys. I think I'll head over to Bella's."

Little frowned. "You just said you weren't getting involved."

"Relax, I'm only saying hello."

Lars cocked his head and peered close to my face. "You could use a brow wax. Ben's due home in a few days, isn't he?"

Little nodded. "And maybe a trim." He lifted a strand of my hair. "Looking a bit ragged."

Double-teaming me was their favorite sport. They'd been too busy this summer to tease me regularly, but made a valiant effort whenever they had the chance. I let go of the guilt about covering up my ulterior motives. Bella would have information about Charley.

Main Street faced the lake and another street of businesses lined the highway. Bella's Beauty Shop was on a side street, three minutes from Little's. Bella had the only beauty salon in Spirit Lake and ran it like a news-gathering organization to rival the Associated Press. If anything happened in the northern part of Minnesota, she could tell you who, what, why, where and how, often before law enforcement or the media.

The bell tinkled when I entered the lavender and white duplex. One side was the salon, with Bella's Beauty Shop printed in black with elaborate flourishes across the window. Bella and her forty-year-old daughter, Violet, lived in the other half of the duplex. Violet did most of the salon work these days. Bella's slight tremor from palsy kept her from cutting hair, giving her even more time to keep abreast of the scuttlebutt.

Bella sat in her rocker by the window. "Violet stepped next door to get something." She peered at me over her glasses. "You really should wear a swim cap. Lake water isn't the best for your hair, especially as much as you're in it." Bella's was not in viewing distance of the dock or my cabin, but she'd never needed to actually see me to track my movements.

I sat in one of the two chairs and waited for Violet. "Thanks, Bella." Not a chlorine-filled pool, seawater, and certainly not lake water would dare penetrate her helmet of permed and sprayed curls.

Violet bustled in, slightly flushed. "Oh, Britt! I hope you haven't had to wait long." Where Bella was compact and taciturn, her daughter was pear-shaped and effusive, given to large gestures and warm hugs.

"I just walked in the door." I smiled, always happy to see her. She'd probably been catching up on her social media habit. Facebook, Twitter, Snapchat, Instagram and Pinterest, several email accounts and her own beauty blog kept her busy between customers. She tried to lure me into her network but so far I'd managed to evade it. I like to be unreachable sometimes. Today, Violet wore hot pink lipstick. She wiggled her matching nails at me. "It's so gloomy, this should perk everyone up."

"It's pretty, Violet."

She snapped out a black cape and fastened it around my neck, pulling my scraggly mane from under it. She stuck her round porcelain face close to mine. "Brow wax for sure. You could use a facial too."

"Go for it." I settled in for the duration.

Bella said, "It wouldn't hurt to take a couple of inches off your hair. You haven't had it cut since you left, have you?"

Had it been three months? "You got me there, Bella. Okay, trim it."

Bella said, "Violet, do one of those lemon rinses. See if you can get some natural highlights since Britt won't join the twenty-first century and let you use your chemicals. What did we send you for that color training for anyway?"

Violet whispered in my ear. "Don't mind her."

Now that the niceties were out of the way, Bella didn't waste any time. "Poor Charley, terrible how you found him."

"Did you know him very well?"

"He was not one to talk, except out at the nursery where he got his supplies. A lot of women tried to get him interested in them when he first moved to town. The church ladies and widows went after him, but he never showed interest. They finally gave up when Helen Farley failed to snag him."

"You'll have to explain that one, Bella."

"Helen was a catch. Pretty, a natural redhead in her day, and rich. Her husband keeled over from an aneurysm and she set her sights on Charley. Tall, handsome, thick head of hair, honey blonde like yours. But he wasn't interested. I think it broke her heart and I know for a fact it wounded her pride. She ended up marrying a real estate fellow from Cooper and moved up there."

Bella kept tabs on everything that happened in the county, particularly Spirit Lake, population five hundred, Cooper, sixteen miles north of Spirit Lake, with a thousand, and Branson, another fifteen miles north, with a whopping fifteen thousand. Those were winter numbers. The county grew exponentially in the summer.

Violet finished my hair and brows, and began painting my face with green mask. I closed my eyes and grunted at key points in the conversation.

Violet whispered. "Some people said Charley was gay."

Because of the silence I expected Bella and Violet were exchanging looks regarding my sensitivity to the situation of Lars and Little.

Violet hurried to add, "Not that there was anything specific."

Bella completed Violet's thought. "He didn't do what most of the men around here are into. Fishing, hunting, drinking, sports. He grew his flowers, and sold most of the plants to garden stores and the flower shop in Cooper before he got too old to drive. People just left him to himself. That's what he wanted, although he was always polite."

Violet asked, "Have Little and Lars figured out who sent that mean letter to them?"

I sat straight up in the chair. "What are you talking about?"

Bella's lips pursed. "Violet, you were not supposed to say anything."

Violet's hands flapped. "It slipped out. I'm sorry."

Toweling the stuff off my face, I raced down the street and slammed through the restaurant entryway nearly knocking over a customer. Lars looked up from handing menus to a family of four. "Whoa, are you the wicked witch?"

Ripping the cape from around my neck, I charged past him. In the kitchen, Little stirred a bubbling pot.

Hands on my hips, I asked, "What mean letter?"

Little put down his spoon. "Who told you?"

"Violet. I want to know right now what it said and why the hell you didn't tell me."

"You have to stop yelling first." He spoke to the second cook. "Chum, could you handle things for a few minutes?" Chum nodded. His slightly protruding eyes always made him look sleepy. His last name was Chumley. I didn't even know his first name.

Little motioned me to join him in his apartment at the back. He shut the door. "Calm down, would you? It's just a dumb letter calling us faggots."

"You told the sheriff, right?"

"Compared to what's been going on, I didn't think it would be a priority, you know?"

I wanted to shake him. "When did you get it?"

"Yesterday."

"I can't believe you didn't tell me." My voice rose again.

"We didn't want to worry you. You're supposed to be taking it easy and besides, this sort of thing happens. It's not the first time."

I dropped onto the sofa. "Have you and Lars touched the letter?"

His eyes rolled up. "How else could we read it?"

"Please bring it to me, only use a tweezers or something."

He went into the bedroom and returned with an envelope held with a tweezers. He handed me a pair of disposable gloves. "Since you're getting all forensic techy on me."

I snapped on the gloves. "This isn't a joking matter. Someone wrote a hate message on Charley's wall. The sheriff doesn't know if it was because they thought he was gay, but you can't take this lightly right now, if ever."

"Those rumors aren't based on anything, but now that he's been killed people have been rehashing the gay thing. We hear the talk in the restaurant."

I used the tweezers to tease the letter out of the envelope. "Did this come in the mail?"

He pointed to the kitchen nook area at the rear of their apartment. "I found it at the back door."

The writing was scrawled in thick black pen. "I'm watching you—Faggots."

Little shrugged. "This is nothing. There's been worse."

"We have to tell Wilcox."

"You can take it to him if you want. I have a kitchen to run."

He hesitated at the door. "Please go to our bathroom and clean up your face. You have green goo hanging from your nose and chin. I don't want you scaring the customers."

I called out after him. "How did Bella find out about the letter?"

He raised his hands, palms up. "Lars and I were talking about it in the restaurant and people probably overheard. You know how it is here."

Ten minutes later, my face washed and wet hair pulled into a ponytail, I dropped off Violet's cape and headed to the sheriff's office. The letter changed everything. Now the case was personal.

Chapter 4

The two-story green building two blocks north of First Street in Branson—the county seat—housed the sheriff, jail, boat, water, parks and emergency management departments. Usually bustling with people trying to buy fishing licenses, at five o'clock most of the offices were shutting down for the day.

A deputy said to go straight back to Wilcox's office. He scowled when I barged in. "You have something to show me?"

I handed him the letter. "Little found this at their back door yesterday."

He removed it from the plastic bag, examined it, bagged it again and blew out a long breath. "Little told you this kind of thing has happened before?"

He pointed to a chair and I took it, leaning toward him. "He and Lars have had to deal with occasional taunts. Lars is a pretty big guy, though, so nothing physical. I wonder if it had anything to do with what happened to Charley."

"A handwriting expert can determine if it's the same as the printing on Charley's wall." He stood up from behind his desk. "We'll find out who's behind this letter, and who killed Mr. Patterson." His eyes narrowed. "Your part is done unless Little gets another letter. I'll want to know about that right away."

I left dissatisfied, but there was nothing more I could do. Wilcox would be happy if I never set foot in Northern Minnesota again. He didn't hate me. It just annoyed him when I got in his way, goaded him into losing his cool, made sure I had my photos and the stories were in the paper on my schedule, not his. Come to think of it, maybe he did hate me.

Thor wasn't in her cubbyhole office at the end of the corridor. I tried the next best bet and found her in her basement space looking at something under a microscope. File cabinets full of past cases and all the equipment and kits she needed for doing her job lined the walls. Her work included taking photos and noting the location of evidence, documenting and bagging it, taking fingerprints and footprints and estimating time of death. A lab in Minneapolis analyzed most of the evidence and autopsies were handled there. They'd already sent Charley's body.

She typed something in her laptop and looked up. "Hey, Britt."

Thor's short spiked hair and multiple piercings didn't even begin to make her look tough. A petite blue-eyed blond with dimples, she was hopelessly cute. Who could blame her for trying to combat the stereotype? She wasn't a sworn officer, but it still surprised me that Wilcox put up with her unusual clothing choices.

"Anything new?" I slumped into a chair.

"Nothing from the lab so far and I hate not being able to work a whole case." She frowned, "Maybe it's time to do what I planned to do six months ago."

"I know you want to work in a big lab." Thor had been ready to complete her degree in forensic anthropology at the University of Minnesota when she and Jason began seeing each other. She'd postponed because it would have meant leaving Branson, and Jason.

"Are you seriously thinking about it this time?"

She nodded and turned back to her notes. "I can tell you the killer tortured Charley before he died. Broken fingers, abrasions and so on."

The idea of someone torturing Charley caused a burning sensation between my eyes. I wanted revenge for the old man who loved flowers and harmed no one. Had the bad guy hurt him for the fun of it, or was he trying to get information?

I joined her at the worktable and poked my face close to the microscope. "Anything else?"

"Wilcox is investigating any family or history on him before he moved to Spirit Lake, but I don't think he's got anything yet."

Her mouth snapped shut when Wilcox showed up at the doorway.

"What are you still doing here, Johansson?"

I moved away from the table. "Catching up with a friend."

"Thor's got a heavy workload right now."

She scooted over to her desk. "Sending that report now, Sheriff." Head down, her fingers flew over her laptop keyboard.

Already at the door, I said, "See you later, Thor. Thanks, Sheriff." I didn't want to irritate Wilcox too much because I needed him to keep me in the loop.

I headed back to Spirit Lake thinking about the letter. It could have been a coincidence Little and Lars got it at the same time Charley was murdered, but I doubted it.

A familiar tension settled in my chest. I'd always looked out for Little. As kids, I was the scary amazon who knocked heads together if anyone bullied my brother. He'd always been small and women would kill for his delicate bone structure and golden arched eyebrows. But that also meant too many boys tried to torment him.

Our father was the worst bully and harder to deal with but we'd come through it, though the memory of the night he died still haunted me. I re-lived it nearly every time I drove on this road between Spirit Lake and Branson.

I was sixteen. I'd picked up my drunk father from the tavern. This time he'd gotten in a fight after someone told him he'd seen Little, then twelve, holding hands with a boy. He threatened to hurt Little when we got home. I couldn't let it happen again. It was snowing hard but I pulled over, reached across the seat and opened the door, put both feet up and shoved him out of the car. As I drove away, my car hit black ice, rammed into a tree and I was knocked out. When they found us, he'd been run over by a truck while wandering drunk down the middle of the highway. He hadn't survived.

Last year when I finally told Little what really happened that night, he'd insisted I would have gone back for him if I could have, but I don't know.

In the years since, the tables have turned and I've relied on my brother's strength of character to get me through my own hard times.

***

Dinner hour at the restaurant was going full throttle. Little didn't even look up to say hello and Lars hurried to seat. Wedged between two people at the packed counter, I ate my grilled walleye and mound of garden vegetables, wishing for a baked potato, but Little said I needed more fiber.

I swallowed my food half-heartedly, missing Ben. We used to be each other's sounding boards, but spotty cell coverage in the Boundary Waters made for frustrating attempts at conversations. I could contact him for emergencies on his law enforcement-issued satellite phone, but I did that only when necessary. We hadn't talked for a week at a time when I was in Syria—that time because he couldn't reach me.

Chloe took my plate away and I went to say goodbye to Lars in the bistro. The guys had created a cozy outdoor seating area under the pines with round tables and bright yellow umbrellas. It opened off the bar on the south side and was the only alternative to Olafson's.

Lars chatted with a group of people I'd noticed before. The group of five usually gathered in the late afternoon and were sometimes joined by a gray-bearded man who wore cargo shorts and a t-shirt with Tenth Annual Spirit Lake International Writers' Workshop printed on it. A woman at the table stared at me. The leering fisherman from the dock sat next to her and three others had their backs to me. Lars looked my way and I waved goodbye. He returned my wave and I headed home, curious about the writing group that included a leering fisherman and a rude woman.

I fed the dogs, but needed something to do to keep my mind off the letter, Charley and the absent Ben. I changed to my swimsuit.

A thick rolling cloud hung above a band of sunlight and backlit the forest along the west side of the lake. A few boaters were out and a couple of jet skis zipped through the waves. Sailboats were heading to shore.

Hoping to beat the rain, I worked through the waves, not so high this time, the rhythm of swimming helping to focus. I pulled myself onto the city dock and watched the sky decide what it wanted to do. The sun hit my shoulders and melted the goose bumps. I squeezed the water out of my hair. Bella would not be happy that I'd subjected it to the elements again.

Footsteps behind me reverberated on the planks. One of the group from the bistro uncoiled the rope from a blue and white speedboat. I recognized the boat. He was the friendly guy from the day before who'd offered me a ride.

He walked over, smiling. "You're the same swimmer I saw yesterday."

I'd noticed him with the group Lars was talking to earlier. Blond-streaked hair hung across one eye, he had a high forehead and long, thin nose with eyes hidden behind aviator sunglasses.

He introduced himself as Peder Halvorsen from Norway.

I reached up and took the hand he offered. "Britt Johansson. I've seen you at Little's with the writers' group. What do you write?"

His shy smile disarmed me. "I write bad poetry, Anke is working on a thriller, another fellow, Neil, is doing a fishing guide book and two students are writing short fiction that I don't understand at all. It's quite interesting."

Thunder boomed in the distance and I stood. "It looks like the rain's coming again. I'd better head back. Nice to meet you, Peder."

"I'd be happy to give you a ride."

"Thanks for offering but I enjoy swimming."

He tossed his book bag in the boat and hopped in. He didn't look like he spent time at the gym working on those abs, but he moved with an athletic spring in his step. With frown lines between his brows and faint laugh lines, I guessed him to be in his early forties.

I dove in. Good thing I was madly in love with my forest ranger. That was one good-looking bookworm.

***

Little's call woke me at five a.m., his voice strained. "Can you come over right away and help us? Some kids spray-painted the windows and we need to get it cleaned off before we open."

I pulled on jeans and t-shirt, grabbed my camera and drove over. From long habit, a camera went everywhere with me, and I usually carried a backup.

My headlights illuminated the black scrawl across the café's lakeside windows—You Will All Die. A small voice inside me tried to deny the magnitude of what it said, and then I realized that Little and Lars were scrubbing at the writing. I jumped out of the SUV waving my arms. "Stop!"

Lars stopped scraping, but Little ignored me and continued sponging away the residue. "There's no time. Help us."

I grabbed the sponge from Little. "Are you nuts? The sheriff will never find out who did this if you get rid of the evidence."

Little backed off while I took photos but said, "After what happened to Charley, people are already freaked out. That's all they're talking about. If they see this, no one will come to the restaurant for the rest of the summer."

"I get it that you don't want to scare the customers, but staying alive is also important for your livelihood, especially if this is the same person who killed Charley."

He picked up the sponge and Lars started scraping again. I called Wilcox, ignoring their protests.

When he arrived, the guys were polishing the windows. Wilcox tore off his cowboy hat, slapped it against his leg and yelled at me. "What were you thinking? Why did you let them scrape it off?"

I'd taken photos of car tracks and footprints, but didn't hold out much hope. Little and Lars had trampled the ground and wiped the windows clean. I lifted my camera as a peace offering. "I have photos. You can see if it's a match to Charley's house, and the letter."

Wilcox settled his hat back on his head and turned to the guys. "What happened?"

They gave him a hurried statement and hustled inside to make sure the restaurant opened as usual.

In a few moments, Thor arrived in a spray of gravel. She lugged her evidence kit out of the car, surveyed the blank windows and scuffed driveway. "Uh, I'll do my best."

Wilcox pulled at the brim of his cowboy hat. "The graffiti guy wasn't foolish enough to leave us a can of spray paint with his fingerprints."

My body had been trembling nonstop since I saw the message. I went inside the restaurant and dropped onto a seat at the counter. Wilcox followed and helped himself to a cup of coffee. He even brought one for me.

"Sheriff, what are you going to do to protect Little and Lars? This is related to Charley."

Wilcox said, "They'll be safe in the restaurant, but they shouldn't go anywhere alone. I'll station a deputy outside at night."

My voice rose. "They need someone in front and in back. There are several entrances and one person can't watch all of them at once."

"Okay, Britt, calm down. No one wants anything to happen to them. I'll put my best deputy on this. I don't have the resources to keep two patrols here."

I forced myself to get the anxiety under control. I'd seen much worse, but perspective went out the window when it came to my brother being threatened.

Wilcox went into the kitchen to attempt to talk to Little as he raced to set up for the breakfast crowd. I slipped outside. Thor was bent over gathering items from the gravel driveway and bagging them.

I asked, "Anything?"

She didn't look up. "Hard to tell. The usual cigarette butts and gum wrappers. I'll bag everything. You never know."

By the time a group of locals trooped in, Lars was ready for them. "We're a little behind this morning, folks, bear with us. Had to get those windows sparkling so you can see the lake. It's supposed to be a beautiful day, my friends. Not a cloud in the sky."

Wilcox came through the swinging kitchen doors.

Jake from the hardware store asked, "Why's the sheriff here? What's wrong?"

Lars faked a smile and poured him a cup of coffee. "The kind sheriff is here to keep the peace in case you get too rowdy this morning, Jake."

Wilcox tipped his cowboy hat and left.

Mid-morning, after the first rush of customers, I joined Little in the kitchen. "How're you doing?"

His chin came up. "I know it was wrong to clean the windows, but everyone seeing that was unbearable to me."

"No one blames you. I sent my photos to the sheriff's so they can see how it matches up to the letter and the writing on Charley's wall." Saying that out loud caused a tight band of fear to grip my chest. Little clutched the slotted spoon in his hand so hard his knuckles whitened.

I said, "You heard Wilcox. He's going to have a deputy guarding you guys tonight, and I'm going to help track down whoever did this."

Little's voice raised several decibels. "No. You promised."

"That was before you became a target."

All color drained from Little's face. Lars came into the kitchen with a breakfast order. His expression mirrored Little's. Among the customers, Lars pretended all was well, but we knew better.

I watched each person who entered the restaurant all morning. Early afternoon, the woman from the writers' group stood outside to finish her cigarette, came in alone and sat at a table for two. She opened her laptop and typed, casting glances at me that lingered too long to be polite. I guessed her to be in her late thirties or early forties. She looked as tall as me but about twenty pounds heavier. She pushed short wavy hair back from her face. The definition in her bare arm told me it was all muscle.

Needing to stretch my legs, I found Lars and told him I was going home to check on Rock and Knute. "I'll be back soon."

He nodded, distracted by a group of people entering the restaurant. I ran my X-Ray gaze over them as he led them to a table in the bistro. The writing group woman's eyes were on me again. I tried to analyze the look. Not friendly or unfriendly. I raised an eyebrow and she turned away to talk to the person next to her.

At the cabin, I filled Rock's bowl but Knute hadn't eaten much. He'd take a few bites and lose interest. I whispered in his ear. "I'm sorry for not promising this sooner. I'll find who did this to Charley and stop him before he hurts the people I love too."

The woman from the writers' group had given me an idea. Instead of sitting at Little's with nothing to do, I'd take my laptop with me and do some research. Full of purpose, I headed back to Little's.

Keeping one eye on the door, I sat at a small table, opened my laptop and began researching hate crimes in the area covering the past five years. Sadly, there were many to choose from—the haters who did it because their god told them to and the white supremacists who went after everyone who was different.

So who was the hater? If it was someone local, why now? Little and Lars had been in Spirit Lake for almost four years. Charley had lived here for forty years. That made me think we had a new hate element in the area. I kept digging, and interestingly, the same name came up several times in my Internet search.

Matthew Willard, kicked out of Branson University at nineteen for gay bashing activities. He started with anti-gay slurs at students who were leaving a gay-friendly bar. He wrote on someone's car in the parking lot of a bowling alley. His behavior escalated and he attacked a student in a bar by using anti-gay taunts, hitting him in the head with a beer bottle and beating him. He was charged with assault and a hate crime. He had been released from prison a month ago so he'd be twenty-two. His parents lived in Iona, a town east of Branson.

I surveyed the restaurant. The bad guy wouldn't dare try anything with all these witnesses. I closed the laptop. Mr. and Mrs. Willard were about to receive a visitor.

Chapter 5

The drive to Iona, eight miles southeast of Branson, took half an hour. Another ten minutes on a twisting two-lane road led me to a turnoff marked by a beat-up mailbox. "Willard" was written on it in black marker.

I turned down the gravel road wondering what I'd find. My intention was to get a visual clue from the kid's family and find out more about him. Wilcox would be furious with me, but I'd fill him in if anything interesting happened. I reached in my glove box for a clipboard with a notepad attached to it.

The weathered gray clapboard house might have been yellow at one time, but was now a dingy gray. I didn't see a vehicle but maybe they'd parked in back. Unsettled air caused ripples on the surface of a stagnant pond across the road from the house. I scanned dark clouds overhead as I knocked on the door. I re-tucked my white shirt into black slacks, waited a minute and knocked again. "Hello, anyone home?"

"Hang on." A woman with stringy gray hair opened the door. She wore a stained tank top with a Bible passage on it. I didn't want to stare at her ample chest too long in order to read it. It wasn't one of the short passages.

Distrustful eyes locked on mine. "We have cable and we're not looking to change to whatever you're selling."

I stuck out my hand. "I'm Britt Johansson and I'm not selling anything. I wanted to ask you a few questions about Matthew."

She squinted at my clipboard. Her sharp chin came up, arms crossed over her chest. "You his probation officer? He hasn't done anything wrong."

"May I come in? I won't take a minute. I just have a couple of questions."

She scowled but stepped away from the door. I followed her into the family room. A 9mm Glock stuck out of the waist of her jeans in back, visible under the thin top hanging over it.

Hesitating, I asked, "Do you always answer the door with a gun?"

"You can't be too careful. I have a permit if you want to check it."

Mrs. Willard still believed I was her son's probation officer. That worked in my favor. She pulled the gun from the back of her pants and I held my breath as she set it on the scarred coffee table. She sat on the couch and pointed to an overstuffed chair.

I perched on the edge of it, conscious of the gun between us. She watched me look at the mantel. It held several photos of a blond-haired boy in different stages of development.

"Matthew's an only child?"

Her mouth puckered, exaggerating the deep lines on either side of it. "The older boy took off a few years ago. We tried to train the homo out of him but the devil had a firm hold."

Wondering what that training consisted of and where he'd gone, I asked, "What's his name?"

"We don't use his name anymore. It's an abomination in a Christian house."

Holding the clipboard in the crook of my arm, I left my chair and picked up one of the photos. A snapshot of Matthew standing next to the severed head of a big buck was tucked into the frame of the larger high school graduation portrait. Medium height, muscular, light hair and skin, even features, sharp chin like his mother, camouflage pants and white t-shirt, no tattoos or piercings. Nondescript in this setting, he'd stand out against the sea of colorful young people showing their style, individuality and character all over Southern California.

"He got that buck just before they arrested him. So what's this about?"

I slipped the snapshot between the pages of my clipboard and set the framed photo back in its spot on the mantel. "Has your son been spending time around the Spirit Lake area?"

She spit out her answer. "He's been working with his dad salvaging. They go all over the county. He goes to work and comes straight home. We go to Bible study in the evenings and church on Sunday."

"What church is that?"

"The church of none of your goddamn business."

Mrs. Willard picked up the gun from the coffee table and stood.

My mouth went dry.

She shoved it back in her jeans. "It appears to me you're on a fishing expedition and you're wasting my time. Matthew's a good boy." Her head jerked toward the door. "I've got laundry to do."

"Thanks for your time, Mrs. Willard." I forced myself to walk at a normal pace out the door and to my car. She continued watching from the porch as I rounded a corner.

I backed the SUV onto a side trail half way between the county road and their driveway, out of sight, but with a view of the house and road.

Forty minutes later, an old pickup passed by with two men in it. The back of the truck was piled high with junk. Following the father and son to their home for another visit didn't appeal to me. If the kid's mother answered the door with a Glock in her pants, what would the father and son be armed with? A hunting rifle sat on a rack in the back window of the truck, but hunting season was long over. Most people around here didn't even lock their doors when they went to bed at night, but this family was well armed.

Time to head back. I shivered and pulled onto the highway heading south. The July air had turned chilly and the dark cloud hung directly overhead. In a few minutes, the sky opened up with marble-sized hail that sounded like gunshots pelting the car.

***

Little's voice carried across the dining room and I halted just inside the restaurant door. Ranting wasn't his style. Lars shot me a look of concern from behind the counter. "I'd better check this out." He headed back to the kitchen and the strident sounds stopped.

Little could be edgy when cooking for a large crowd. He wanted everyone to leave happy and satisfied. Sometimes his striving for perfection caused him to be gruff with the staff, but they understood and loved him anyway. This sounded different. The hail had come and gone quickly, but the outside tables were still wet and raindrops clung to the umbrellas and dripped from the trees overhead. Chloe went out to wipe down the tables.

I sat at the counter and in a few minutes, Lars brought coffee and sat next to me. I asked, "How's he doing?"

"I wish we weren't so busy. We need to get away from here for a few days. This thing with Charley and the window threat has upset him more than he lets on."

"Couldn't your staff take over for a while?"

"Little would be more stressed over that." Lars ran his hand over his bald dome, ruffling the fringe of curls around the edges.

I held out the picture of Matthew standing next to the buck's head. "Have you seen this kid in the restaurant or in town recently?"

"He looks like half the kids around here." He peered closer. "We get so many new people coming through in the summer, it's hard to say. He got himself a big buck there."

A customer held up his cup and Lars moved away, refilling coffee along the counter before coming back to me.

"Where did you get that picture?"

"I checked online to see if there were recent hate crimes in the area, and this kid showed up from a few years ago. Three months ago he was released from prison for aggravated assault against a gay man."

"That didn't answer my question about where you got the photo."

I tried for an innocent tone. "The family lives east of Branson and I dropped in for a visit today. I was looking at the picture and forgot to put it back."

His lip curled at my lame explanation. "Jaysus, Britt, don't show that to Little." He leaned in close to my ear. "Seriously, the less he knows, the less he'll worry."

"I won't tell him, but there's no way I'm letting this go until Wilcox has the killer behind bars."

Lars shot a glance toward the kitchen. "Promise me you won't disturb our customers by showing that picture in here. We're safe during the day and Wilcox has someone coming to watch the place tonight." A group of customers came in, and Lars hustled away with a smile plastered on his face.

Lars didn't want me to show the photo in the restaurant so I hit the street, aware that Wilcox wouldn't look into the coincidence of Matthew's recent release from prison and the Spirit Lake hate crimes without evidence or facts.

People were milling around town, entering and leaving the tourist shops. The back of my neck itched as if someone watched me. It wasn't unusual for me to get a few curious looks. My height and the camera around my neck attracted attention. I disregarded the itch.

After an hour, I'd shown the picture in nearly every business in town with no luck. My last stop was Erickson's Hardware. The store had the largest square footage of any business in town. People around here were do-it-yourselfers. If they couldn't figure out how to fix or build something, a neighbor offered assistance. I passed the photo around to the staff. They said the same thing at every stop. Hard to tell, the kid resembled half the kids in the county. But everyone admired the deer head.

They all shook their heads when I asked if anyone had been spouting any anti-gay comments recently. They'd get the occasional question from tourists or hunters about Little and Lars. Most of the business owners would simply say, "You like the food and the service is good, right?" Haters sometimes showed up, but murder, especially the horrific murder of Charley, was different.

Not expecting anything, I pushed open the door at Bella's. The familiar bell tinkled above me. Violet had one customer in the chair and two others in line. Bella stood at the register running a credit card for a woman. When the woman left, Bella peered at the picture through her bifocals.

"Sure I know who that is. He just got out of prison and he's living with his parents up in Iona and working with his dad. I remember when he went in. His folks were associated with one of those white supremacist cults, but they haven't been in any trouble that got them on the police logs. They usually get younger and stupider people to do the dirty work. Their older son's not around."

She plumped down into her rocker, picked up the remote and switched the channel on the wall-mounted television to CNN.

Violet bent over the photo. "Look at the size of that rack."

***

According to Mrs. Willard, Sunday was church day. I wanted to see this church of none of your goddamn business. Could it be a front for anti-gay activities and possibly a connection to Charley's death? I set out early in the morning with my binocs, camera and backup equipment. The only time I didn't carry a camera was in the shower. Sometimes I couldn't see clearly unless I was looking through a rectangle.

I backed the SUV into position in my hideaway on the Willards' road and waited, sipping from a giant coffee and working my way through a bag of Little's blueberry muffins. This was a fishing expedition. When the family left for church, I'd follow, and maybe even slip into the services unnoticed.

Shortly before ten, a caravan of two pickups and one battered Ford passed my spot heading toward the Willards' home, carrying mostly men, a couple of women and two or three children. The church must be on the property.

After making sure no one else was coming, I hiked up the road keeping close to the woods. The vehicles were not in the driveway. Scouting the area behind the house, I found car tracks leading down a dirt road barely wide enough for one vehicle. Tufts of weeds and grass covered parts of the rutted path. The recent rain meant muddy going for those cars. The quarter-mile trail led me to the cars and trucks parked near a weathered outbuilding. Rifles were mounted above the back windows in the pickups. I photographed several license plate numbers.

Lots of these old homesteads had outbuildings. This one was the size of a one-room cabin and surrounded by woods on all sides except for the driveway area. The building had one open window, maybe three by five, and the door was closed. No dogs barked. If there were dogs, I'd run like the wind back to my SUV.

I wondered how long services lasted. I made my way to the back, then sidled around to the open window. Cigarette smoke wafted out. I stifled a sneeze. Mrs. Willard talked about me. "She was no parole officer. I described her to Matthew here and he said his parole officer was a man for one thing."

Several people spoke at once but I couldn't catch their words. Mrs. Willard said, "She could be from one of the groups that try to keep us from spreading the word."

"Until we find out, everyone watch your backs." That might have been Mr. Willard or someone else from the congregation. "Dale, did you di*strib*ute those flyers like you were supposed to?"

A younger male voice spoke. "I stuck a bunch up at that gay bar on Fourth Street and put some up at the community college. I'm all out now."

"Good for you. We need to get to them before it's too late and Satan has them in his claws." That sounded like Mrs. Willard.

"This has nothing to do with that woman checking me out, but didn't we agree to cut back on the small stuff for a while? Me and dad are working on a bigger project." That had to be Matthew.

A nasal male voice. "We're all in this together. Since when did you and your boy go off and do your own thing?"

It sounded like Matthew's father again, "It's not like that, Orin."

I couldn't distinguish any specific voices after that comment. Everyone started talking at once, loud and agitated. Matthew's father said, "Margery, jump up there and make more copies for everyone before we leave. The parade is tomorrow and the fair is next week. You can pass out the literature, just no vandalism for a while. That's all we're saying. Be strategic, people."

The sound of a copier chugging surprised me. I didn't see any electrical lines. Maybe they used a generator. A six-foot-high pile of junk sat a few feet from the shed. The generator could be hidden there. I'd have to check it out. What were they printing that was so secret they couldn't keep their printer at the house?

Someone made a hate-in-the-name-of-the-lord speech and wrapped it up. Matthew's father spoke, "Okay, folks, let me know if you see a tall, long-haired blond woman hanging around. If she found Matthew here, she might be watching the rest of us too. Be wary."

A woman's high-pitched voice responded. "They can't keep us from doing our work."

"That's right, sister. Remember, let the other Church of the Creator groups handle the rest of it. Our mission is to eradicate the homos and that's what we need to concentrate on."

The hair stood up on the back of my neck, signaling it was time to leave, but before I could go, chairs scraped back, feet shuffled and the group spilled out.

Flat against the back wall, I waited until everyone pulled away. After the dust settled, I walked around the building, taking photos from all sides. The junk pile was made up of old car parts, farm machinery, piles of brush and wood, toasters and blenders, all blasted by the elements. Several cans of black spray paint with no caps lay in a heap on one side of the pile. I shot photos of them, picked one up with a Kleenex and set it aside to take back with me.

They'd shut the window, closed the curtain and padlocked the door before leaving. A black cable partially covered by debris snaked around the building to the back of the junk pile. I followed it to a generator tucked between a wringer-type washing machine and a sprung easy chair.

A sound came from the woods in the direction of the Willards' house. I stopped breathing and peered into the trees, nervous about being cut off from my SUV. Nothing else disturbed the quiet and I drew in a deep breath. Maybe a deer had stepped on a fallen branch. I wanted to look through the window, and then I'd get out of here. The place made me edgy.

They'd wedged a stick in the window, an effective enough lock to keep it from sliding more than a quarter inch. I reached around to see if there was wiggle room to pop it out of its weathered tracks, and heard the unmistakable crack of a pump-action shotgun behind me. I froze.

"We shoot trespassers here. Turn around."

I turned in slow motion. The rest of the group materialized out of the woods, standing with legs spread and guns pointed at me.

Chapter 6

I recognized Mrs. Willard's Glock—the rest carried rifles. Matthew held a big hunting rifle. The buck's head popped into my mind.

The man standing in front of me was mid-fifties, mid-height and weight, and the mean stare meant business. He moved closer, keeping his shotgun pointed at my chest. "What are you doing here?"

"I want to join your church." My effort to speak with confidence came out sounding more like a scared mouse.

"You're trespassing on my property. I have the right to shoot you for that."

My throat closed. "That seems a little extreme."

Matthew pointed to my camera. "She's taking pictures, Dad."

Mr. Willard spoke to the group. "What we have here is that *StarTribune* photographer who was plastered all over the news about five months ago on that trafficking thing over in Spirit Lake."

He turned his gaze to me. "Frankly, I was all for what you did, keeping foreigners out of the U.S."

Even though his take on it was skewed, I hoped it would keep him from shooting me. I'd helped rescue four Vietnamese girls from being trafficked through Canada into Minnesota. That particular ring had been shut down, but trying to stop the sex trade was like trying to hold back a raging river with a beaver dam.

My knees trembled, but I looked directly at the elder Willard. "Tell them to put down their weapons before someone blows my head off and I'll explain why I'm here."

He nodded to the others. They dropped the weapons at their sides but moved in closer.

The problem was I didn't know what to say. I'd taken photos in the past of some of the physical damage hate factions like this did to the groups they despised. They liked to attack with bats and beatings. My cell phone rang and I jumped, thankful it hadn't done that while they were inside the building and kicking myself now for not turning it off. I studied the screen. Maybe the call could save me. "My editor in Branson knows I'm here. She's checking on me."

"Tell her you're having a chat with the nice people out here who just finished their Bible study and I might let you out alive."

I hit answer. "Hi, Cynthia." I listened, then said, "Thanks for checking. I'm still talking with the Willards out in Iona but I'm heading home now."

Lars was sputtering when I hung up. I muted the sound in case he called back. This group didn't need to know I no longer worked for the *StarTribune*.

Mrs. Willard put her hands on her hips, presenting a good view of a Ban Gay Marriage slogan on her gray tank top. "Why's the paper doing a story on us? We haven't done anything."

I turned to Matthew. "Actually, it's you we're interested in. We're doing a follow-up since you recently got out of prison. I wanted to take your photo and ask if our reporter could get an interview with you."

Mr. Willard said, "My boy works with me. He's not talking to any press to bring more media attention to our home. Now, get the hell out of here. Next time I catch you trespassing on my property, I *will* blow your head off."

I raised my camera. "I'd like to take a picture of your group."

"What you can do is hand me the camera."

Stepping back, I said. "I'll press charges if you damage it."

He yanked the strap from around my neck, nearly taking my head with it and took out the memory card.

"Give it back to me." I mentally slapped myself in the head. Never knowing when to quit is a problem I'm still trying to overcome.

He tossed the camera at me, raised his shotgun and blasted a round into the air. "Now get out."

I moved fast down the lane, grateful for my long stride.

They followed me all the way to my SUV. Mr. Willard stood aside for me to back out of my not-so-great hiding place. "Don't bother bringing the cops. By the time they get here, there will be no evidence of what you think you saw. Anything you say will be the word of a trespasser against our word as God-fearing members of the community."

He held the shotgun in one hand and pointed it at me. "We are strategic and now we will be watching you."

I wanted to stomp on the accelerator but drove away at a normal speed, swallowing several times to keep my breakfast from coming up. When that was under control, I checked my phone. Missed calls from Lars and Little. I returned the call from Lars first to get my story straight with him and find out what he'd said to Little. "What's up?"

He sounded relieved to hear my voice. "Little was nervous that we didn't know where you were. I figured you'd done something stupid, especially after you called me Cynthia."

"I checked out an anti-gay group in Iona and wanted them to think I still worked for the bureau."

"Jaysus, be careful. Does Wilcox know what you're doing?"

"No, and you better not tell him."

What would be a sigh coming from most people was more like a blast when it came from Lars. "Hurry back. Little won't settle down until he sees you."

"Tell him I didn't have cell service." I'd kept a lot from Little when he was too young to understand things. Even though he was a grown man now, I continued to protect him from being upset. Early conditioning is hard to shake.

My trip to Iona had turned out to be dangerous, I'd learned nothing incriminating about them and now they knew about me.

At least by not telling Wilcox, I saved myself from another tongue-lashing. The sheriff wasn't interested in my gut feelings.

***

A late lunch crowd packed the restaurant. When Little saw me he tore out of the kitchen. "I've been worried about you."

I slid onto a stool. "Sorry, I lost track of time."

His hands went to his hips. "That happens with you a lot."

My nerves were still jumpy. It's not every day people point guns directly at me. Before he could go into his usual spiel about how inconsiderate I was, I put my hand on my stomach and tried to look pitiful. "Any lunch left?"

He disappeared into the kitchen, returning with a giant plate of something purple alongside brown rice. I sniffed. "Smells like Thai."

"It's called Eggplant Delight."

Little's didn't have a food theme. My brother cooked whatever captured his interest. It pleased everyone, and the locals were grateful for the variety. He hurried back to the kitchen. Mouth full, I called after him. "Thank you. It's delicious."

I sipped tea and watched the open air bistro begin to fill. People were coming in off the lake after a day of recreation on one of the rare sunny afternoons this summer. I waved at Lars, busy pouring wine and beer at the bistro bar. He'd created his own specialty cocktail for the summer folks—the Sun 'n' Fun. I no longer drank alcohol but the beverage smelled citrusy. It was a big hit even when the sun wasn't shining and no one was having fun.

Peder, the blue and white speedboat guy, sat at a bistro table. He caught my eye and made a welcoming gesture indicating the chair next to him. I snagged a couple of cookies from the baked goods display and joined him.

He moved a yellow writing pad out of the way. "Not swimming today?"

"Not yet, but it's a good idea." The lake was in full view from our vantage point on a little knoll under the birches. I offered him a cookie.

He bit into it. "Very good." His accent was heavily Scandinavian and reminded me of my great aunts, who'd never lost that lilting speech pattern. I nibbled my cookie. Lemon, my favorite. "Where's the rest of your group?"

"Vik often sends us out to do writing on our own."

"Is Vik your workshop leader?"

"Yes, also Norwegian, although he's like you, born in the U.S."

Lars brought a pitcher of iced tea to our table. "Refill for you, Peder?"

He looked at his watch, pushed his glass toward Lars and thanked him. "I've finished my piece and have half an hour left until we meet back at the cabin."

Lars said, "I didn't know you two had met, or is Britt harassing the customers now?"

I said, "We met at the city dock."

Lars clapped Peder on the back and headed to another table. "You two scandahoovians enjoy yourselves."

Peder tilted his head. "But isn't Lars also Scandinavian?"

"Half. His mom was Swedish but his father is Jewish. His name is Jacob Lars Weinstein. He used to be a history prof at the University of Minnesota but since moving up here with Little, he's definitely embraced his inner Swede."

Licking cookie crumbs from my fingers, I stood. "I need to check on my dogs. Thanks for inviting me over."

Peder gathered his things. "And I need to get back for the reading." He held the door for me on the way out. Chatting with Peder almost made me forget the Willards.

***

A flash of fear slid through me as I opened the door my cabin. I should start locking it now that I'd stirred up the anti-gay haters.

I stepped in the shower, hoping to wash away the image of guns pointing at me. My cell phone rang and I reached out to grab it from the counter, but the caller had hung up.

It was Ben. Maybe he was coming home. I hurried to finish showering, put on a t-shirt and shorts and stepped out to the deck, shaking my hair like Rock shook water from his fur.

Knute slept in the grass, his old bones warming in the sun. Most likely not a great watchdog. I whistled for Rock and in a minute, he dashed through the trees. He never strayed too far. Surely, he'd bark if a stranger showed up.

I sat on the porch swing outside my bedroom to let my hair dry in the evening air, punched in Ben's number and settled against a cushion for a romantic chat. I still couldn't believe my luck that we were back together again. He was the one true love of my life. I didn't care how schmaltzy that sounded. It took me far too long to realize it and in the meantime, I kept trampling all over his feelings and causing misery for both of us. For a thirty-four-year-old professional woman with a lifetime of experience in the way humans behaved toward each other, I was unaccountably clueless when it came to my own personal life.

Ben sounded grim. "Lars called me. You should not mess around with the World Church. Those people are ruthless."

So much for romance. "Lars is such a tattle-tale. I can't trust him with anything." My feet pushed the porch swing back and forth.

"He wanted me to talk some sense into you, but everyone knows my record in that regard."

The swing banged against my calves when I stood. "Do you want to lecture me or do you want to hear about why I did it and what I found?" I left the porch and Rock trailed me to the lake's edge.

Ben's voice calmed. "Sorry. It's frustrating to be so far away and find out Little and Lars are in the sights of a nutcase or some fringe crazies. Tell me why you're looking at Matthew Willard."

Everyone valued Ben's opinion. Smart, deliberate and wise, he rarely spoke unless he had something useful to say, unlike me, who never had a thought I didn't blurt out the second it hit my consciousness. Spontaneous would be a kind way to describe my actions. I was more intuitive than smart and more determined than wise. We were made for each other. I filled him in but left out the part about nearly getting my head blown off.

"He's the only person who showed up when I did a search on hate crimes in the county. Matthew left prison a month before Charley's murder. It seemed worth checking out. Maybe he heard the rumor about Charley being gay when he was in town collecting junk. It's not a secret about Little and Lars."

"Talk to Wilcox about this, let him contact the Iona police to see what's going on."

"You know Wilcox won't listen to me, especially now that I'm not working for the *StarTrib*."

Ben didn't reply to that because it was true. I said, "Matthew and his dad do salvage work all over the county. Charley has several rusted out heaps of iron behind his house that look like giant insects. Maybe Charley contacted them to pick it up, they'd heard the gay rumor and saw an opportunity."

"You're talking about an old combine and maybe some tractor parts. It's still a stretch that they would do anything that violent."

"I'm so worried about Little and Lars. You do realize the same message was on the restaurant window as the one on Charley's wall."

"I did. 'You Will All Die.' His voice deepened. "Britt, stay away from those people. I'll talk to Wilcox."

"I don't want to go near that place again. They mentioned a Fourth of July disturbance in Iona but I didn't hear details. You might want to tell Wilcox about that, too."

"I'll tell him, but it doesn't sound like you found anything that connects them to Charley's death or to what's happened at Little's unless you're thinking that because they talked about vandalism, that ties to the hate message at Charley's."

When he put it like that, it sounded thin even to me. "How's your project going?"

"I should be back home in a couple of days."

The 'should' didn't sound promising. "That's great. I really miss you, Ben."

"It sounds like you're wasting no time missing me with that Swedish tourist to keep you company."

He teased, but I didn't want to strain our relationship now that it was going so well. "He's from Norway and he's part of that writer's retreat group that hangs out at Little's."

"I know. The event is being held at my resort this year."

My voice low and sexy, I said, "It's you I want, Ben. Hurry home."

"I'm hurrying."

***

I ate the last piece of chocolate meringue pie as the guys went about their closing-up routine. Little sat at the opposite end of the counter, making his meal plan list for the following day. He called to Lars. "Tomorrow's the Fourth. How's the float coming along?"

Lars wiped down the counter. "Chloe and the kids finished it. All ready to go."

Little grumped. "I'm not even excited about it this year with everything that's happened."

As I licked the last sweet morsel of pie from my lips, Lars picked up my plate and wiped the counter in front of me. I snatched the towel from him. "I can do it."

"What's the matter with you?" He set the plate in a bin.

"How come you ratted me out to Ben about the World Church people?"

He looked at the ceiling. "He asked about you."

I stood up from my stool and stretched. "I'm taking off. Be sure to double-check all the locks tonight."

I waved at the patrol car sitting in front of the restaurant and headed home to bed.

After tossing and turning for hours, I gave up on sleep and jumped back in my car and cruised over to Little's. I pulled into the driveway next to the deputy on duty, recognizing him from the sheriff's office. "Hi, Jerry, how are the kids?" A few years older than me, he had three young boys and coached hockey.

Jerry rubbed his eyes and yawned. "The boys are a handful as usual. What are you doing here? It's two a.m."

"I just came by to say hello."

56

He frowned. "You're checking up on me. Go on back home." He squinted at my passenger seat. "Are you carrying a weapon?"

"That's my camera." A camera was my weapon. It had brought down murderers, rapists, fraudsters and tyrants. "C'mon, Jerry. I can't sleep worrying about the guys. Let me just sit there for a while."

"You've got me over a barrel. If I tell Wilcox you're here, he'll be pissed as hell for waking him." He considered for a moment. "If anything happens, stay in your car."

I nodded and pulled over to the bistro side.

At five a.m., the lights came on in the residence. Time to begin their work day. I waved goodbye to Jerry.

Chapter 7

The weather didn't cooperate on the Fourth of July either. But even with an overcast sky and a murderer in our midst, life went on. Businesses shut down during the parade, tourists lined the streets and children chased treats tossed from the floats.

Jerry stayed at the restaurant to protect it from vandals. He said Wilcox believed Little would be safe riding with Lars in the parade.

I tried to talk my brother out of going. "You'll be too exposed."

The groove between Little's brows deepened. "I always ride in the car with Lars. People expect to see me." The staff had been working after hours building their best-ever float for the annual parade. And it was true, the crowd always cheered loudest for my brother.

I found a good vantage point on the post office steps and photographed the Shriners weaving in and out in their miniature cars, the skittish horses, high school bands, balloons and hoopla, alert to anyone or anything out of place.

The same uncomfortable feeling that someone watched me put me on edge. I scanned the crowd. Anke, the woman from the writers' group was across the street with her eyes on me, more insolent than furtive. She stood slightly apart from the crowd, smoking, with the same dour expression I'd noticed at Little's. If I hadn't needed to keep the guys in sight, I'd have confronted her right then.

A few people threw irritated looks at her. No one liked smokers. Her eyes slid away and back to the high school marching band making its noisy way up the street. The two students, one wispy female and dark-haired male stood nearby with their workshop leader.

When the Little's Café float rounded the bend and started up Main Street, I pushed past the tourists and loped to meet it. I continued to take photos, but my real purpose was to keep an eye on my brother.

This year the theme included a round table with a yellow bistro umbrella. Lars pulled the float behind his SUV. Little waved from the passenger seat. Staff dressed as tourists sat at the table sipping wine. I moved to the back, shooting. Chloe, her dark hair free of its ponytail, and wearing a red, white and blue swimsuit with a tiny apron, waved and tossed candies. Kids flew at the treats from all directions. A photo from this year would hang in the restaurant alongside the ones from the last two years.

My peripheral vision caught a stranger in a straw cowboy hat staggering up to Little's window. He grabbed Little's shirt. I jumped on him in an instant, yanking him away from the SUV. He slipped from my grasp and fell backward on the ground with a thud. Everyone gasped. Lars stopped the float and he and Little jumped out, yelling at me. "What are you doing?"

Lars helped the guy up and brushed him off. "Sorry, Louie, are you okay?"

Louie blinked. "What the hell just happened?" He straightened his hat and wobbled down the street.

His face purple, Little's loud whisper blasted my ear. "He's obviously had too much to drink. What's the matter with you?"

I stammered, "I'm sorry. I'd never seen him before. His actions looked aggressive."

Little spoke through clenched teeth. "He wanted to tell me how much he loves my peach pie."

Lars told the crowd everything was okay, they got back in and the SUV continued up the street. I slunk back into the crowd but kept up with the float from a distance until the parade ended and Little was back in the restaurant. I wouldn't hear the end of that for a while, but looking foolish was a small price to pay for keeping my brother safe.

To avoid the hordes of tourists that overtook the town after the parade, I headed to Branson to have lunch with Thor and my former *StarTribune* co-workers.

We met at Luigi's Pizza, a Branson institution for thirty years. Waiters wound through tables delivering beer and pizza to noisy students, locals and tourists. Cynthia and I talked newspapers and Jason watched the door until Thor showed up. Her dimpled baby face radiated wholesomeness beneath the oversized ball cap. Thor hardly acknowledged Jason when she slid into the booth next to him. His expectant smile dimmed. Maybe she meant it about going back to school this time.

Jason, Cynthia and I ordered a pizza to share, loaded with everything. Thor ordered a personal-sized one for herself. Her specifications hadn't changed since the last time I'd been with her at Luigi's. "No cheese, veggies only, heavy on the spinach, and a Hef." We all stared at her. Her cornflower blue eyes popped open. "What? Who has pizza without beer?"

We caught up on what everyone had been doing in the three months since I'd left the bureau. The waiter brought Thor's Hefeweisen and the pizzas came shortly after.

I asked Thor, "How's Wilcox doing on finding Charley's family?"

She sipped her beer. "No luck so far, but he's been following up on a business card we found in Charley's jeans at the scene." She looked sick for a moment but composed herself. "And he's checking calls from the same St. Louis number that's on the card."

I leaned in. "Whose card?"

Her fingers flew to her mouth. "I did it again. I'm not supposed to tell you anything."

I almost grabbed her arm. "What did the St. Louis person want with Charley?"

Her teeth clamped down on a slice of pizza.

I remembered watching Charley pick up that business card and tell me he had to cancel our coffee because something had come up. And that was the last anyone had seen him alive. I'd work on Thor later. Reaching in for a slice, I told the group I'd stirred up a World Church of the Creator offshoot in Iona and why.

Cynthia said, "I can ask the *Iona Weekly* editor to keep an eye on them, although I'm sure they already do."

Jason took his eyes off Thor for a minute. "You want me to do some research, see what I can find?"

"Thanks guys, it would be a huge help." I enjoyed watching the way the couple glanced at each other out of the sides of their eyes. Jason in navy polo and khaki shorts and Thor in her American flag t-shirt seemed mismatched, but opposites do attract. Although, Thor wasn't smiling at him today.

I missed the camaraderie of this trio. An inner voice nagged that I'd made a mistake in quitting the bureau to jump back into the fast-paced and competitive *L.A. Times,* but I dismissed it. You have to give up something to get something else.

Back in Spirit Lake, I passed the packed Little's and drove home. Rock and Knute barked from the porch at an older pickup idling in my driveway. It took me a second to place it. My instinct was to back out of the drive and call Wilcox but curiosity got the better of me.

Rock ran to my car as I pulled up next to the truck. Matthew Willard sat in the driver's seat. Ready to stomp on the accelerator if necessary, I leaned across my passenger side. "What can I do for you?"

His eyes flicked at me and back down at his steering wheel. "I came by to talk but I don't have much time. I'm supposed to be collecting junk."

The kid didn't look scary to me. "Sure, let's sit on the dock." We got out of our vehicles and I pointed to my dock, waiting for him to go first. If he messed with me, I'd throw his scrawny body into the lake.

My dock widens into a T at the end. I'd bought a table and chairs set in anticipation of sitting there with Ben, watching the sunset. Wondering if we'd be together soon, I let the wistful image go and followed Matthew. I pulled out one of the chairs at the teak table. "Have a seat."

A fisherman in the cove next to my place cast his line. I waved, hoping he'd stay and fish until Matthew left. He waved back and I saw it was Neil, the creepy guy from the writers' group. The last thing I wanted was his attention.

Matthew wore the same type clothes I'd seen him in before. Dusty jeans, plain t-shirt, work boots, buzz-cut hair. "How did you know where I live, Matthew?"

He darted a look at me. "After you were at our place, my Dad got on the computer, and made a couple of calls. He can always find out stuff."

"He sent you?"

His head snapped up. "Uh, no, he told me to keep away from you."

"And yet here you are. What's on your mind?"

He looked troubled. "I'm here because I didn't think it was right that they were trying to scare you yesterday."

I could feel my eyebrow shooting up. "You're not part of the anti-gay faction of the World Church of the Creator?"

"I don't want to be."

"But you did those things that got you sent away."

"Yes, but that was before. In prison, they had me talk to therapists and social workers and I got that what I did was wrong."

This didn't sound like the Matthew who had a gun pointed at my head the other day, but maybe he'd been putting on a show for his parents. "What makes your folks so hate-filled?"

He shrugged. "They've always bashed the government and minorities. They didn't single out gays until they found out about my brother." He bit his lip.

Did he mean to say that? "Your mother said he left home and hasn't been back."

"Trevor ran off about three years ago."

He faced the water so I couldn't look in his eyes. "What did you think about your brother?"

"I always looked up to him but I wanted to be a tough guy like my dad. I wanted my mom to respect me. They both said the devil had hold of Trevor."

My voice measured, I asked, "Did your group kill Charley?"

He shook his head. "We didn't even know about him until we saw it on the news."

I stood over him, louder now. "Did you write the message on my brother's restaurant?"

His head tilted. "Huh? I don't know who your brother is or what restaurant you're talking about."

My hand gripped the back of his chair. It would be so easy to tip him into the water, but I didn't. Instead, I leaned close to his ear. "It's not something they talked about in your meetings?"

He checked his watch. "I gotta get back." His neck craned to scan the yard. "You got anything around here I could toss in the truck so the old man doesn't give me a bad time for slacking off?"

I toned down my rising anger. "I have a small pile behind the cabin."

He didn't need help tossing the rusted hand-mower, broken toaster oven and a few other items into his truck. The kid was stronger than he looked, wiry.

"Would you do me a favor, Matthew? If you hear the group talking about coming to Spirit Lake to do anything, please let me know."

"I can do that."

In case he was being sincere, I said, "And you need to figure out how to get away from your family and that group. I know it won't be easy, but you're a man now, and you ought to go your own way."

"I know I do." He got in his truck.

"If you want to talk to anyone, you can call me." I gave him my number and asked for his. He hesitated, but I waited him out until he told me. I tapped his cell number into my contacts, then focused the phone's camera on him. "Okay if I take your picture?"

"I guess so." He ran a hand through his hair.

His ordinary face framed by the truck window, Matthew turned to the camera, and grinned. I clicked and stepped back a few paces.

He pulled away, and I sat down hard on the porch steps. People will show themselves to a camera every time. His gaze had been everywhere but on me as we were talking, but he'd looked directly into the camera for his photo. I studied the close-up.

Matthew's grin revealed a mouth full of too many teeth jammed against each other every which way, long eyeteeth grazing his lower lip, tobacco stains in the crevices. The look in his eyes reflected pure meanness.

I walked to the edge of the lake, wanting to jump in and wash away the feeling that I'd been in the presence of something diabolical. Was that act to lure me in or keep me away? Had my arrival caught him about to do something to my cabin? I didn't know, but I was sure he had not seen the light in prison.

I ruffled Rock's fur and patted Knute's head. "Good watch dogging, doggies." Neil, the fisherman, had moved away from the cove. Now he knew where I lived.

***

I sometimes used Gert's mini-office between the cabin's laundry room and garage. The five-by-eight-foot office space was tight for someone my size, but there were some connections I preferred not to make on my own laptop. A rack of clothes hid the office door and even Ben didn't know about his aunt's secret office. I hated to keep secrets from him, but he was in a branch of law enforcement as a forest ranger and that meant following the rules. That didn't always work for me.

Gert's computer was useful for connecting with Sebastian, a young hacker from Minneapolis. She had rescued him from freezing to death in a fish house two winters ago. He'd gotten in trouble with his folks for a hacking prank that cost them a lot of money to fix.

Sixteen, depressed and guilty, he'd run away. While staying with Gert, Sebastian helped her figure out who embezzled from the Dreamcatcher casino. Gert's financial sleuthing got her killed. That was nearly two years ago. I found his email address on a sticky note on her computer and contacted him. Since then, he'd helped me a couple of times.

I booted it up. Usually nocturnal, I was surprised when he responded right away.

–Hey, Britt, what do you need?

Sebastian didn't do chitchat. I said hello and got to the point.

–It's not an emergency, but could you put your tentacles out and see if you can find a twenty-seven-year-old kid named Trevor Willard? He used to live in Iona Township, Minnesota. His parents are big into the World Church of the Creator.

–What are you doing messing with those haters?

–As little as possible, believe me. And one other thing I know is a longshot. I'm looking for background on a ninety-year-old Spirit Lake guy who moved here forty years ago. We don't know anything about his life before that or any family. His name was Charles Patterson. He was murdered.

–No problem. It's relaxing to kick back with this low-level stuff.

–Please tell me you aren't behind the collapse of the world economy.

–What's the challenge in that?

–How's college life?

–On summer break, doing security work for a bank.

His security work didn't mean he was the guy wearing a badge, positioned at the door to protect customers from bank robbers.

–That's ironic.

I couldn't see the smirk, but it was there. Sebastian signed off.

He was likely deep into figuring out how to prevent more hackers from breeching major financial institutions. I'd asked him details about how he worked, but understood when he brushed off my inquiries. If someone asked how I achieved a certain effect on a photo I usually said I just point and shoot. They wanted to hear what settings, lighting, lenses, all that. But after all these years, I don't think I could break it down anymore; that part was automatic, like driving a car. You use what you've learned and instinctively make the right moves at the right time.

I shut down Gert's computer and rolled the rack of plastic-covered winter clothes in front of the low doorway.

Too tired to attempt another nighttime vigil at the restaurant, I brought the dogs in and locked the front door. Then I closed the sliding door leading to the deck from my bedroom and locked it. That was a first; I loved falling asleep to the sound of waves against the shore. Wilcox had better find this guy quick. This was turning out to be a scary, depressing and lonely summer.

***

At five-thirty a.m. my phone woke me. Wondering if it was a dream repeating Little's call about the windows from two days ago, it took me a minute to answer. Lars' voice rose several octaves higher than a choir boy's. "You have to get down here right away. It's the bistro."

I could hardly push the words out. "Is Little hurt?"

"He's hyperventilating, but he's not hurt."

"What, then?"

"Just hurry."

Chapter 8

I rounded the corners on two wheels, slid into the restaurant driveway and ran toward the bistro. A deputy with his phone at his ear held up a hand. "You can't go in there."

Barreling past him, I stopped short just inside. In the eerie dawn light, the severed heads of a dozen squirrels, weasels, rats and an opossum hung from umbrella spokes. They smelled as if they'd been dead a while.

I wanted to run from the sight of their contorted grimaces, but I needed to get photos before Wilcox arrived and banned me from the scene. Little and Lars were together and safe, so I hurried back to the SUV and grabbed plastic booties and gloves. From long habit, I always kept extras in my camera bag.

The deputy, in his twenties, razor haircut and jaw thrust forward stood with his legs in a wide stance.

I asked, "Who are you? Where's Jerry?"

"I'm Riley. We changed shifts a couple hours ago."

"You didn't hear anything?"

His arms crossed over his chest. "I wasn't asleep if that's what you're suggesting." He shot a nervous glance at the parking lot, likely not looking forward to Wilcox's arrival.

I swept the area with my hand. "This took more than a few minutes." I stepped around Riley and raised my camera, ignoring the nausea and began documenting the scene.

Deep in concentration shooting close-ups of the cord used to tie the creatures' heads to the umbrella spokes, the sound of cars braking on gravel alerted me that my time was up. Doors slammed and Wilcox, Thor and Erik walked through the archway. Eddy, Spirit Lake's night watchman, pulled up shortly after, bleary-eyed. Everyone knew he nipped at a bottle during his rounds.

Wilcox was so busy tearing into Riley, he didn't have time to tell me to get out of there. Thor gasped when she saw the bistro. "This is twisted. I'd say creepy kids' prank if it wasn't for what happened to that old guy."

Wilcox registered my presence. "You have no business back here."

Normally, I wouldn't let him dismiss me without a fight but I turned without a word and went into the restaurant. I'd gotten what I needed and wanted to see my brother.

Little sat in a booth with his hands wrapped around a mug of hot tea. His whole body trembled. Lars sat next to him with his arm across Little's shoulders.

"Hey, Little," I said. His eyes didn't quite focus on me. I moved in close to his face. "The sheriff and all those people need coffee and something in their stomachs. I could use some coffee too."

Lars said, "Jaysus, Britt. Leave him alone. Can't you see he's upset?"

Little nudged Lars to move and scooted out of the booth. "Lars, put the coffee on and make it strong. I'm going to the kitchen to bake cinnamon rolls. That should mask that awful smell."

Lars threw a look at me over his shoulder on his way to make coffee. "I guess you know him better than I do."

My brother was wired for taking care of people, especially with food. Little gave me an order, too. "Tell Wilcox I'm opening at noon today so they'd better finish investigating fast so we can clean up that mess."

Lars' face turned green. "We're not going to serve out there today, are we?"

"Not today. We'll make a sign that says, 'Reorganizing Bistro. Open tomorrow.'" He vanished into his magic realm of pots and pans and ingredients.

It was still too early for the restaurant to open so we didn't have to explain what happened to any customers. I went to the bistro to tell Wilcox that Little wanted the creatures out of there ASAP so he could get the place cleaned up.

Wilcox narrowed his eyes at me. "I'm not cutting corners so his customers don't get upset."

I put up my hands in surrender. "Just the messenger. You noted the theme, right? What's this maniac doing?"

Wilcox took a minute to think it through. "He wants them too scared to open the restaurant. He might want them dead, but he has to get his kicks first."

The words Little and dead in the same sentence sent my system into the same catatonic state my brother had been in earlier.

Wilcox tugged the brim of his hat forward, his way of saying he was all business. "Anyone this crazy will show himself. I don't suppose we could get the guys to shut down the restaurant and leave the area until we find him?"

"Not a chance, Sheriff. Besides, how are we going to smoke him out if his target's gone?"

"It's not how *we* are going to find this guy." He jabbed his finger toward my chest. "You stay away from it. What *you* can do is stick close to Lars and Little."

Lars set a tray of coffee on the waiter's station just outside the door of the bistro. "Cinnamon rolls coming up."

Thor picked up a cup and thanked him. "I'm nearly done with fingerprinting and photographing. Erik is collecting the, uh, victims for me to check out at my lab."

I tried not to grimace. "You're going to autopsy rodents?"

She glared. "Their necks were all severed with a sharp instrument. I want to see if I can identify it, if the same one was used on all of them, and also what he used to tie them. It looks like ordinary fishing line, but we want to know for sure."

I asked Thor and Wilcox. "Do you want me to send my photos to you?"

Protecting her turf, Thor had bristled last year when the sheriff asked for my photos on a case, but we'd since resolved that issue. Two sets of eyes were better than one.

"Yes, send them." Wilcox didn't want to give me an opening to be involved in his case, but he wanted the photos.

I stared him down until he said it.

"Thank you." This time he stuck his finger in my face. "But this crime scene does not get in the paper."

"If it gets in the paper it won't be my doing. Little would be furious if customers were scared away." I took my coffee into the restaurant.

Wilcox came in half an hour later. "Let's talk."

Lars, Little, Wilcox and I had coffee refills and cinnamon rolls in front of us. I couldn't eat but the aroma was comforting.

Wilcox went through the drill, looking us each in the eye. "Have you seen anyone or anything suspicious, out of the ordinary, or had unusual conversations with people?"

Thinking of Matthew, I had trouble making eye contact with the sheriff.

Little said, "It's summer. Of course there are strangers and odd conversations with people."

Lars jumped in. "Summer people like to get to know the locals. They want to feel like it's their home away from home so they ask personal questions. They seem to want a relationship with us."

Little nodded. "The restaurant becomes their special place that they discovered and they go back home and tell stories about, in our case, the great restaurant run by the gay guys and how quaint we are and all that."

Lars said, "They like my fishing stories. I always tell them the best spots to go."

Little smiled at Lars. "We like it too. We get more customers and face it, it's good to be a popular destination."

Wilcox cut them off. "Okay, I get it." He turned his gaze on me. "You're not telling me something."

I plunged in. "Do you know anything about a hate group in Iona that's an offshoot of the World Church of the Creator?"

Wilcox's eyes bored in. "Only the bulletins we get from around the state when there's a flare-up of activity. You going to tell me why you're asking?"

I left nothing out, even the mysterious big project Matthew and his dad were keeping from the rest of the group, and that I'd seen several cans of black spray paint on a junk pile near their meeting place. "Then they caught me and I told them I wanted to interview Matthew for the paper."

Wilcox broke in. "You misrepresented yourself."

"They were pointing guns at me."

Little gasped. "You didn't tell us about that."

Wilcox paced in front of the booth. "They might not have even known about Little and Lars."

I ducked my head. I'd aroused the beast and now, even if they weren't involved before, they might retaliate. Hitting a popular restaurant would get the World Church lots of publicity. "Sheriff, I have the license plate numbers of some of the group if you want me to send them to you."

He nodded. "What else?"

"Yesterday, Matthew came to my cabin. He said he wanted to get out of the organization and he apologized for the way they treated me."

Wilcox looked like he needed an antacid. "You bought that?"

"At first I kind of did but then he did something that changed my mind." A shiver ran up my spine.

"And that was?"

"He smiled for the camera." I found the photo on my view finder and showed it to Wilcox and the guys.

Little recoiled. "That's not a smile. That's a tiger ready to pounce."

Wilcox blew out a frustrated sigh. "You can't condemn a kid because he's not photogenic." He pointed to Little and Lars. "You guys have never seen this kid in here?"

They said they couldn't be one hundred percent sure of it. Lars said, "It can be a zoo in the summer. People become a blur."

Wilcox jammed his cowboy hat lower over his forehead. "I'll assign a deputy inside the restaurant."

Little protested, but Wilcox put his hand up. "He'll be in civilian clothes. Britt, you'd be smart to stay with the guys. It will be easier for us to protect you if you're all in one place. I'm already shorthanded."

"What if they vandalize my cabin? Burn it down?" I wasn't sure how I could stop someone, especially if it was a group of the World Church people, but refused to leave the place unprotected.

"Why did I know you would say that, Johansson?"

"I'll ask Eddy to drive by my cabin a few times on his nightly rounds. With a deputy parked on the corner at Little's, the rest of the shops on Main Street should be safe, right? It wouldn't be leaving his usual rounds unprotected for long."

"If you won't budge, that's what we'll do."

"Plus, I have two watchdogs now," I said to the sheriff's retreating back.

Little eased out of the booth, his face drawn. He straightened his shoulders and said to Lars. "We're behind schedule. We'd better hustle if we're going to have the main café open for lunch." He walked to the kitchen like a drunk trying to appear sober.

Thor and Erik left with the bagged heads and other possible evidence. A van arrived and two men wearing jumpsuits walked toward the bistro. Thor used a discreet cleaning crew for situations like this. She said it was only the second time she'd had to call them.

Some of the staff arrived to begin their shifts and wanted to know what was going on. Lars said, "Someone vandalized the bistro. We won't be serving out there today."

By midafternoon, my mood matched the gloomy drizzle. The place was jammed with tourists and locals, who didn't know what to do if they couldn't swim, fish or race around the lake in speedboats. A few local fishermen would be out, but there were differing opinions about whether fishing was better or worse when it rained. That's what the subject at the counter was all about, with Lars right in the middle of it. The fisherman from the retreat sat next to him, gesturing and spouting off about his vast experience, arguing with everyone. It occurred to me that he might be riling up the group to get better information for his book. His presence annoyed me since the leering incident. People will show you who they are instantly if you're alert enough to catch it.

Little was in the bistro with Edgar, a nearly blind Ojibwe elder, who performed a cleansing ceremony to clear out the bad vibes. Native American culture was Little's specialty when he had taught anthropology at the University. Little visited the old guy and listened to his stories whenever he could get away from the restaurant and they'd become friends.

I slipped outside and stood under the awning next to Little. Edgar sang and waved a bundle of smoking sage. They estimated Edgar's age to be mid-nineties—but to me he was timeless. I wasn't even sure he was a mortal.

His grandson Henry, a big moon-faced man, guided him among the tables and chairs. Today, Edgar's waist-length white braids were tied off with simple red bands. Depending on which great-grandchildren did his hair that day, the braids might have colorful elastic bands or even sparkly bows at the ends. He wore his usual button-down denim shirt, his jeans held up by a concha belt.

After the ceremony, we trooped into the restaurant and crammed into a booth. Little brought Edgar's favorite chicken-wild rice hotdish to the table and excused himself to get back to the kitchen. We ate in silence.

Edgar was ready to talk about the bistro after Chloe cleared the dishes. The creases in his face folded in on themselves. "I'm troubled. The anger seems new and yet old."

That's exactly what I expected from Edgar. How was that supposed to be helpful? We had a bit of a history. He'd guided Ben and me to solve a couple of bad crimes but he was maddeningly nonspecific.

Still, I listened when he spoke. Edgar had lived on the reservation for so many years he was tuned into its land and people on levels I couldn't comprehend. If Edgar was disturbed by something out of the ordinary in Spirit Lake, people needed to pay attention.

Sometimes I could swear I saw a small group of ethereal Indians hovering behind him. He called them his ghost ancestors and seemed tickled that I'd sensed them. I kept trying to get a photo but they were never there when I checked the viewfinder. I didn't try to figure it out. It gave me a headache.

I trusted what I saw through my camera. Edgar believed what he saw when his eyes were closed, and sometimes our visions were not that far apart. That's as deep as I wanted to go on the subject.

Lars stopped to refill coffees. "Henry, how are things going at the Dreamcatcher?"

Henry had an MBA and was both tribal chairman and casino business manager. His eyes disappeared behind his cheeks when something amused him, and that was often. "The bad weather this summer has been good for business. In fact, I'd better take Edgar home and get back to work."

I rose from my seat. "Time for me to go home, too." Edgar's claw-like hand clamped over my wrist. "Be careful. Trouble is seeking you from more than one direction."

A chill snaked up my spine. "I'll be careful." Little had gone to the kitchen when Edgar tossed that one at me or he would have had an instant panic attack on my behalf.

Once again, Edgar had spooked me. I kept glancing into the woods on the drive home.

Chapter 9

Ben's green Forest Service truck was in my driveway. He waved to me from the dock when I pulled in. I jumped out of my SUV, raced across the wooden slats and threw myself at him, almost knocking us both into the lake. "Why didn't you tell me you'd be here?"

The corners of his eyes crinkled. "I wanted to surprise you."

I couldn't take my eyes off him—wide-shouldered, short brown hair, lean, taller than me, hawk nose and eyes that slanted down at the outside, a fan of fine lines around them. "You look great, Ben."

He held me close and whispered into my ear. "It's been a long three months." I put my arms around his neck for a real welcome home kiss.

Our arms circling each other's waists, I led him across the porch and opened the sliding door to my bedroom. We made love to the sound of gentle rain and waves lapping against the shore, making up for the months apart.

Later, still wrapped together in bed, he stroked my hair and I burrowed into his side. We talked about going out for dinner but weren't ready to untangle. We were so relaxed and happy when we were horizontal but often clashed in our vertical lives. It was my fault. I'd left him twice, once for twelve years and again last year when I'd briefly gone back to my philandering ex-husband.

Still, cozy as we were, something was on his mind. He'd always drawn inside himself when upset. Ben wasn't talkative as a rule, unless it was about the latest technology gadget that helped catch bad guys. Then you couldn't shut him up. He hated that too much of his time as a forest ranger was spent going after the two-legged animals, when all he really wanted to do was take care of the creatures and natural habitat of the forests. But he did like the gadgets.

This was a different quiet. Curled against him, loving his warm, bare skin touching mine, breathing in his woodsy male scent, I said, "You've started to say something twice now and then stopped. What is it?"

He disengaged from my web of limbs and hair. "Are you spending so much time with Edgar you're taking on his skills?"

"Today was the first time I've seen Edgar since I got back. He warned me about being careful, but he always warns me about that. Don't change the subject, what's wrong?"

His thumb traced a strand of hair falling across my eye. His hazel eyes, warm with love only moments ago, now were almost black, unreadable. "I want to be here now to protect you and the guys and work with Wilcox to find out who's doing this."

A huge weight lifted. "That's what I want too. I'm so glad you're back." I'd spent my entire career in precarious situations with no Ben and managed to handle it so far, but this thing with Charley unnerved me.

He left the bed and stood facing Spirit Lake. "I want to be here, but there's been a breakthrough on that border trafficking ring, and they need me back in the Boundary Waters."

I went to him, my fingers trailed down his chest and almost holding my breath, said, "It will never be finished, will it?"

He caught my hand in his and brought it to his lips. "It's an impossible task. It would take armies of rangers, police, FBI and ICE to stop them. All we can do is slow them down." His jaw tightened. "But we're close to containing this one cell."

I went into the bathroom and turned on the shower, dreading the lonely summer ahead. "When do you have to leave?"

He followed with a heavy sigh. "They expect me tomorrow." We undressed and stepped in, holding each other as the water streamed over us. I wanted to throw a tantrum or at least whine, but since I left him three months ago to begin a new contract for the *L.A. Times*, I swallowed it. It was hard for him too and I didn't want to make it worse.

Ben soaped my hair and massaged my back and I groaned in pleasure. We made sudsy love, only this time as if outside forces were tearing us apart and this was our last chance together.

We went to Little's for a late dinner. Little, Lars and Ben chatted about subjects unfamiliar to me due to the gap in years when I'd been away from Spirit Lake. It made me regret what I'd missed.

Ben had a beer and I sipped tea as the guys closed up. He urged me to stay at his place in Branson until Wilcox caught the killer. "This guy is sick. You live by yourself in the woods. Think about it."

"Nobody has threatened me. I want to help keep an eye on Little and Lars, and your home is too far away." He bit off his response and we didn't talk about it anymore.

After the restaurant closed, the four of us went to their apartment in back. Lars and Little sat across from Ben and me on the sofa.

We talked about Charley. Little said, "He never got close enough to anyone to be actual friends, other than our dad."

Ben nodded. "I remember rhododendron plants showing up on Aunt Gert's step in the summer. I think she stopped in to see him once in a while."

The guys were exhausted from the harrowing morning and long, busy day. We said goodbye, making sick jokes about what they might find next in the restaurant. Laughing about it helped keep the fear at bay.

They said goodbye to Ben. "We wish you didn't need to leave right away."

His face clouded. "Me too. Take care of yourselves."

When we were outside, I bee-lined for Jerry's car, stationed at the front of the café. "Hey, Jerry, can I get your cell number?"

Jerry said, "That was Riley who messed up last night. He's on desk duty now. You don't need to call if that's what you're thinking. Wilcox will end my career if I let anything happen on my watch."

He gave me his number anyway. "You should have it in case."

Ben's arm settled on my shoulder. "Let's go home. I wouldn't be surprised if Wilcox calls him every hour."

At the cabin, I brought in Rock and Knute and locked the door. Ben and I talked for a long time. He'd been my best friend when we were kids and sharing everything with him now came naturally. Our romance was a fairly new development and we were still finding our way.

With his arms wrapped around me, I slept, almost at peace. Car lights flashed across the cabin several times during the night, waking me each time. A peek out the window reassured me that Eddy was on duty. Earlier, he'd said, "Don't you worry about anything, Britt. I got you covered."

***

Sunlight slanted across the bed, waking me. I squeezed my eyes shut against the glare and stretched like a cat, still tingling from the night with Ben. How had I lived for so many years without him, and how was I going to manage our long distance romance in the future? I tried to keep from thinking about how cold and barren my bed, and life, would be again.

I reached for him but touched only twisted sheets. My eyes fully opened. Had he left already? In a moment, the aroma of brewing coffee reached my nostrils. Kitchen sounds reassured me.

I needed to hear Little's voice and picked up my phone to tap in the café's number. From the pans clanking and the whir of his industrial mixer, I could tell he was already in the restaurant. My shoulders lowered in relief. "How'd it go last night?"

"I got up early to fix Jerry breakfast before he signed off. He said nothing happened except for Wilcox's voice on his phone every couple of hours."

"Ben said he'd do that." I laughed, thankful that nothing had happened during the night, although a voice in the back of my mind warned that the killer would wait until the authorities relaxed their vigilance then strike again, and it wouldn't be when anyone was watching.

"Wilcox has a guy coming to babysit us inside the restaurant. Enjoy your time with Ben. I gotta go, I need both hands."

Little's calm attitude helped, and his advice about enjoying what little time I had left with Ben sounded like a good idea. I pulled on a t-shirt and tiptoed into the kitchen. He stood at the sink, his back to me. I slipped up behind him and kissed his neck, but instead of taking the hint, he turned away to pour a cup of coffee for me.

I said, "Your mind must be on something other than last night."

He handed me the cup, his jaw set. "I'm going up to the Boundary Waters this morning to turn the case over to another investigator. I'll be gone two days max. I'm not leaving Spirit Lake with a murderer after Little and Lars, and I can't be worrying that you'll be in the middle of it."

My mouth dropped open. I wanted him to stay but the trafficking case was his project. He'd been lead on it for more than six months, eating, sleeping and chasing down every thread. They'd cut off the tentacles and most of the Hydra heads but there were still a few left and this was supposed to be the final push to stop this cell. Without this final blow, the organization would build itself back up and soon be running at full throttle again, all that time and effort a waste.

"There's no way to get someone else up to speed in time." I couldn't believe my own words. "It's your project. You have to see it through."

"I'm not going."

I was familiar with the look, head lowered like a bull, subject closed. This time I used my brain before my mouth. "You're always telling me Wilcox is as good as they come. He's got a task force working on this. The Minnesota Bureau of Criminal Apprehension might get involved if they decide it's a hate crime."

"The BCA investigator is working with us in the Boundary Waters. Their teams are spread pretty thin now, too."

That wasn't surprising news since the BCA covered the entire state. "Well then, the FBI. Just do your own job, you shouldn't have to do the sheriff's."

His head snapped around to look me full in the face. "That's funny coming from you, the crusader who has to take charge of everything, including Wilcox's job."

He had me there. "Please, Ben, I promise I won't do anything but wait for Wilcox to handle things. You know you need to go."

I eventually convinced him to leave, but asked a favor before he went. "Wilcox won't tell me what leads he's working on. Someone left a business card at Charley's two days before I found him dead and he'd gotten calls from that same person. Do you know anything about that?"

"We've talked. He's checking out someone who was trying to buy Charley's place. So far there's nothing suspicious."

"Do you have a name?"

He kissed me. "Morris Bolger, but if Wilcox gets anything, he'll deal with it."

I moved away from him. "You must know more than that."

He set his cup in the sink. "There are allegations in St. Louis of strong-arm behavior, but so far he's avoided any criminal charges. His attorney contacted Charley a number of times and Bolger's been to Charley's house. But they haven't been able to put him together with the hate stuff."

"What else? The sheriff must have other leads, since he's not that interested in the Willards."

"He's been to the resort interviewing the people in that writers' group."

That caught my attention. "Why them?"

"They hang out at Little's a lot. It's just routine."

"What are their stories?"

"I've only met Vik Baaker, the workshop leader. He's a prof from Northwestern. Older guy, staying at the big cabin with the two students from his class, a kid from India and a young woman from Illinois. Vik says they usually have about ten to twelve, but half of them canceled this year because of the bad weather."

"What about that tall woman?"

"Anke Schmidt. She's from Germany." He rolled his eyes. "Patty says she smokes in the cabin. That's not allowed."

I said, "I think Peder stays on my side of the lake. I don't know where the fisherman is staying. He's a creep but he and Lars are friendly."

"Neil stays at his friend's cabin on the north shore. Wilcox is watching him. He has anger issues and his ex-wife's got a restraining order on him in Duluth."

Pushing it, I asked, "Did Wilcox come up with any evidence from his interviews with them?"

"It's been hard for Wilcox to pin down alibis because Vik doesn't schedule regular sessions. They come and go. He says he likes to keep it 'loose and creative.' Now, no more questions."

He left within an hour. To watch him go even though I sent him away left me miserable. I'd done the right thing, although seeing Ben was my most important reason for coming back to Spirit Lake. I'd missed him so much. Of course, Little and Lars, Rock and my friends meant a lot to me, but it was Ben I ached for all those months. The summer was going much too fast. He had to come back before I left for South Sudan.

I sat on the porch swing and wallowed. Knute made his arthritic way up the few steps and put his white muzzle on my knee, taking my mind off Ben. It was time to find out what an old bachelor and the guys had in common other than that the old man might have been gay.

Lars answered this time when I called the restaurant. "Has Wilcox's inside guy shown up yet?"

"The sheriff said he's finishing up another job and will be here tomorrow."

Someone should be watching them today. I dressed, secured the windows and was out the door in ten minutes. I locked the front door and then stared at the key in the palm of my hand. Did I really expect a thumb-sized piece of metal to protect my cabin?

Rock jumped into the SUV and I boosted Knute in behind him. "Let's go keep an eye on the guys."

A slice of sunshine peeked through the café windows—customers lifted their heads like flowers bending toward the light. Lars was in the bistro, setting up the waiters' station with water pitchers, glasses and menus. I came up behind him. "Let me do that, Lars."

He hesitated, waiting for the catch. Okay, maybe I hadn't readily offered in the past. He cringed at the umbrellas above the tables. "I don't even want to be out here."

"Why open it?"

His head tilted toward the kitchen. "Little insists and the customers love it. They don't know what happened. Some of the townspeople saw the police over here but assumed it was kids vandalizing, nothing serious."

I stuck my hands in my jeans pockets. "I'm planning to hang around so anything I can do to help, let me know."

Lars still looked at me like I was an alien but handed me an apron with long strings. "You could bus tables and refill beverages, but try to stay out of the staff's way."

He wasn't being rude, the people who worked at Little's zipped around at warp speed. He pointed at my head. "You'd better borrow a hair band from Chloe to tie that back. You know how Little feels about loose hair."

This wasn't the time to argue. I pulled it into a single braid and wound a rubber band around it. Hair dutifully subdued, I grabbed a bin and started clearing empty tables. I knew how the process worked and handled tasks that brought me close to each customer.

I checked out everyone who entered, looking for someone suspicious, or maybe one of the Willards' crew. Even without the worry over Little and Lars, due to years as a photojournalist, I generally looked at people with distrust. Most of them were in the news for a reason—bad behavior.

Lars sidled up after an hour. "Smile at the customers. Your hard stares are scaring them."

I nodded with no intention of letting up on my surveillance, but the next few hours of filling water, tea and coffee, fetching doggy bags, answering questions and setting tables made me lose concentration. I'd even graduated to schlepping plates of food. Little didn't tolerate customers getting cold food.

Edgar's cleansing ceremony must have worked. Groups of families drank their sodas and iced teas outside in the sunshine. Moms spooned ice cream into the open mouths of toddlers. At another table, three ladies were having an animated conversation. The writers' group showed up mid-afternoon and sat at their usual table. Neil followed Lars around complimenting him and trying to talk about fishing. Ben's admission that Wilcox checked them out made me feel better about the sheriff. Just because he didn't share his investigation with me didn't mean he wasn't moving forward.

For a moment, I almost believed whatever evil had blown into Spirit Lake had blown back out.

My brother didn't surface until four in the afternoon when he plunked down beside me at the counter. I had slipped out of my gym shoes and was resting my aching feet.

"I've been watching you. Want a job? Of course, we'll have to give you a few more pointers on being pleasant to the customers, but you have the work down. I could use more like you."

That was a huge compliment coming from him. Lars dropped onto the seat next to Little. I asked, "Where's your shadow?"

Lars grinned. "Neil's going to use what I've told him about my best fishing spots in his book." He looked wistful. "I haven't been on the lake in a long time."

Little stretched and headed to the kitchen. "Time to prep for dinner." Lars raised an eyebrow at me. "You staying for the dinner shift or have we worn you out?"

"I'm staying."

"Why don't you take off for a while? We're fine."

I unwrapped myself from the apron. "The dogs could use some exercise."

I'd left Rock and Knute snoozing in the grass behind the restaurant, but both dogs were barking at a pickup sliding around the corner. It looked like the Willards' truck and I ran to get a better view. It was gone. Rock and Knute trotted back to me.

Neil and another fisherman stood outside the restaurant entrance. Neil's words carried back to me. "Just because I talk to Lars about fishing doesn't mean I'm one of them. I need to pick his brain."

The evil in Spirit Lake hadn't blown back out after all.

Chapter 10

Knute slumped by the restaurant's back door and wouldn't budge but Rock danced around, itching to go for a walk. I put Knute inside, took off my gym shoes and slipped into my flip flops to give my aching feet some air and locked the door.

Rock and I started toward the lake when someone called my name. Peder came up behind me carrying two bags of groceries.

"I'm making my own dinner tonight for a change." His sunny smile was almost an antidote to the events this week.

"Would you like help with those bags?"

He passed one over to me. "I was hoping you'd ask. It's awkward with two."

I took the bag and he bent down to pet Rock. "Interesting coat."

"People say he looks like someone splashed him with black and white paint. His name is Rock."

Peder ruffled Rock's fur again. "I miss my Sasha and Tasha."

"Your dogs?" I shifted the bag to my right side.

He reached into his book bag, opened his wallet and showed me a photo of two identical Siberian Huskies. "They are my children." The silvery dogs stared from the photo with ice-blue eyes.

"They're stunning." They looked like him, especially the eyes.

"Sasha and Tasha were all I wanted from the divorce."

"I'm a divorced dog lover myself." I smiled. "How's your poetry coming along?"

"I'm having a bit of writer's block at the moment, but tea at Little's helps me forget about it for a while. I noticed you working and tried to catch your attention to say hello."

"We were all busy today."

"You must be close with your brother. That's nice. I don't have any siblings."

"Little's well-being is the most important thing in the world to me. And that includes Lars because he's the best thing that's ever happened to Little."

Peder's head tilted and I stopped speaking. The tension in my voice even scared me. I'd have to try harder to relax. Peder was so cheerful.

He smiled. "Your brother's lucky."

"Coming back to Spirit Lake and opening a restaurant were huge risks for him but with Lars behind him, he did it. So Lars is right up there on my list of people I love." That was better. More upbeat.

Peder stowed his bag under a seat, teetering as I handed him the other one. His hand touched mine as he took it from me. "So there's no boyfriend on your list of loves?" His smile was teasing and testing.

It had only been a few hours since Ben and I were together, and I still felt the warmth of his arms around me. "I do have someone. We have a long history."

He tucked the bag next to the first one and hopped back out of his boat. "We hardly talked the last time we had coffee together. Please join me." He sat on the edge of the dock. "It's the writer's block. I can't face the computer just yet."

I stepped out of my flip flops and dangled my feet in the water. "So you're using me to procrastinate."

"Maybe, just a little."

His shy smile won me over. I took my camera from my pocket. "Let me take your photo."

He got to his feet in one graceful motion. "I'm honored, but I'm not a very good subject."

I stood up too. "No need to pose. Just look into the camera for me, only please take off the dark glasses." I wasn't above a bit of flattery to get what I wanted. "Your eyes are blue with a bit of sparkle like the lake, and I'd like to catch that."

He turned away mid-click. "You said you and your boyfriend have a long history?"

Lots of people are camera shy, especially with close-ups. I put it back in my pocket and gazed across the lake toward Ben's resort on the point. "Ben and I have known each other since middle school. I hadn't been back to Spirit Lake for years and had lost touch with him, but I came back here to work for the *Minneapolis StarTribune* and our connection was still there. Unfortunately, with our jobs that connection gets tenuous at times."

"And now you work for the *L.A. Times*?"

Rather than going into the whole story, I simply nodded. "That's right."

"Where's this Ben now? I haven't seen you with him."

I hesitated, not wanting to encourage Peder's personal interest, but I liked his easy manner after all the tension. "He was here yesterday. He works for the forest service and is on a project in the Boundary Waters area."

His brow furrowed so I explained. "The Boundary Waters Canoe Area Wilderness is a million acres of forest, with more than a thousand lakes and streams that borders Minnesota and Canada. People refer to it as the BW."

"Impressive." Peder looked closely at me. "Ben means a lot to you, but not as much as your photojournalism work. Do I have that right?"

I slipped into my flip flops. "That's apples and oranges. You can't compare." I called to Rock. "Time to go, buddy."

His smile faded. "I've said something wrong. Sometimes I don't quite get the nuances of the English language. I just assumed that since you left here, your *L.A. Times* job was your priority. I'm sorry, please don't leave."

I softened. "It's not you, I really do need to get back to the restaurant." Over my shoulder, I said, "Good luck with your writing."

Opening up to a new acquaintance was rare for me, but Peder's chatty teasing and questioning made me forget my worries. Still, he didn't get my relationship with Ben at all.

Several cars were pulling into Little's parking lot, the dinner crowd already arriving. I herded Rock into the back door, patted Knute's head and put food in their bowls before returning to the restaurant.

The staff had changed from the morning crew. A different cook's helper and dishwasher were in place in the kitchen. The only ones who worked from opening until closing were Lars and Little. I'd always thought the winters must be rough for them when business was so much slower, but they probably welcomed the rest.

Little waved as I walked through the kitchen. Mostly all females worked at the restaurant. Lars told me once that even though the townspeople loved the restaurant and liked them, they didn't want their sons to be unduly influenced. Boys didn't want to be thought of in that way, so few applied anyway. Small prejudices over time are as hurtful as the blatant ones. The guys overlooked a lot of it, but what they had to endure infuriated me. I had to alert Lars that Neil was using him. Lars thought he'd made a new friend.

Bella and Violet showed up for dinner and I took waters to their booth. Bella picked up a menu. "We wanted to see you in an apron." She peered at me above her glasses. "Ben must have made quite an impression last night. I hope you didn't wear your hair like that."

My hand involuntarily tucked a loose strand of hair behind my ear. At Little's insistence, I'd pulled my braid into a bun at the nape of my neck.

Violet made a face at her mother. "It's nice you're helping out, Britt. You look quite regal with your hair like that."

By the time the customers were gone and the place cleaned and readied for morning, it was after eleven. "How do you guys do this every day?" I took off a shoe and rubbed my sore foot.

Lars pointed to my feet. "I can fix that. Come on."

I followed them back to their apartment. Little sat in his recliner and I moved a pile of linens from the sofa, grateful to be off my feet. Lars left the room, returning in a few minutes with an electric foot spa filled with hot water. "This always helps."

He brought one for Little and another one for himself. Little dumped in what he called special rejuvenating herbal essences, and the three of us stuck our feet in the bubbling tubs and cranked up the television volume to hear the news.

Happily percolating, I asked, "Do you always keep an extra foot bath for guests?"

Little said, "We bought new ones but Lars wanted to keep one of the old ones for emergency backup."

"I'm glad Lars is a hoarder. This is heaven." Rock stuck his nose too close to the bubbles and snorted. Knute wasn't having anything to do with it.

Lars said, "I suppose we won't see you tomorrow. Too much work for an old gal like you."

Ready to shoot back with a rundown of my daily routine of swimming, squats, situps, pushups and weights to keep myself in shape for the physical work I did as a photographer, I saw the twinkle in his eyes and stopped. He was using reverse psychology, and it worked.

"I'm not taking my eyes off you guys during the day."

Little frowned. "We want to keep an eye on you, too, but why don't you just hang out? We have enough help."

"From what I could tell, there's never enough help. It's a bottomless pit of customers. You know I'd lose my mind sitting at the counter all day."

Our banter was almost forced, as if we were pretending everything was normal. The threat out there kept it from being the cozy scene we all craved.

I took my spa into the bathroom, rinsed it and left it in the tub. Little was nodding off. He had to get up at dawn again. I peeked out the window. "Jerry's on duty so I'm taking off."

A loud sound outside like a firecracker made us all jump and Rock started barking.

My phone was out in an instant. I tapped in Jerry's number. "What happened out there?"

"Everything's good, just an old pickup backfiring."

I told the guys what Jerry said but Little chewed on his lower lip, a sign he was nervous. I said, "The dogs can stay with you guys. Rock's the best security around."

Little said, "What about you?"

"This guy isn't targeting me but if it makes you feel better, I'll ask Eddy to swing by my cabin when he's doing his rounds."

He bit his lower lip. "If you're sure."

"Of course."

I double-checked all the doors, waved to Jerry and went home. Toes still tingling from the foot bath, I pulled into my driveway. Last night with Ben had been wonderful, but not exactly restful. I needed a good night's sleep.

***

Eddy didn't answer my call so I left a message. At the cabin, I listened to Norah Jones as I undressed, stepped into the bathroom and turned on the shower.

Warm water rolling down my back carried the tension away. I closed my eyes, nearly falling asleep standing up, then reached for the shampoo with a sigh. There was no hurrying up the washing and rinsing process with long hair.

I paused at a slight sound above the music. It wasn't Rock and Knute roaming around, they weren't with me. Prickling at the back of my neck made me uncomfortable enough to turn off the water and listen. Nothing. I stepped out. The hair on my arm raised. I always left the bathroom door open to let the steam escape but it was closed. I turned the knob and pushed. The door didn't open. That made no sense since it locked from inside. I jiggled it but it wouldn't budge. I rammed the door with my shoulder and it gave slightly. Something was jammed against it from the other side.

The music stopped. I stiffened. A door closed and I yelled, "Who's out there?" I scrambled for my cell but it wasn't on the sink where I'd set it. Only my camera was still there.

I slammed against the door until my shoulder and hip ached, then stopped to catch my breath. The bathroom had one tiny window set high, ten inches by twelve, just big enough to let in fresh air. Even though the closest house was a mile away, I stood on my tiptoes and screamed anyway.

When my voice was too hoarse to yell anymore, and terrified that the killer did this to make it easier to get to Little and Lars, I kicked the door with my bare feet until they were numb.

Toward morning, I wrapped a towel around my body and slid to the floor holding my hair dryer for a weapon, waiting for him to come for me.

Chapter 11

My land line ringing in the living room woke me. It rang, stopped and rang again. Shortly after that, my mobile phone chimed from somewhere close. Maybe the bedroom. He hadn't taken it, only moved it out of my reach. The caller tried several times, then silence. Whoever was on the other end would guess I wasn't home and when my cell didn't work, assume I was out of range and give up. Little and Lars would eventually miss me and come looking. If they were okay. A chill crept up my spine.

I rubbed my bruised shoulder and splashed cold water on my face. Haunted eyes ringed by dark circles stared back at me from the mirror. A beam of light shining through the tiny window told me it was morning.

Not long after the phones quieted, I stiffened at the sound of a door banging open. Then Little and Lars called my name. Relief flooding my system, I rewound the towel and banged my fist against the door. "I'm locked in the bathroom."

Feet stampeded through the bedroom, the door opened and I threw myself at them.

Little said, "Are you okay? You said you were coming to work this morning and when you weren't there and didn't answer your phones, we knew something was wrong."

"I'm fine, and relieved that you and Lars are okay. I was worried he might try something at the restaurant."

Lars showed me a metal pipe with a rubber grip on the bottom. "He wedged this against the door."

The top part was forked to fit snug under the door knob. I'd seen them in the hardware store—the poor man's security system.

I grabbed Little's shirt, thinking arson. "Who's watching the restaurant?"

"Seth is there and Jerry's with us. He's keeping watch outside," said Lars.

Little pried my hands from his shirt and headed toward the kitchen. "Why don't you sit for a minute? I'll make you a cup of tea."

Lars cleared his throat. "Wilcox will be here soon. Maybe you want to get dressed?"

They were treating me like a delicate two-year-old and I was grateful but couldn't sit down. "I'll have tea later, Little." I tossed on jeans and a shirt, grabbed my camera and walked through the cabin, looking for anything out of place. Wilcox would be angry that I was destroying evidence by moving around in the space, but the guys had already run through it looking for me.

The intruder had unlocked every door and left the windows wide open. He'd broken the back lock to get in. Nothing else was disturbed. Then I saw the message and froze, camera half-way to my eyes. The words "You Can't Protect Him" were laid out on the table next to my laptop. The slight breeze moved a few of the letters out of line but it was readable. I swallowed and raised my camera.

Little stood beside me looking down at the message, his face white. "Does he mean me?"

Lars put his arm around Little's shoulders. "Jaysus."

When the sheriff's car screeched into the driveway, I was outside taking photos and looking for footprints. Wilcox barked. "Thor's on her way. She'll take care of that. What happened here last night?"

"I didn't hear or see anyone, Sheriff. I'd locked all the doors and windows, but he sneaked into the bathroom while I was showering, took my phone and locked me in."

Wilcox walked around the side of the cabin and returned in a few minutes. "The back door lock was broken."

I'd already taken a photo of the broken lock. He went inside and checked the bathroom first, and then the rest of the house. I followed. He stood in the doorway of the former guest bedroom. "What's all this?"

I'd stored the guest bed in the garage and filled the room with weights, jump rope and resistance band and installed a pullup bar in the doorway. "I don't think anything's been touched in here," I said.

He pointed to a thirty-five-pound kettle bell. "You're lucky he didn't bash you with that."

Thor showed up wearing a graphic comics t-shirt and camo pants, her ears loaded with an assortment of skull studs. She hauled her fingerprint kit and bag of tricks into the cabin.

I showed her the pipe and she bagged it. "We'll see if we can get any prints from it. The sheriff will check hardware stores. Maybe a clerk will remember someone buying it."

Wilcox stood behind her. "Thank you, Thor."

She stammered. "I'll do the bathroom first." She'd told me the sheriff didn't like having to remind her that her job was to collect and preserve evidence, analyze it later if possible, and write reports. Period.

He stood at my table, his finger jabbing at the words. "He was sending a message that he could get to you any time he wanted."

I pointed to a photography magazine on the table. "He cut the letters from this."

"We'll see if he left fingerprints on it, but he's been careful so far." His eyes narrowed at me. "You're staying with Little and Lars. No argument this time. What the hell were you thinking leaving the dogs at Little's?"

I lifted my shoulders. "I didn't think I was on the killer's agenda, but I left a message for Eddy to come by on his rounds. Maybe he didn't get it."

Little and Lars went back to work and I followed an hour later. I dropped my overnight bag on the sofa in the guys' apartment for my sleepover. Wilcox didn't get an argument from me this time. Staying by myself at the cabin had lost its appeal.

Cynthia called as I filled coffees along the booths. "You're not going to like this. Wilcox convinced me to hold the piece on Charley and the vandalism and threats."

I was used to law enforcement holdback on specifics to keep the bad guy from finding out how much info the police had, but in this case Wilcox wanted to stop the entire story.

Walking into the bistro where it was quieter, I whispered. "If I were the killer, I'd be more suspicious if nothing was in the paper. They'll know Wilcox thinks it's a big deal. What if we treat it like a rash of break-ins and vandalism in Spirit Lake, but don't connect them to Charley."

Cynthia said, "That's not big enough news for the *StarTrib*. What we'll do is give it to the *Branson Telegraph* for their weekly crime log."

That had to satisfy me and I got back to work clearing tables. We'd had our one sunny day of the week and now the sky threatened rain again, bringing tourists inside. When one group left, another hovered, waiting to be seated. My arms and feet ached as I hustled back and forth from kitchen to dining room.

Eddy showed up looking contrite. "I swear I drove by your place a couple of times but it looked okay."

"Don't worry about it. He was in and out fast." Eddy wasn't part of the police or sheriff's office. He might not even carry a gun. The town hired him as security a few years back, after kids broke into Olafson's and stole a case of beer.

At the end of the lunch rush, the three of us had our own late meal at a table near the kitchen. Little pointed out the dark circles that ringed our eyes. "We look like a family of raccoons."

Wilcox came in and sat with us, leaning in and speaking low. "My plainclothes detective is here. I don't want to scare you, but from past experience I believe whoever's doing this is about to escalate."

Little and Lars gulped in unison.

A man with graying facial stubble, wearing shorts and a t-shirt advertising Baywater Resort walked into the restaurant with a newspaper tucked under his arm. Wilcox said, "That's

Gene. He's familiar with the situation. Seat him so he's facing the door and has a good view."

Lars grabbed a menu and walked over to him. Little hurried back to the kitchen.

Gene couldn't have come at a better time. Now that he was watching the guys, I intended to find out why the Willards' truck was hanging around Little's yesterday. I whipped off my apron.

Wilcox pointed at my plate. "You didn't finish your lunch."

"I don't have time to sit around when someone is trying to hurt my brother. What are you doing about that hate group in your back yard?"

He leaned back, half-smiling, like he'd gotten the information he wanted without having to work for it. "You're planning to run out there and stir them up again." He pointed at the chair.

I plunked back down and we glared at each other. Lars seated Gene and came back with coffee for us. His eyes darted from me to Wilcox. "Keep it low, would you. No need to upset the customers." I forced a smile and he moved on to another coffee drinker at the counter.

Wilcox lowered his voice. "We're watching them and you could trample all over the headway we're making."

"You do think it's them."

"I don't speculate." He pulled his cowboy hat low over his forehead and slid out of the booth. "I'll know if you show up in Iona. I'm heading there now."

I rose from my seat. "Let me go with you." The guy had me sniveling in terror on my bathroom floor last night but now I was ready to go after him. If it was Matthew Willard or any of his group, they'd better watch out.

"No."

"A ride along. I'll take pictures." Action was the way I worked. I shot photos, asked questions, researched.

"Forget it." He leaned toward me, his hands splayed on the tabletop. "I don't have to remind you to stay here at the restaurant tonight, right? This guy would like to drag it out because he gets a kick out of scaring people, but what he might really want is instant gratification."

I sat back down. "I'm sleeping here tonight, Sheriff."

"Good." He left and, holding my temper in check, I retied my apron, cleared our table and moved on to others, hatching a plan. I hadn't checked Gert's computer for word from Sebastian.

After the dinner crowd, I told Lars I was going for a swim.

"Didn't you hear anything Wilcox told you?"

"This guy had a perfect opportunity to harm me last night. He only wanted to scare me."

"At least take the dogs if you're going." He walked away shaking his head.

***

Wilcox would call my coming back to the cabin alone reckless, but I didn't get this far in my chosen profession without learning to trust my instincts. I knew how to take precautions and defend myself. The sheriff had to go through all the proper channels. He'd talk to the Branson hate crime task force, keep the Iona police in the loop as a courtesy, have a guy unobtrusively questioning and watching, and it would take too long.

I opened the car doors and Rock bounded out and ran to the woods behind the cabin. I helped Knute, my mind churning. Questions about some of the people connected with the writers' group and that developer who was after Charley's property muddied my mental waters.

The water looked inviting. A swim would work the aches out of my body and clear my mind, but that would have to wait.

The dogs weren't agitated and I took that as an all-clear sign, but my stomach clenched when I walked in the cabin. I'd had a locksmith fix the back door but tested it anyway. Everything was in order.

Satisfied there'd been no visitors, I headed for my secret office and noticed the message light flashing on my land line. Ben had called. Hoping he was coming home, I listened to the message. "Hey Britt. It looks like I have to stay with it here.

You were right, no one is willing to take the lead on it after this much time."

My shoulders slumped, but I tried to keep the disappointment from my voice when I called him back. "It's okay. Wilcox is on it."

His voice dropped. "He told me about your cabin. You really should stay with the guys at night. Think of yourself as another layer of protection for them if you won't do it for yourself."

I stepped onto my deck. "So they got you to do their dirty work."

"Britt, this guy cut off Charley's head and stuck it on a stake. He took the time to capture and decapitate those animals and strung them up in the bistro as a warning. Wilcox doesn't have enough resources to post a deputy at your place too."

My skin crawled at the memory of those images. "I've already promised Wilcox I'd stay at Little's tonight."

"One other thing. I know you don't like to use a weapon, but now might be a good time to start carrying that SIG Sauer you keep in the closet."

He knew I hated guns and he wouldn't have suggested it if he wasn't seriously worried. "I'll think about it." I had already been thinking about it.

Hoping the conversation would turn personal, Ben cut it short. "I've got to go but you should get back to the restaurant."

"I'm almost out the door."

His voice lowered. "I miss you and I'm worried about all of you. Be careful."

I promised and we ended the call, both knowing he wouldn't stop worrying and I wouldn't be his version of careful.

Being alone in the cabin made me nervous, but I wanted to check in with Sebastian. With the dogs inside and the door locked, I loaded my SIG Sauer and carried it with me to the secret office between the laundry room and garage. I moved the rack of clothes camouflaging the doorway and entered the small space.

When the computer booted up, I checked for news from Sebastian using Gert's sign in. His reply was waiting for me.

—No hits on the missing Willard brother. The family hasn't been in contact through emails. They talk in code about meetings. Nothing overt on the emails. Re: Charles Robert Patterson, the birthdate on his driver's license is May 2, 1922. No fingerprints on record for him, no criminal charges. He didn't apply for his social security number until 1946 when he was hired at a nursery in Cleveland, Ohio. He moved to Spirit Lake in 1967. No family background info. Need more to go on. Later.

I sent an email thanking him and signed off, but continued to stare at the blank computer screen, wondering if Wilcox already had that information. Rock put his paw on my knee. Startled, I woke from my daze. "Right, let's go, buddy." I tucked the gun into my jeans, locked the room and drove back to the restaurant.

Chapter 12

My ringing cell phone jarred me awake. I jumped up to answer it and tripped over Knute, banging my knee on the coffee table. It was Jason, talking fast. "I'm in Cooper. There's been a fire and a guy's dead inside. A firefighter said something about accelerant."

Did every emergency have to happen at this ungodly hour? This was the third time I'd been called before dawn in a week. I rubbed my knee. "How'd you hear about it?"

"I bought a police scanner to have at my apartment. The fire call came in at four a.m."

My bleary eyes registered that the sun was just starting to rise. "Nice work, Jason." He'd clearly figured out that the best way to see Thor was to go where she went, and she was always at a death scene. "Who's the dead guy?"

"They don't know for sure, but probably Rob Jenkins, a local attorney."

Rob had handled Gert's will. He'd been the one to officially tell me Gert had left Rock, her cabin and a mile of lakeshore to me. I blinked the sleep out of my eyes. "Why are you telling me this, Jason?"

"Cynthia hasn't been able to get a stringer to come out this early."

I recalled the paunchy photographer in the green hatchback, too sickened to shoot Charley's murder scene. "Cynthia's calling me now." I hung up with Jason and answered. She got right to the point. "I doubt if this is anything the *StarTrib* will want, and I can only pay you the usual rate, but we need to cover all the bases in case this is a murder. The wolf is at the door."

She meant that management rumbled about shutting down the bureau every few months. They'd whittled the staff to nothing and expanded the coverage to the entire upper half of the state. It was no secret the bureau was on borrowed time. "I'm on my way."

Little and Lars watched me from their bedroom door. Little whispered, "What happened?"

I pulled on my jeans and threw a shirt over my tank top. "Rob Jenkins' law office burned down. They think it's his body inside. Cynthia wants me to take photos."

"How did the fire start?" asked Lars.

"I'll call you as soon as I find out."

The guys hustled to begin their day as I let the dogs out, brushed my teeth and grabbed my equipment bag. I joined Lars in the restaurant. He'd already made coffee. "Bless you, Lars." I filled a to-go cup, snagged one of yesterday's muffins and headed out the door. "Lars, would you bring the dogs back in for me?"

He nodded. "Be careful out there."

I stopped at my cabin, dug through a drawer for my old *Minneapolis StarTribune* ID and hung the lanyard around my neck just like old times.

The drive to Cooper, sixteen winding miles north of Spirit Lake, took barely fifteen minutes. An acrid stink assaulted my nostrils as soon as I hit town. Rob's office was on a side street near Nordic Souvenirs and a flower shop. A few people gawked from the post office parking lot across the street, as close as Wilcox would allow. Firetrucks, sheriff's vehicles, local police, ambulance and Thor's car were parked haphazardly, blocking the street. I pulled in behind them.

The shops that flanked Rob's office had suffered some damage, but the lawyer's office was nothing except charred remains. Jason stood outside the cordoned area talking to the fire chief. I took as many photos as I could until Wilcox stalked over to me. "What do you think you're doing?"

"Cynthia hired me."

"Not funny. Get back."

"Seriously, she wants me to get photos. Her guy's unavailable." I held up my *StarTrib* ID, glad I'd taken the time to grab it.

The fire chief called to Wilcox and I used the distraction to scoot under the yellow tape. No one stopped me. They must have seen me talking to Wilcox and assumed he sanctioned it. It would only last until he turned around so I worked fast.

There were no standing walls. Metal file cabinet carcasses lined one area. Hundreds of files had turned to ash. A melted computer and printer were lying on the ground above the remains of a desk. It was all sodden and reeked of smoke. I squatted and shot from that angle, then moved to higher ground to capture the big picture.

Thor joined me, her forehead smudged with soot. Her hand swept toward the burned office building. "This is way out of my league. An arson investigator from the Cities is on his way now."

I pointed to an ambulance leaving the scene. "Is that Rob?"

She nodded. "The body is on its way to the lab down there. Dental records will tell us for sure, but his car was the only one out front."

Everyone in Spirit Lake knew Rob. He'd been around forever and it wasn't unusual for him to work late hours. No one had mentioned a Mrs. Jenkins or kids.

I tore my eyes away from the scene and suppressed a smile at Thor's outfit. She wore a Laplander cap, plaid golf shorts and a striped shirt under her jean jacket. "How long have you been here?"

She covered her mouth with her hand and yawned, leaving another soot smear on her cheek. "Wilcox called me at ten after four this morning."

I was still circling and shooting. "What do you think? Arson, murder or accident?"

She followed, whispering. "Just between us, not an accident. The gasoline smell was really strong when I first arrived. Whether it was murder or not, I couldn't say. Maybe he did it himself."

Wilcox coughed behind us. "You in the speculating business now, Thor?"

"No sir, sorry." She edged away. I'd been on the other side of that Wilcox sarcasm in the past. The only difference was that it didn't bother me.

Before he could order me to leave, I asked, "Who called in the fire?"

"A post office employee. We're talking to him now. And no, he says he didn't see anyone—just the flames."

"I saw that melted mess that used to be his computer. Are you looking for back-up files at his residence? Maybe that would lead to a motive."

"Now everyone's an investigator. The only problem with your great detective work is that no one has said this was arson or murder."

I pressed my luck. "Suicide?"

Wilcox pulled the brim of his cowboy hat low over his brow. A warning, but I still didn't stop. "Do you think this has anything to do with what's happening in Spirit Lake, Sheriff?"

"Why would I? We don't even know what that is yet." He turned on his heels.

I called after him. "Why was Rob in his office at four in the morning?"

An hour later, sitting at my old desk at the bureau, I downloaded my photos and worked on captions. Cynthia came out of her office and said out loud what I was thinking. "You look comfortable in that chair, Britt. Maybe you want to stay?"

The bureau still leased the tiny office space above Lakeshore Realty, with a view of Branson Lake. I flipped through my file of photos. "Part of me would like to, but I'm locked in to the *Times* on a year contract."

"There's no limit to how many contracts you can be working on as a freelancer. Interested?"

"Sure." I rarely turned down a photo gig and could use the legitimacy of working for the *StarTrib* while looking into Charley's murder. Without the ID, I was nothing but a nosy onlooker.

"Let me talk to management." Cynthia went back to her office.

I asked, "Are you really doing better, Cynthia? You look healthier, that's for sure."

Her eyes filled. "I wish I could go back to the way it was before Alex got sick, but I can't bring him back. Some days it's really hard but this job helps, and friends."

Jason stomped in and tossed his notebook and pen on his desk. "Investigators are going over Rob's house but they wouldn't let me near it."

"Did you get any more information at the fire?"

He kicked his chair and it rolled a few feet. "No one would answer my questions."

"Keep at them, Jason. Go on back and hang around until they forget you're there."

He grabbed his stuff and left. "Waste of time."

Too bad he was having difficulty with Wilcox but his reaction pleased me. When I first met him, he wouldn't have gone back.

It was noon already. I drove to Spirit Lake, glancing at the thunder clouds lying in wait. Did the entire region have a dark cloud over it this summer?

***

Trussed up in my apron, I started schlepping dishes. The job didn't require my full attention, a good thing, because my mind was on Charley and Rob. Would Wilcox forget about the old guy now that he had Rob's death to deal with? Had he followed up with the hate crimes task force yesterday? One thing, he wouldn't have time now to watch my movements.

The World Church often used arson as a way to get their messages across, but what, if anything, did Rob have to do with them? Was Rob gay? Were they hunting gays up and down north central Minnesota? Lars would say I was getting ahead of my skis and he'd be right.

I'd researched online statistics for hate crimes in the country. Most of the time, a gang would pick one or two gay people to harass. Occasionally, it would escalate and the gang would go into a hate-frenzy and beat the person, sometimes to death. Sometimes, they did worse—tying them up and dragging them, or other atrocities. But what happened to Charley was a new one.

We were all tense and by midafternoon, Little had burned a batch of rolls, Lars dropped a tray of dishes and the staff snapped at each other. One of the locals said I scared her granddaughter. I raised my hands, palms up. "I only suggested she make up her mind about what kind of cookie she wanted."

Ever the diplomat, Lars came over with a cookie. "How would you like a snickerdoodle, Megan?"

She nodded and grasped it with both hands. The grandmother pursed her lips at me.

Lars took me aside. "Britt, you're going to have to work in the kitchen if you can't stop snarling at the customers."

"I'll do better." I tilted my head toward the kitchen. "I'm not going in there. Little's on the warpath."

We were coming unglued. I called Wilcox. "Have you checked where the Willards were at four o'clock this morning?"

"We checked, and you're wasting my time with questions like that. If you'll recall, your job is staying close to your brother and Lars."

"Thank you, Sheriff, I didn't mean to bother you. I'm just worried that they're hanging around Spirit Lake."

"My deputy reported that father and son are on the east side of the county picking up junk, nowhere near Spirit Lake. Mrs. Willard headed to town a few minutes ago."

He must have had a weak moment. That was much more information than I usually got from him, and just what I needed to hear.

Gene sat at his usual table at the back, newspaper and cup of coffee in front of him. He could see anyone who entered the front door and had a good view of the bistro. I took off my apron and said to Lars. "I'm taking the dogs out."

With both dogs in the SUV, I barreled to Iona, shrugging off the guilt. I hadn't said we were going for a walk. I wanted to get another look at that meeting place at the back of the Willards' property.

***

Wilcox's info was accurate. No cars were in the drive. My SUV bumped along the single lane path to the out-building. I let Rock loose but left Knute in the car in case we had to make a hasty getaway.

They'd changed a few things. Across from the junk pile, a rectangular area had been plowed and tiny plants sprouted in neat rows. Expecting it to be locked, I tried the shed door. It opened. I checked the woods to make sure no shotguns were trained on me and entered. Garden implements and fertilizer took up the space where the copy machine and chairs had been.

Rock ran to the junk pile. I whistled to him, not wanting to draw attention in case the Willards had come home, but he'd found a good digging spot. That dog loved creatures that burrowed. A rat scuttled from under a crumpled fender and darted into the weeds. Rock took off after it, barking. I chased him down, grabbed his collar and dragged him away.

The commotion unnerved me and brought me to my senses. Mr. Willard had threatened to kill me if I showed up again.

I drove too fast on the rutted lane, bouncing the dogs like jack-in-the-boxes and breathed a sigh of relief when we sailed through the Willards' still-empty driveway. I didn't take a full breath until we were back on the highway. One thing was obvious to me. The Willards must be hiding something important to have gone to so much effort to remove all traces of their church.

I checked in with Thor on my way back to Little's. "Have you found out for sure if the burn victim was Rob?"

"Wilcox hasn't issued a statement yet, so just between you and me it was Rob. The arsonist might not have done it on purpose if he didn't know Rob was in the building. I mean, it's still manslaughter or whatever, though."

"Has Wilcox mentioned what Rob was doing in his office at four in the morning?"

"No, and we won't hear from forensics for a few days about what they learned from the body. But why do that to a seventy-year-old man?"

106

"Revenge? Maybe someone blamed the messenger at a will reading or believed Jenkins cheated him."

She said, "Jason told me Mr. Jenkins had a good reputation."

"Has Wilcox mentioned finding any clues at Rob's house?"

Thor let out a gust of air. "The sheriff doesn't trust me with information now that I'm dating Jason. You know how he hates to see stuff in the papers when he's working on a case. I'd never tell Jason anything Wilcox asked me not to but the damage is done."

She asked me to hold on, talked to someone on the other end of the line, and Jason came on.

"You work at the sheriff's office now?" I asked.

He huffed. "I'm over at Thor's lab working on the story."

"I was teasing, Jason." I enjoyed watching love in bloom but was a little jealous. I missed Ben.

He said, "I wanted to tell you I did some checking on hate crimes in Iona in the period since Matthew got out of prison, and they've actually decreased."

That surprised me. "Where did you get your information?"

"Crime logs are open to the public if you know how to access them."

I thanked him and hung up, remembering that Mr. Willard had told the World Church group they were working on a big project and to hold off harassing the gay community.

The sheriff was his usual helpful self when I called him. "You're determined to connect all this to that group in Iona, but we don't work that way. We go where the evidence leads us."

"Did you find any clues at Rob's house about who did it or why?"

"We're still going through his papers."

"Was Rob gay?"

He emphasized each word. "Not that we know."

I pressed for more information about Charley. Wilcox said he'd let me know when they had something and hung up. He probably didn't have much more from using his law enforcement channels than I'd gotten from Sebastian. Past ninety, Charley pre-dated Internet technology.

Back in Spirit Lake, I locked the dogs in the guys' apartment. Little was in the restaurant kitchen, looking haggard. He might not have even known I was gone. I walked through the swinging doors and stopped short at an angry conversation taking place.

Neil leaned across the counter toward Lars. "You've been sending me to crap fishing spots. I haven't caught anything. So much for your so-called expertise."

A couple a few seats away hurried to finish their coffee.

Lars stepped back. "Those were all great locations."

"More like wild goose chases. You've been messing with me this whole time."

Lars' face flushed. "Maybe you're not the fisherman you think you are."

Neil pointed his index finger at Lars. "I challenge you. Let's see you catch a damn fish in one of your secret spots. He walked to the door talking loud. "Or maybe you like hiding behind that apron."

Neil saw me and lifted the right side of his lip in a lecherous smile. "Well, hello Britt."

I wanted to wipe the look off his face but ignored him and slid onto a seat across from Lars. I said, "That guy's a jerk."

If Lars polished the glass in his hand with much more force he'd break it. He scowled at me. "You said you were taking the dogs for a walk. You've been gone over an hour again."

"I figured we'd be safer away from town."

His head rotated in a circle to get the kinks out. "I need to get out of here. I can't take this much longer." I followed his gaze out the window. Neil headed across the street to his boat.

I touched his arm. "You know it's not safe for you to go off on your own."

Chapter 13

Lars stared at the lake like a prisoner plotting an escape. A chilly rain began to blow into the open windows. Lars and I hurried to close them, his mouth stretched in a fake smile to calm the agitated customers. "Now we're nice and cozy."

But the restaurant turned steamy and claustrophobic, a far cry from cozy. Lars glanced at the lake again and went to the kitchen. I cleared a table and carted a tub of dishes to the kitchen. Little and Lars stood just inside the swinging door, whispering. I reached them as the discussion escalated from a whisper to an argument. Lars scowled and Little's chin tilted up. Lars said, "I'm going fishing and no one's stopping me." He stalked toward the back. Little went after him and I set my tub down and followed. Lars' hand was on the door to their apartment when we caught up to him.

Little said, "You can't. It's too dangerous."

"I can't stand to be cooped up anymore. Gene and Britt are here. You'll be fine."

Little grabbed his arm. "I meant it's too dangerous for you."

Lars pulled away and walked through the apartment with us on his heels. He reached for his rain jacket on the peg at the back door and headed out to the garage.

Little pushed me. "Britt, stop him."

"You know he won't listen to either of us. Go on back to the restaurant. I'll make sure he gets into his boat and safely onto the lake. Once he's out there, he'll be okay."

"But what about coming back?"

"I'll ask him to call my cell so I can meet him at the dock."

Little nodded. "You're right, there's no stopping him when he gets stubborn like this. He needs to get away for a while." He bit a fingernail. "Ask if you can go with him."

"I don't want to leave you."

"Gene's here. I'll be fine."

I grabbed a rain jacket from the peg and hurried out to the garage. Lars already had his tackle box and fishing gear ready to go.

"Let me go with you."

"No way. I'm counting on you to keep an eye on Little for me." His eyes pleaded. "I have to get out or I'm going to lose my mind."

"I'm driving you to your boat."

"That's silly. It's a block away."

"Humor me. My SUV's parked outside the garage."

I started the car and waited. He rolled his eyes and got in. As we passed the restaurant, Little darted out with a waterproof bag and thermos. He handed it to Lars. "It's a sandwich and coffee."

Lars attempted a grin. "No cookie?"

Little made an effort to return the smile. "Chocolate chip."

Seated in the boat, his hand on the tiller, his back straightened as if the weight of the world had fallen from his shoulders. He even sounded like the old Lars. "Don't worry about me. I'll only be gone a couple hours."

"Don't let that idiot Neil get under your skin if you see him out there, and call me as soon as you're heading back. I'll meet you here."

He gave me a thumbs-up and started the motor. I surveyed the area with a nervous wobble in my stomach. At the playground, a mother hurrying to her car, pulled her son behind her. The kid whined, "This place sucks. There's nothing to do."

What the tourists wanted on a day like today was an indoor shopping mall where the kids could run around or maybe go to a movie. Few cars were parked in front of the shops but Olafson's Bar parking lot was full. Cars had spilled over to the lot across the street. The casino would do good business today too.

It turned out to be a prophetic thought. I pulled into Little's parking lot and watched a bus of rowdy seniors from St. Paul jostle to get inside and find good seats. I hurried in to help.

Chloe told me the group came through town every few months on their way to the Dreamcatcher Casino. Stopping to eat at Little's was part of their itinerary. In addition to the seniors, the place had filled up again. Everyone showed up at once. It often happened like that, similar to the way a flock of birds takes off and lands at the same time and same spot. I had to do double duty, seating them and clearing up after. Even though I'd never have Lars' way with the customers, I was speedy.

One of the oldsters grabbed my arm. "How's about a smile, hon?"

I made an effort but it didn't have the right effect. He threw his hands up in the air. "Just kidding."

Note to self—practice sweetness. Second note to self— forget first note. I didn't care what other people thought of me.

Little was a Samurai, chopping, stirring, flinging spices into sauces, ordering us around like he was sending his troops into battle. "Get those people moving along the window booths; customers are stacking up at the door. Hustle!"

Busy as he was, Little had to chat with the seniors before they'd leave. A pink flush spread across his cheeks at the attention. After they left, we settled into a more normal pace. I noticed Peder sitting in a back booth across from Anke. Their heads were bent over notebooks and they were busily writing. For once, her eyes weren't on me.

I checked the clock and did a double-take. Nearly four hours had passed since Lars left. I hadn't had a minute to think of him the entire afternoon and we were well into the dinner hour. I punched in his cell number. No answer.

Lars' long absence must have occurred to Little at the same time. He pushed through the swinging kitchen doors, eyes wide. "Why hasn't he called? He promised not to be gone long."

He fished his phone out from under his apron. Lars didn't pick up for him either. Even though my radar was pulsing, I said, "He always loses track of time when he's fishing."

Little's eyes were saucers. "But why didn't he answer?"

"There's no signal in some of those coves."

Little didn't buy it. "Something's happened. We have to find him."

I whipped off my apron. "I'll borrow a boat. I know most of his spots."

Chloe tapped Little on the shoulder. "I have some orders." She didn't know what was going on.

Little snapped. "They can wait. No, I'll do them, but would you get Chum to come in for the dinner crowd? I need more kitchen help."

She nodded. Chloe understood Little better than most. "What's wrong?"

Not wanting everyone to panic, I said, "Lars is playing hooky from work, so I have to haul him in."

She said, "I'll handle the front desk."

Little twisted the towel hanging from his apron, rooted to the floor. I grabbed a rain vest from the hook by the kitchen and tucked my camera into a pocket. "I'm going to Winter's Resort to borrow a fast boat."

Peder and I reached the door at the same time. He looked from me to Little. "Is something wrong?"

Little said, "Lars has been out on the lake longer than we expected. I hate to ask, but could you help Britt look for him?"

Peder said, "Of course. My boat goes very fast."

I didn't want to bring him into the drama but was close to panicking. "Thanks, I appreciate this."

On the way to the dock, I called Winter's Resort. Patty, who managed the resort for Ben, answered. I told her we were worried about Lars and asked if her husband, Daniel, was available to help look for him if we needed him.

"Of course. Let me know."

"I imagine we'll find out Lars was so busy enjoying himself, he lost track of time." That's what I hoped anyway.

The rain stopped and a steamy fog hung over the lake as we sped from one cove to the next. For an hour we zigzagged back and forth and still no Lars. I kept trying his phone. Little called several times and I told him we were still looking, but the fact that I could receive Little's calls made me even more frantic. I tried to tell myself that Lars could have dropped his phone in the lake. It happened to tourists all the time, attempting a selfie with a hooked fish.

Peder quietly waited for my directions, steering the boat wherever I indicated. My respect for him rose when he didn't badger me for details.

We'd been to every fishing hole and cove I knew, with no luck. Twenty-eight miles of shoreline covering about six thousand acres was too much for us if he wasn't in his usual spots. I called Patty again, trying to keep my voice steady. "I need to take you up on that help."

"I'll send Daniel out right now and spread the word. What's Lars wearing?"

"He wore a yellow rain jacket when he took off, but it's stopped raining. He has a Little's Café t-shirt under it and is in an eight-foot aluminum fishing boat with a ten hp motor."

"Don't you worry, we'll find him."

I'd feel foolish for raising such a panic in everyone if Lars putted around a corner with a basket full of fish, but I'd take that embarrassment any day just to see his face right now. It was my fault if something bad happened to him. I'd let him go.

My phone rang and I grabbed it, hoping it was Lars. Ben's voice on the other end sounded worried. "Patty told me Lars is missing."

"Ben, I'm scared. I can't find him."

"You aren't alone out there, are you?"

"Peder offered his speedboat."

"Good. I'll check with Woz. If he's not guiding, he can fly over the lake with the Beaver."

Summers were Woz' busiest month, just like everyone else around here. The Wozniaks ran an outfitter store in Ely, an entry to the Boundary Waters area, where Ben was currently hunting his traffickers. Woz helped him whenever he could with his amphibious plane. He'd gotten me out of a serious jam shortly before I left for L.A., even though I hadn't trusted the black-bearded man at first. Now, I'd trust him with my life.

Ben called back in a few minutes. "Woz is unloading a group of backpackers. As soon as they're off the Beaver, he'll fuel up and head over."

I called Little with the news. He was relieved that Woz could help, but frightened at the implications. It had been six hours, but it didn't get dark until nearly ten o'clock in July. We had a few more hours of daylight.

A log bobbed up in the water in front of Peder's boat and he swerved to miss it. Fear weakened my knees. What if Lars had hit something and capsized? I didn't like to think of how deep the lake was—two hundred feet in some places. I gazed out at the vast expanse of water around me. He could be anywhere. We'd mostly been looking along the shoreline.

My cell rang. Please let it be Lars, I prayed. A familiar voice bellowed in my ear. "When were you going to tell me Lars was missing?"

I'd forgotten Wilcox. I thought of him as landlocked and scrambled to explain, ending with, "Woz is on his way."

He cut me off. "I know. That's good. Our helicopter is up in Federal Dam." Wilcox had one parting shot. "Can't you people follow directions? I told you no one goes anywhere alone."

I had nothing to say. I should have tried harder to convince Lars not to leave.

Shortly after Patty's husband was on the lake, several neighbors took out kayaks, fishing boats, speed boats—whatever worked on water. Jake from Erickson's Hardware shot by on a Jet Ski.

Peder, concerned but calm, helped keep me from a full-blown freak-out. He offered reassuring smiles. "He probably ran into another fisherman. Lars can talk fishing for hours at a time."

What he said was true. "I'm sorry for taking advantage of you, Peder. I expected to find him right away."

He held up a gas can. "I'm glad I could help but we're running out of gas. I forgot to fill the backup."

"We can stop at one of the resorts for gas, but first can you pull around closer to the island and follow the shoreline?"

Linda Townsdin

A narrow road bordered by a few trees connected the land to the island, so technically it was a peninsula, but it had always been known as the island and was part of the Ojibwe reservation. The tribe built a rehab and diabetes center on the shore side of the peninsula and kept the island as wilderness.

A certainty gripped me that something terrible had happened. Peder interrupted my dark thoughts. "Didn't we already look here? We really are running low on gas."

We'd have to turn back soon or they'd need to send someone out to rescue us. I said, "Maybe he got out of his boat and slipped on a rock. Please, get as near shore as you can."

He pointed at the rocks below us in the shallow water. "Any closer might damage my propeller but I'll try."

Peder slowly guided his boat into the shallow area. Weak sunlight had finally shown its face, and something silver glinted on shore. I pointed. "Stop!" He throttled down, I jumped into the knee-deep water and stumbled toward the object.

My legs turned to jelly when I saw what had caught my eye. It was the hull of Lars' boat hidden under brush. I yelled to Peder. "There's his boat. I'm going to look for him."

His voice floated back. "Be careful."

My fingers were clumsy as I punched in the sheriff's number but the signal was too weak. I followed a sketchy trail toward the center of the island calling to Lars.

Through a break in the trees, a streak of yellow on the ground caught my attention. I ran. "Lars!"

The breath left my body when I reached him. He lay unmoving under a stand of birch, upper body curled in a fetal position, arms protecting his head, his right leg splayed in an unnatural angle. I froze. He couldn't be dead. The barest groan came from his mouth and I dropped on my knees next to him. Whispering past the boulder in my throat, I said, "Hold on Lars. I'm getting help." I didn't dare move him. It was impossible to tell if other bones were broken. I could see cuts on his hands and face but no giant pool of blood showed unless it was under his body.

I raced back to the shore, branches biting my skin and tearing my hair. I tripped over a fallen tree trunk and sprawled on my stomach. Catching my breath, I ran again, screaming for Peder. He stood in the boat, his hands at his ears.

"I found him! He's hurt!" I pointed to the mainland connecting the island and yelled louder. "Go to the building on the north side. It's a rehab clinic. Get the doctor. Tell them to call Wilcox. Hurry!"

Peder nodded, carefully turned the boat away from shallow water, and when he was deep enough, sped off. It wouldn't be long. The peninsula was only a half mile away.

I made my way around the perimeter of the island until I found a weak signal, and called Wilcox. My voice was thin and high. "Did the rehab center reach you?"

"No. Have you found Lars?"

"He's barely breathing!" I told Wilcox exactly where I was and that I needed a medevac to get Lars to the hospital.

He said, "Woz is almost there. I'll alert the hospital. Medics and an ambulance will meet you at Branson Lake. We're heading to the R & D Center now. We'll walk from there to the island."

I stuttered, "Sheriff, I don't know if he's going to make it."

Wilcox said, "Goddammit, you hang on Britt. Get back there and document the crime scene."

Numb, I nodded at the phone, made my way back to Lars and leaned in close, barely detecting a breath. With trembling hands, I pulled my camera out of my vest and focused. That calmed me enough to start shooting the trampled brush, footprints and Lars lying motionless. As the camera clicked, I kept up a constant one-sided conversation. "Hold on, Lars, help is coming. You have to stay with me for Little. He's waiting. We all love you. We all need you."

The minutes dragged before the buzz of Woz' float plane penetrated the air. The woods were too thick on the island for him to see me so I ran to the shore and splashed into the water, arms flailing. He saw me and came in for a landing. The plane bounced twice and skimmed toward me. In a few minutes, Woz waded to shore with a backboard balanced on his head. Daniel's boat pulled up, Jake on his Jet Ski right behind him. The three of them followed me.

When we reached the clearing where Lars lay, Jake stumbled backward. "What in hell happened to him?"

Woz fastened his deep-set eyes on the two men. His black eyebrows drew together. "Don't talk, just do what I tell you."

We were quiet after that. Woz checked Lars' breathing, then pulled a cervical collar from his backpack and fastened it around Lars' neck. He told us how to lift without causing more trauma. Daniel and Jake were on one side and I stood next to Woz. He counted to three. We all lifted at once and slid Lars onto the backboard. Woz strapped him down and the four of us waded to the Beaver holding Lars above the water.

I got into the plane. Jake and Daniel watched as we taxied out and lifted off. I whispered to Woz. "He's going to make it, right?"

He turned to me, his eyes filled with compassion. "Bad head wound, there could be internal bleeding. I don't know."

Chapter 14

A team of medics was waiting to transfer Lars to the ambulance when the Beaver touched down on Branson Lake. Shaking from head to toe, Little arrived at Branson Hospital shortly after Lars was admitted and found me in the intensive care waiting room. "Where is he, I have to see him."

We told the desk nurse who we were and asked when we could see Lars.

She frowned at her paperwork. "I'm sorry. You're not listed as family. A sister has been notified. Once he's been stabilized, she can see him."

Little took off down the hall and pushed through the doors to the intensive care unit looking for Lars' room. I followed, but he'd already been stopped by two orderlies. One on each side, they brought him back, still struggling. Nurse Connie hurried toward us. She led him to a chair, saying something to him in a soothing tone. I edged closer. When he was calm, she suggested he take a sedative. He nodded. Connie waited until he relaxed against the chair before leaving.

It was futile to argue with hospital rules but that didn't stop me from haranguing the desk nurse, demanding Little's right to information as Lars' partner. My ranting didn't work any better and I wasn't offered a sedative.

Little turned inward, refusing to talk to anyone. I called Lars' sister Sarah. She said she'd booked the next flight from Chicago. Their mother passed away years ago, and their father lived with his other daughter, Margaret, in St. Paul. He had Alzheimer's and she couldn't leave him. We could do nothing but wait for Sarah.

Ben called me. The sound of his voice triggered a mild hysteria. My voice wavered. "I don't know what's happening here. They won't tell us anything about Lars."

"I know. I just talked to Wilcox. I can be there in a few hours."

I wanted Ben but what I wanted more was to go after whoever did this. Ben would be on Wilcox's side and try to keep me away. I took a deep breath and calmed myself. "There's nothing you can do. Little and I are just waiting to hear about Lars. I'll call you if anything changes."

He argued but eventually agreed. "I'll talk to Wilcox again in the morning and let you know what they found at the island. They're out there now."

Wilcox came in at eleven o'clock, three hours after I'd found Lars. He spoke with the desk nurse, then joined us, hat in hand. "We've done what we could, but it's too dark now. We don't want to trample over evidence. We'll go back at first light to continue processing the scene. Ray's deputies are guarding the site."

He was referring to tribal police Sgt. Ray Stevens. Anything that happened on reservation land was his jurisdiction. Ray and Wilcox weren't exactly buddies, but they respected each other.

Little nodded and focused his gaze back on the corridor. Wilcox put on his hat. "We'll get this guy."

He turned to leave and I followed him. Out of Little's earshot, I asked, "What caused his injuries?"

"Right now all we know is it was a blunt instrument. Best guess is that it was someone five-nine or ten, right-handed, strong."

"Now will you take the World Church and Matthew Willard seriously?"

"We're checking their alibis and we've talked with everyone at the rehab center. No one saw anyone going to the island, although it would be easy to miss if they had a boat. They have twelve-step groups in the afternoons and the usual diabetes regulars and visitors to the hospital section. But with the rain, people hurried in and out of the building."

"That's all you have?" The feeling of helplessness was more than I could stand.

"You can tell me everything Lars said to you before he got in the boat." He looked over at Little. "I'll talk to him later."

I told him about Neil's angry taunting of Lars, and that he'd left by boat.

"I'll bring him in. Maybe that argument escalated." Wilcox cast a worried look toward the closed doors to the intensive care unit and left the building, his usual ramrod straight back slightly stooped.

Peder called an hour later. I jumped on him before he had a chance to say anything. "They said you never showed up at the rehab center."

"That's what I wanted to tell you. My boat ran out of gas and I drifted until one of the boaters looking for Lars saw me and hauled me to shore."

"Why didn't you use your oars?"

He sounded sheepish. "I've never put them in the boat. They didn't seem necessary with a motor."

"Did you at least try to reach them?"

"Yes, of course, but I couldn't get a signal. I'm sorry I let you down."

What he said was true about cell service, and I'd assumed all Norwegians would know about boats. Clearly, that wasn't true. I dropped the strident tone. "Sorry I snapped at you. You were a huge help."

"I feel terrible about this. How is he doing?"

The lump in my throat made it hard to answer. "We don't know anything yet."

Peder apologized again and said goodbye.

Near midnight, Dr. Fromm stood before us, chart in hand. "All I can tell you is that Lars is still unconscious."

I moved close to Fromm, forcing him to take his eyes from his chart. "You know us. Tell us if he's going to make it."

He took off his round glasses and wiped the smudges with the hem of his white coat. "I wish I could tell you more, but we have to talk to his family first."

Blinking back tears, Little said, "I'm his family too. Let me see him."

I ached for my brother and for all of us. Dr. Fromm really did look troubled that he had to follow the ridiculous rules. He motioned to Nurse Connie. She took Little aside and asked if he'd like another sedative. "You really should try to rest."

He nodded, haunted eyes straying to the corridor where Lars was lying close to death.

In the past, I'd made fun of Dr. Fromm and Nurse Connie, or Nurse Cranky as I'd nicknamed her, but they were the best medical team in the area. They wore identical round glasses and had worked together so long they communicated without words. I just wished they'd communicate with us.

The restaurant staff had heard what happened to Lars. Little asked me to call Chum and have him take over. Little said, "Chum doesn't like to work hard or make decisions. He tried to manage a burger stand on the outskirts of town and couldn't handle the stress, but you have to convince him. I can't deal with it."

Slumped against the waiting room wall, I called Chum and asked him to handle the kitchen without Little for a while.

He tried to turn down my request. "I don't know, Britt. What if, like, we get real busy?"

I pushed myself away from the wall, trying not to lose my cool. "Just do the best you can. It won't be for long."

"How's Lars doing, anyway?"

"He's a tough guy and he knows how much we all love him." The words caught in my throat. "He'll get through this."

"Okay, I'll try."

Little sat slumped on one of the waiting room couches. I sat beside him. "Chum said he'd do it."

Little didn't respond. He spoke slowly—the sedative's effects. "Lars was the reason I had the strength to move back to Spirit Lake to the house I hated because of the way Dad treated me."

"I was surprised when you said you were leaving the classroom. You loved anthropology."

He rubbed his eyes. "I did, but my stomach clenched up every time I taught a class. I dreaded standing in front of the students."

"I had no idea." A pang of guilt at how much I didn't know about my brother's recent history made me wince. At one time, I'd known every detail.

Little gazed toward the intensive care corridor. "He'd been there teaching history a few years already. All his students loved him. He's so outgoing and friendly. We had coffee one day and that was the beginning."

Little's words drifted away. His face clouded. I didn't want him to brood in silence again. I prodded. "You were going to explain why he was the reason you came back here."

"We began seeing each other and he raved about my cooking. He said I was a different person when I cooked, that it was clear I loved it. He said I should open a restaurant."

"So you quit and moved to Spirit Lake."

"Not right away. I thought he was just being nice. But he said he'd grown up in a Minneapolis suburb and lived for the summers when their family would go up north to the lake. He loved to fish and hike and intended to move to a small town on a lake when he retired."

"That's a long time to wait for a dream to come true."

"Exactly. After Mom moved to Palm Desert, Lars and I spent a summer in our house and that's when the restaurant plan was hatched. After that it was a whirlwind. You know the rest. Back then you'd made it clear you had no interest in coming back here, and neither did Mom, so she let me have the place. We got a loan to renovate it, and here we are."

I moved closer to Little and put my arm around him. His eyes filled. "We were so happy. How could anyone do this to someone as wonderful as Lars?"

He lifted agonized eyes to me. "And the worst part is that I wanted to get married when gay marriage was legalized, only he was concerned it might keep people from coming to the restaurant if we drew too much attention to our relationship."

I squeezed his arm. "I'm so sorry, Little. Sarah will be here soon."

122

He eventually fell asleep. I paced again, furious. Why hadn't Wilcox gone to Iona sooner? Maybe it would have stopped this brutal beating. I was angry at everyone, the Willards, Wilcox, Peder, the doctor, and especially myself.

Toward morning, I sprawled on the couch across from Little and dropped off to sleep.

***

Sarah arrived at noon. Small and dark-haired, she looked nothing like Lars. She rushed to hug Little. He gripped her hands. "We can't find out anything from Dr. Fromm. Please make them tell you if he's going to be all right."

"I'll get you in to see him. Don't worry." She hurried to the nurse's station and asked to see the doctor. They handed her a form and when that was filled out to their satisfaction, Dr. Fromm arrived and spoke into her ear as he guided her down the hall.

We waited an interminable fifteen minutes. Little rocked back and forth and I paced. Both of us kept our eyes on the hallway waiting for the first glimpse of Sarah.

When she returned, she clung to Dr. Fromm's arm as if she might collapse. He eased her onto a chair. Little and I waited, our eyes on the doctor.

Fromm cleared his throat. "Ms. Weinstein has authorized me to tell you about her brother's condition." He nodded at Little. "You will be allowed to see him."

Little jumped up, ready to go, but Dr. Fromm held up a hand. He gave us the details, most of it in layman's language so we got the picture. Lars could die, or never come out of the coma, or wake from the coma and be brain-damaged and not know any of us, or a miracle could occur and he would heal and be the same Lars he always was.

I breathed. "When will we know?"

"We won't know the extent of damage to his brain for a while. He's in an induced coma until the swelling lessens."

"What about his leg and the rest of him?" I asked, inwardly cringing at the image of him lying in the woods.

Dr. Fromm referred to his chart. "Someone beat him with a blunt instrument on multiple parts of his head and body. His leg was broken. He'd been kicked repeatedly in the ribs and kidneys."

He noticed our stricken faces and hurried to add, "Those we can fix and they will heal in time."

Little stepped forward. "Thank you, Doctor. I want to see him now." I knew what he would find, but there was no way to prepare him for the shock.

Dr. Fromm checked his watch. "He's scheduled for more tests, but you have about ten minutes."

Little's face was drained of all color when he returned, as shaken as Sarah had been. He turned away when I went to him. "I can't talk now."

Sarah and Little took turns sitting with Lars for the rest of the day. There was no change. Little told the restaurant staff he wasn't leaving the hospital until Lars came out of the coma. "If it's too difficult, you can close."

To me, he said, "I don't care about the restaurant. All I care about is Lars."

That evening, Wilcox passed through the waiting area with Jerry. I stirred from a fitful doze. "What's going on, Sheriff?"

His head tilted toward the deputy. "I'm stationing him outside Lars' room. Lars might have gotten a look at his assailant. If the individual believed he killed Lars and found out he's alive…"

"I get it, Sheriff." A chill moved up my spine. "What about the restaurant?"

"We'll keep one guy on during the day and one at night." Wilcox walked toward the exit and I followed. "Can't you tell us anything?"

He kept walking. "We believe one person did the damage. One set of rain boots—the same brand everyone in the area wears."

"The weapon?"

"We've narrowed it down—one weapon, not a bat or a log, but wood. Dr. Fromm gave us bits of wood taken from Lars' head and torso. Thor kept slivers to work on and sent the rest to the lab in Minneapolis. We're hoping to identify the source."

"Thanks, Sheriff." He rarely shared information with me and I appreciated it. "I know you think I'm a broken record, but Matthew Willard was in Spirit Lake on two occasions that I know of. He came to the cabin to convince me that his group had nothing to do with killing Charley, and I'm pretty sure I saw his truck turn the corner by the guys' garage two days ago. He could have been waiting for his chance to get one of them alone to do this."

He stopped. "How did he follow Lars in his boat if he was in a truck?"

"It's not hard to steal a boat around here."

He pushed out the door. "We'll check to see if anyone reported a stolen boat."

He looked skeptical, but if he said he'd check, he would.

***

The next morning Lars was still in the coma. Sarah went to her hotel to sleep while Little stayed with Lars.

I paced the hospital waiting room. I'd already worn out my welcome with the sheriff, but he did tell me he'd spoken with the Willards. Matthew had been working with his dad all day. I'd like to know if the people who provided his alibi were World Church members, but Wilcox would have checked. He was experienced and skilled. The only thing hindering him was that he had to go by the book. But I didn't.

I called Henry at the casino. "I'm going to see if I can find anything the sheriff's people might have missed. Do you have a car or truck I can borrow for a few hours? The killer knows my SUV."

Henry said, "Bad idea."

"This guy passed up a chance to kill me. The message he left on my desk said, 'You Can't Save *Him*.' I don't think he's after me."

The tone in Henry's voice told me he wasn't happy, but he said to meet him at his grandfather's place.

Edgar's garage was open and I pulled in, then walked over to him, waiting in his doorway with his arms crossed. I said, "I suppose you're going to try to talk me out of this, too."

He said, "If he goes for you in the woods you'll be okay, you know it better than most."

I nodded. I was familiar with the trees and bushes, the underbrush, the rise and fall of the ground, the loamy, soft spots that would wrap around a shoe and suck you down to your knees, where it was good to sleep. I'd spent summer nights camping not far from where I'd found Lars.

Henry arrived shortly in a rusted red Ford truck. I hurried to him with my camera bag over one shoulder, the SIG Sauer tucked in a side pocket. "I really appreciate this, Henry." No one would pay attention to the old truck rumbling through the reservation's rehab and diabetes center grounds.

Henry stayed behind the wheel. "I don't get this. The killer was after Lars?"

I shook my head. "Right now I'm so confused. I don't know what Lars has to do with Charley, or Rob, or even if there's a connection."

I waited, impatient for him to get out of the truck. "Thanks, again, Henry. I'd better get going so I can be back before dark."

He faced forward, chin up. "I'm going with you. Ben would be mad if I let you go off and get yourself killed."

The big man would slow me down, but I didn't want to be disrespectful. I slid into the passenger seat. Now *I* wasn't happy.

Chapter 15

The Rehab and Diabetes Center main building looked more like a resort lodge than a medical facility. Henry parked among a dozen cars and trucks. The center ran twelve-step groups and a mostly out-patient medical service.

I tucked a camera into my camo jacket, transferred the gun to my waistband and left the camera bag and other equipment behind. Henry took his rifle from the gun rack and we walked down the narrow trail leading to the island. It was reservation land, a mile across, and there were no houses or businesses on it. As kids, we'd canoe from town and have picnics or camp here. But today it didn't feel welcoming or safe. It was hard to admit it, but I was grateful for Henry's solid presence as we entered the dense woods.

My ears were tuned to every sound and there were plenty of them, but they were familiar ones. If the forest creatures got suddenly quiet, I'd know something was wrong. We walked in silence to the place where I'd found Lars. I shuddered at the memory and once again used the camera eye to record the scene. We fanned out from the spot and spent the next two hours traversing every inch of ground.

Henry stayed apart from me, his eyes scanning back and forth through the terrain as I stumbled through swamp and brambles, poison oak and ivy and the nearly impenetrable rocky shoreline surrounding the island.

From his vantage point a few yards above me, his rifle in one strong arm, Henry pointed to something in the water. A chunk of splintered wood was wedged between two rocks a couple of yards from shore. No more than six inches long, a diagonal sliver of blue ran across it.

I waded out, slipping on the rocky bottom in my gym shoes. Afraid the tide would whisk it away before I could reach it, my gaze stayed riveted on the piece of wood. When I was close enough to grab it if it slipped away, I shot from all angles, and then tugged the wood free of the rocks.

A twig snapped and I swung toward the sound, my hand on the SIG Sauer at my hip. Henry pointed his rifle toward the woods, his body taut. The entire island held its breath.

In a moment, normal sounds started up again and the hairs settled on the back of my neck. It could have been a deer out for an afternoon snack or maybe a creature waddling through the underbrush. My jeans were soaked to the knees and my shoes sloshed as I hurried back to Henry and showed him the piece of wood.

We turned it this way and that. If there was blood on it, all traces had washed away. I said, "Thor will find out if the splinters taken from Lars match."

Henry nudged me forward. "Let's get back to the truck. Someone's out there."

Wordless, we hurried through the woods the way we'd come. I felt like a sitting duck as we crossed back over the narrow trail to the rehab center parking lot, but we made it safely. Henry secured his rifle and got behind the wheel. I reached inside my camera bag for a plastic envelope, touched wet fur and snatched my hand back. The severed head of a raccoon stared up at me with its bandit eyes. "Oh, shit, Henry, look."

He took one look, grabbed for his rifle, jumped out of the truck and trotted across the parking lot faster than I'd ever seen him move.

Henry was back shortly, shaking his head and panting. "I have a better idea."

He called Ray Stevens of the tribal police and asked him to send someone to check out the island. "There might be someone hiding out there who doesn't belong. He could be armed."

He got off the phone and pointed at my camera bag. "The sheriff has to see that."

I hedged. "I doubt our head hunter is anywhere near here by now and Ray might not appreciate the sheriff charging in."

His eyes narrowed. "You'd better take that thing to Wilcox."

I wanted to toss the raccoon head into the bushes but Henry was right, it was evidence. "I will."

He rooted in the glove box for napkins and handed a wad to me. I cleaned my hand, and swallowed to rid myself of the squeamish feeling in my stomach. "What's with this guy and heads, Henry?"

One thing was clear to me. He wasn't going to detach my head or Little's or Lars' from our bodies if it was the last thing I accomplished. If I could live through some of the things I'd seen and done, I could handle one sicko with a head fetish and a vendetta against anyone connected to Charley. I kicked the side of the red truck and my shoe tore through a rusted spot.

Shocked at what I'd done, I turned to Henry. "I'm sorry!"

He frowned toward the island again. "Don't worry about it. Let's get out of here."

Henry dropped me off at Edgar's. I apologized again for the hole in the truck. "I'll have it repaired."

Henry said, "Don't worry about the truck, it's not my good one. I'm just relieved I don't have to tell Ben *your* head was in that bag."

***

I found Wilcox and Thor in her basement lab peering at the computer. The sheriff's eyes flicked up at me and back at the screen. "We're busy here."

Holding the camera bag away from my body, I edged closer. Now was the time to ask questions, before I opened the bag. "I'm curious about what you found out about Neil."

Wilcox straightened. "We're holding him, checking his alibi. He said he didn't see Lars after he left the restaurant. He said he fished a while and then went to a bar in Cooper. So far, no one remembers seeing him at the bar."

"Thanks, Sheriff." He hadn't had to tell me. I steeled myself for what was coming, handed him the chunk of wood and told him where I'd been, leaving Henry out of it. No need for him to suffer through a Wilcox tirade as well.

The sheriff blasted me—I was reckless, the last thing he needed was another murder to deal with, and so on. When he wound down, I swallowed and set the camera bag in the middle of the table. "If you're upset about that, wait until you see this." I stepped back.

Wilcox looked inside and reared back. "What the hell?"

The raccoon head set him off again. I was almost sorry I'd brought it back. He was about to march me off to a cell for interfering with a criminal investigation when my cell rang. I checked the caller ID and held up my hands in surrender.

"Excuse me, Sheriff. It's my brother. Maybe he has news about Lars."

It wasn't about Lars. Little wanted me to check on the restaurant. I'd planned to stop there anyway. Chloe had been feeding Rock and Knute and letting them out for brief periods, but I wanted to see them too.

Thankful for Little's good timing, I left Wilcox still fuming and made a hasty getaway to my car, dodging the rain. My phone rang again as I pulled into the restaurant parking lot. This time it was Marta, my *L.A. Times* editor and best friend, likely with an update on my Sudan assignment. The trip was still a month and a half away. I let it go to voice mail. My fingers tapped the steering wheel. She never called just to chat.

***

The crew at Little's moved in slow motion. Chloe had worked double shifts since Lars was hurt and now even her perky ponytail drooped. She'd been with the guys for two years and had assumed the role of temporary manager, a big job for an eighteen-year-old.

Anke and the two students sat at a table drinking coffee. I could feel the tall woman's eyes following me as I went through the kitchen to the guys' apartment.

Rock shot out as soon as I opened the back door. Knute creaked to his feet and limped behind him. Rock blasted through puddles like a puppy and Knute even wagged his tail.

Hating to end their fun, but needing to get back to the hospital, I put them back inside and locked up. I toweled them down and added an extra helping of food to their bowls. Rock's muzzle bumped my hand. He knew something was wrong for his routine to be so disrupted.

On the way to my car, I detoured across the parking lot to the deputy on night duty. "Stay alert, Seth, there are two loved pets inside." I also reminded him the arsonist at Cooper had killed someone.

His jaw tightened. "I don't need you to tell me how to do my job. Wilcox rides my ass day and night."

Another reminder I needed to work on my people skills. Seth was in his thirties, a little cocky the few times I'd seen him, but Wilcox wouldn't have him here if he didn't think he could do the job. I went back into the restaurant, poured coffee in an insulated cup and grabbed a bag of cookies.

Outside again, I passed them through his open window. "I know you're on top of it, Seth."

He thanked me and reached into the bag. "Don't worry, Britt. I'm ready for this guy."

On the drive back to Branson Hospital, I scanned the woods on either side of the road and kept one eye on the rearview mirror.

Little spent the night in Lars' room. I made myself as comfortable as possible on a waiting room couch and prepared myself for Marta's voice mail. No doubt she had been juggling twenty things at once, brown bangs hanging in her eyes, big glasses pushed up on her head. I pulled the phone from my pocket and listened to her message.

Her voice came across at warp speed, as usual. "Hey, Sudan is being fast-tracked. Knowing you, I'm sure you're ready for action, and frankly, I don't know how you can live in a place with no Peet's Coffee. Call me. This is time-sensitive."

Time-sensitive was her way of saying she wanted me there now. A strangled laugh erupted from my throat as if a hyena had control of my vocal cords. How much more messed up could this month get? I flopped back on the hard couch and stared at the ceiling. South Sudan was the biggest challenge of my career. Everything I'd ever done led up to this. I wouldn't miss it.

Sarah hurried through the waiting room in the morning, her dark curls still damp from the shower. "I'm sorry. I slept right through my alarm. I only meant to be gone a couple of hours." I assured her it was fine. Little never wanted to leave Lars for a second anyway.

Little and I grabbed breakfast in the cafeteria. His fork made circles in his eggs. I sipped my coffee. "You know those eggs are already scrambled, right?"

He made a face and set the fork on his plate. "I should get back to Lars."

"Do you mind if I take off for a while to run a few errands? I want to find out what Wilcox is doing to find this guy."

"Don't worry, Wilcox will get him." Little didn't sound as though he was a hundred percent sure.

"If he doesn't, I will." The familiar heat between my brows meant reason had taken a back seat. Revenge and the need for speed drove me now.

He leaned forward. "Can't you just stay with me and let Wilcox's people handle this? I need you."

I reached across and squeezed his hand until he yelped. "I need you too, little brother, and that's why I'm not letting anybody take you away from me."

I called Wilcox on my way out the door. "Why isn't Matthew Willard behind bars?"

"Good morning to you, too. We can't place him at Charley's murder or Lars' beating or the arson and murder in Cooper. We have no motive and no evidence."

"Why, because his dad says he was scavenging junk with him?"

"Watch it now."

"Sorry, Sheriff."

He spit out the words. "At the time Lars was beat up, every place where they said they stopped on their route checked out. We got the autopsy report from Minneapolis with Charley's time of death. They were not in the area when he was killed, and we have no evidence they had anything to do with the arson and Rob's death."

He hadn't seen the deranged look in Matthew's eye, though. "Have you questioned all the World Church members? Maybe one of them is the killer."

He waited a beat, likely getting his temper under control. "We've questioned them." The phone went dead.

Pleased I'd gotten Matthew to give me his number, I called and asked him to meet me at the Country Kitchen on the outskirts of Branson. He put me on hold, most likely to check with his father. He came back on and half-heartedly agreed to meet me in half an hour.

Camera around my neck and gun in the glove compartment, I set out determined to get some answers from the kid Wilcox said had alibis. I wanted to see if the diabolical look on his face had been a trick of the light, and find out if he'd really meant it when he said he wanted to get away from the World Church people and his parents. I could have had it all wrong. I cringed. That had happened before.

Matthew was already seated at a booth when I walked in. I checked the restaurant for the rest of his posse, didn't recognize anyone and slid in across from him.

A young waitress came to take our order, smiling at Matthew. I ordered a BLT. He asked for a Coke, and his gaze followed her back to the kitchen.

I said, "I'm wondering why you agreed to meet me."

Too busy ripping up his napkin and shoving the shreds to the floor to make eye contact, he said, "The sheriff's been asking us a lot of questions. Like what I was doing in Spirit Lake that time I went to your house. I had a hard time explaining that so my dad wouldn't get mad."

He hadn't answered my question. "He tell you about our poor friend, Lars, who might not live after he was brutally attacked?"

"It wasn't me. The sheriff hasn't taken me in so I'm in the clear on that."

"What about your father?"

The right side of his mouth twisted. "He's more like a general who sends the troops to battle."

Was the son tired of doing Daddy's bidding?

The waitress set Matthew's Coke in front of him with another smile and water for me, no smile.

I asked again. "Why did you agree to meet me here?"

"My dad's group doesn't want the police nosing around and thinking we're responsible for everything bad that happens."

"So you're on a good-will mission?"

He darted a sly look at me. "More or less. For one thing, you can't blame me for anything when I'm sitting right here in front of you."

I crossed my arms. "Okay, you're a good guy, who no longer wants to be associated with an organization that beats up gay people and you insist it wasn't you or the World Church. So do you have any idea who did it?"

He shrugged.

I leaned in, dead serious. "Lars is a great guy. My brother loves him. They've been partners for years. I *will* find out who hurt him."

He slammed his glass on the table and I jumped. The mean look was back in his eyes, his helter-skelter teeth bared in a snarl. "This is bullshit. I can't sit here and listen to you talk about how your homo brother and this guy Lars love each other. That purely makes me sick. He deserved what he got."

He stalked out of the restaurant. I tossed cash on the table and followed him to the parking lot. He reached for his door handle, I twirled him to face me and stuck my finger in his chest. "You stay away from Spirit Lake."

He was strong enough to twist out of my grasp but I stayed with him, my face in his. "If anything happens to my brother I will hunt you down." He stepped back and I wasn't sure if he was scared of me or of returning to prison.

The waitress stood in the doorway holding up a slip of paper. "You left too much money."

"Keep it." I waved her away.

She bit her lip. "You want me to wrap up your BLT?" To her, the scene probably looked like I was attacking an innocent kid.

Not taking my eyes off him, I said. "No. Thanks."

"You sure?"

I turned to her and he jumped into his truck, laying rubber when his tires hit the asphalt. I considered following but let him go. As far as I was concerned, it was mission accomplished. I had gotten Matthew to show who he really was. He didn't confess to attacking Lars, but as much as admitted he could have.

***

Little snoozed in a chair by Lars' bedside. I changed the water in vases of flowers sent by well-wishers, tossed out deflated balloon bouquets and told Lars Norwegian vs. Swede jokes, hoping he'd wake up and crack a smile. Late afternoon, Nurse Connie wheeled him out for more tests. Jerry followed to stand guard and we returned to the waiting room.

Sarah answered emails and talked to her office in Chicago, Little had turned into a stone and I paced, until Dr. Fromm came toward us from the corridor an hour later. Slightly less grim than before, he said, "The swelling in his brain is down. We can bring him out of the coma tomorrow."

Little shuddered. He'd been holding on, waiting to hear those words. The three of us hugged each other. This was the first good news since the beating and it had been a long time coming.

Dr. Fromm said, "You should get some sleep in your own beds tonight. This is far from over and he'll need you at your best."

A shower and stretching out on a real bed sounded great to me. Little wanted to spend a few minutes with Lars before leaving for the night, and Sarah was on the phone with their older sister in St. Paul sharing the hopeful news. I let Wilcox know that we would both be sleeping at Little's. He said he'd have another deputy watch Lars and send Jerry to the restaurant.

***

The staff gathered around as my brother told them about Lars, and then they headed back to their duties. Chum whispered to Little, they huddled for a moment and went to the kitchen. I asked Chloe what that was about. Her lips made a straight line. "Customers grumble that Chum's cooking isn't as good as Little's and it hurts his feelings. We've been trying to keep Little from worrying and now Chum's in there whining to him." She started to say something more but bit her lip.

"What else, Chloe?

She blurted it out. "The customers want Little's cooking and Lars' personality. We can't duplicate that. Business is down."

A late coffee-drinker raised his cup. Chloe threw an apologetic look at me, grabbed the coffee and headed to his table. Knowing Chloe wouldn't think of complaining unless the situation was really bad had me worried. We were all at the brink.

Little had already gone to the back. I stepped out into the night to tell Jerry I'd be bringing out the dogs. Puffy eyes looked back at me. "Thanks for the heads-up."

"Everything okay?" I asked.

He wiped a hand across his face. "Elise is ready for me to come home. The boys are getting hard for her to handle."

I tried for an encouraging smile. "I know, it's been a long haul."

He half-heartedly snorted. "We'll be happy for the overtime pay at Christmas anyway."

I circled around back, feeling like an anvil was crushing my shoulders.

Little stood at the back door, frowning. "I thought you said Rock and Knute were here. Did you mean the cabin?"

He saw the look on my face.

"They're not at the cabin, are they?"

Chapter 16

I ran to the woods and back to the garage calling to Rock and Knute. Jerry hurried toward me. "What happened?"

My legs continued pumping, arms flung out in a wide circle. "My dogs are gone!"

He kept up with me. "I've been watching both front and back and checking inside all evening. He'd have to have been really fast."

I slowed to a walk and Little caught up to us. I said, "Rock wouldn't have willingly gone with a stranger. What if one of the staff went to that bedroom you use to store supplies, stepped out back for a cigarette or to make a call and left the door open?"

Little said, "You think they got out and went to the cabin?"

My SUV was parked in front of Little's garage. I fished the car keys from my pocket and jumped in. "I'm heading there now."

Little hurried toward the restaurant, talking over his shoulder. "I'll ask the staff about the storeroom."

Jerry put up a hand to stop me but his job was to watch Little and the restaurant. He said, "Let me know right away if you find them. I don't want to get Wilcox out here for no reason."

I took the corners on two wheels to my cabin and went through the same routine—racing into the woods, back to the lake, across the road and calling until I was hoarse—but they didn't come. I walked to my front door with legs filled with lead. The cabin was locked as I'd left it. I went in. No letters from the killer on my desk this time. I re-locked the house and scanned the woods from the porch knowing they were gone, but yelled one last time, my voice echoing in the trees. "Rock, Knute!"

Slumped over the steering wheel of my SUV, I called Wilcox and Jerry, trying not to picture the creatures hanging in the bistro that horrible morning five days ago, then drove back to Little's.

Seth pulled up at the restaurant the same time I did and we went inside together. "The sheriff's on his way. I would have been here sooner, but I was on a domestic dispute. It's crazy busy in the summer."

"Did Jerry tell you what happened here?"

"Yeah, I'm sorry about your dogs. He wants me to contact the staff."

Everyone but the clean-up crew had gone home. His hand trembling, Little wrote down all the info on his contact list and handed it to Seth. "That's everybody who was on today, first and second shift."

Wilcox found no evidence of a break-in. He, Little, Jerry and I sat at a table near the kitchen. Jerry said, "Seth questioned the staff. Chloe let out the dogs mid-afternoon, they did their business, then she locked them back inside and fed them."

Wilcox flipped through his notes. "No one heard anything suspicious. No one went to the back for supplies. They insisted no one could have slipped through the kitchen and into the guys' apartment without being seen."

I said, "But they were focused on cooking or picking up or delivering food to tables and bringing in tubs of dirty dishes. How could they be so sure?" I turned to Jerry. "An intruder couldn't have gotten in without the dogs barking."

He scratched his head. "The deputy might not have heard it."

Little gestured toward the kitchen and dining room. "The dishwasher, people talking, music playing in the background, traffic."

I turned to Wilcox. "He took a big chance getting the dogs into a vehicle. Someone could have seen him."

He shoved his cowboy hat back from his forehead. "He might have sedated them."

I shook my head. "Sedated, Knute would be difficult to get into a car."

Jerry said, "He could have monitored my routine and calculated how much time he'd need to get the job done."

"Sheriff, the guy would have had to pull into the garage driveway or on the street, walk several yards to the back door, get the dogs into the car and leave before Jerry made his rounds and returned."

Eyebrows knit together, Wilcox looked into the distance as if trying to visualize the abduction and not having any success.

Even though my voice was calm, my body vibrated. I could only think about getting this demon who had infiltrated our lives. I asked, "What are we going to do, Sheriff?"

"We?" Wilcox started his usual lecture about my not being law enforcement and to let his team handle it, but I put my hand up. "Don't."

We stared hard at each other. He broke eye contact. "I'll find out if Matthew has an alibi for this one. We've already asked everyone up and down the street if they saw him, but you know, this time of year all shop owners see is the customers and all they care about hearing is their cash registers ringing." He clamped his hat down on his head.

Little touched my elbow. "I can't be here. I have to be with Lars."

Wilcox asked, "You're both staying at the hospital tonight after all?"

We nodded.

"Good." Wilcox's back crackled when he stood up. "Seth will follow you."

We waited while Little gathered a change of clothes and toiletries. I followed his example and stopped at the cabin to fill a backpack with a few items. On the drive to Branson, Little glanced at me a couple of times.

"What?" I kept my eyes on the road watching for deer, a constant hazard on this forest-lined highway. Seth kept a steady pace behind us.

He asked, "Have you told Ben?"

My throat closed. "I'm going to get them back." I couldn't tell Ben I'd lost his aunt's dog. Rock was our connection to Gert. Talking to him would make me feel better but wasn't fair to him. He couldn't do anything.

Seth peeled away when we walked through the hospital doors.

Little said, "I'm going to Lars." He turned back at the corridor. "I'm so sorry, Britt."

I nodded. "I can't just sit here. Maybe Edgar can see what connects all this."

Little frowned. "It's eleven o'clock."

"He likes to watch late night TV. He'll be awake."

That was the one argument that would get to my brother. He believed in the old blind guy's reputation, but in my past experience, Edgar only saw enough of a situation to pull me in, then he let me figure out how to apply his cryptic comments. Last year he'd dreamed about crying girls on the reservation but he didn't know where they were, or what they were crying about. I had to find that out on my own. Still, Edgar pointed me in the right direction.

"Keep in touch, Britt. I can't be worrying about you, too." Little's eyes misted. "Really, I can't."

I squeezed his shoulder. "I'm not going to do anything foolish."

***

Little thought I was going to Edgar's and I intended to, only not right now. Guilt crept in and gave me a nudge, but right now I needed concrete information more than guidance. I pulled out of the hospital parking lot with one eye glued to the rearview mirror. No suspicious headlights came into view behind me, and I made it to Spirit Lake confident no one followed.

I parked the SUV on a side street up the street from Olafson's and dug through the glove box for my SIG Sauer. I pulled my black hoodie from the bag of clean clothes I'd picked up earlier, zipped it over the camera hanging against my chest and hid my hair under the hood.

Gun in hand, I checked all directions, crossed to the Paul Bunyan Trail and sprinted the mile to my cabin with a sliver of moon to guide me.

I watched the cabin from behind a pine tree, sniffing its familiar scent, listening to the night. When on some silent and parched desert, I liked to recall the peaceful sound of waves lapping and breeze rustling in the birches, but the reality is that a night by the lake is anything but quiet.

The creatures were having a party in the marsh across the road. The cacophony of frogs and crickets, owls hooting and night creatures rooting for food used to seem joyous to me, but now I worried that it masked a killer's footsteps. Trickles of fear raced up and down my spine. The killer could be watching me right now.

With a deep breath, I stepped from behind the tree and slid along the back of the cabin to the garage door. I stuck the gun in my back pocket and unlocked the deadbolt, the keys jangling like cymbals. The seldom-used door creaked on its hinges. Heart thumping, I slipped in and locked it behind me, then waited to let my eyes adjust to the blackness.

Holding the gun in front of me, I moved silently through the cabin. Small electronics beamed illumination from the rooms—the time flashing from the microwave display, a bathroom night light, the Bose in my bedroom winking its pale blue light.

I crossed to the kitchen and laundry room and unlocked that door, eased it open and peeked in. No movement, no scent out of place, except for the overripe apple on the counter. I moved the rack of clothes hiding the door to my secret office, fished the key from the detergent box and let myself in. I turned on the light in the cramped windowless space and booted up the computer. In a few minutes, I typed out my message to Sebastian.

—Can you see if there are any connections between Charley Patterson and my dad Jan Johansson, Rob Jenkins, Matthew Willard, World Church of the Creator, Jacob Lars Weinstein, Jan Johansson Jr. or me?

A minute later he pinged back.

—On it.

—If you get a chance, could you check on connections to these names too?

He said he could. I typed in the names, attached a photo and we signed off.

I closed the door to the cramped secret office, and made my way to the living room. I'd wait half an hour to see if Sebastian came up with anything.

Seated in a dark corner with the gun pointed at the door, I half-hoped the killer would come. I'd make him tell me what he'd done with my dogs and why he killed Charley and nearly killed Lars, and then I would shoot the rabid beast between the eyes.

I hadn't slept except for brief moments of dozing at the hospital and on Little's sofa, but my system was used to sleep deprivation. It was part of my job—I stayed awake and on the story until I got the shot. I put down the gun, unzipped my hoodie and reached for my camera. The familiar shape in my hands steadied my heartbeat. For a couple of years I'd substituted holding a glass of vodka for comfort. Most of the time now, I didn't miss the alcohol other than to wonder how I had gotten so dependent, how easily it had escalated until my life spun completely out of control. Or was it the other way, my life got out of control with a bad marriage, I became a workaholic to keep from dealing with it and then drank to blot it all out?

I put the unwanted thoughts away, zipped the camera back under my hoodie and picked up the gun. This time I wanted a different kind of shot.

A tapping noise that wasn't the wind blowing branches against the roof had me out of my chair and pulling the curtain back just enough to peek out the front window. After sitting in the dark cabin, the crescent moon shone like a spotlight as my gaze swept across the yard and driveway. The wind had picked up causing the waves to slap harder against the dock and shore, but nothing caught my attention.

I moved through the cabin, checking every window, then stood watch out the sliding door in my bedroom, straining to hear. Curious, and unwilling to feel like a scared rabbit trapped in its warren, I slid the door open and stepped onto my deck, gun in one hand and the flashlight in the other. Cool night air washed over me. It had been stifling in there.

Frogs with their nightly din, waves, birch leaves rustling were all familiar but they obscured a sound I couldn't place. Listening hard, I stepped into the yard.

A rhythmic bumping came from the dock, like a boat knocking against it. But there was no boat. I walked along the wooden planks to the T-shaped end and the bumping sound became louder. The teak chairs and table were stable, umbrella snapped closed.

A gust of wind caused the sound to speed up. I looked down at the water and saw what was making the sound. A trapped chunk of wood banged against the dock. My breath came out in a whoosh. I put the gun in my jeans, squatted and pulled up the wood.

It wasn't a loose chunk of driftwood. A slab of old barn wood was attached by a chain that looped around a boat tie-up. Its rounded top reminded me of fake grave markers dotting lawns at Halloween. Something was written on the wood. I unhooked it and brought it closer, training the flashlight beam on the words.

RIP was carved in the top section. Under the RIP were the names, Rock and Knute. He had stapled their collars to the bottom of the marker. I fell to my knees. On my knees clutching the marker to my aching chest. "Oh, God, no." My gaze took in the expanse of lake. His message was that they were out there somewhere.

I leaped up, planted my feet wide apart, faced the woods and raised the grave marker, my rage ricocheting off the trees. "If you're out there watching me, know this. I'll get you."

With quaking hands, I called Ben. My cell phone weighed a hundred pounds. The call went to voice mail. I didn't leave a message. Next, I called Wilcox.

"Get back in the cabin and lock the door. We're on the way." His voice sounded urgent, but I couldn't move.

I was still on the dock when he arrived. He pried the wood marker from my arms and helped me to my feet. The sheriff studied it for a long moment, shoved his cowboy hat back and shivered in the pre-dawn mist. "What a sick sonofabitch."

He tried to tell me it could be a trick, the dogs might still be alive, but neither of us believed it. He said, "Why don't you sit down over there?" and guided me to the cabin. I sat on the porch with my back against the front door, legs splayed in front of me, needing to be anchored to something solid.

Thor showed up shortly after Wilcox. He showed her the marker. She ran over and threw her arms around me. "This just sucks."

Wilcox coughed. She ducked her head and grabbed her case. "I'd better bag that thing." Thor took her flashlight and equipment and crossed the yard. Later, I saw her light moving through the trees.

Wilcox was easier on me than usual, even gentle. "He could have gotten to you, Britt."

I stared into the distance, my eyes empty black holes. "He expected me to find this."

"You're lucky he wasn't ready to stop toying with you." He pointed to a deputy waiting in the driveway. "He'll take you to get your car, wherever you stashed it. Then he'll follow you to the hospital. Do not go anywhere by yourself."

Depleted, I said, "Whatever you say."

He hesitated. "We won't stop until we find this guy."

It was nearly light when Erik's car turned into the driveway. He'd stay with Thor. The big Swede would scare anyone away. He had the temperament of a puppy but whoever was out there wouldn't know that.

Wilcox's tires threw gravel when he left. The deputy walked over to me. "We should go."

"Give me a minute." I tracked down Thor at the back of the cabin. "Has any evidence shown up this time?"

She frowned. "I found Marlboro cigarette butts outside Little's when I was collecting evidence on the window graffiti and those heads. They belonged to that woman from the writers' group. She smokes out there before she goes in to meet the group, but others do too." She pointed to the woods. "I found her brand of cigarette butts in those trees. Wilcox will want to check her out."

My brain buzzed with that information. I said a quick goodbye and got into the deputy's car. He looked like a teenager. I didn't ask his name. "My SUV's near Olafson's.

When he pulled up next to my car, I said, "I'll follow you."

The deputy didn't argue. I stayed with him through town keeping as far behind as possible without causing suspicion, then made a quick left and shot down the shortcut to Winter's Resort. Patty was just opening the office as I pulled up next to her. "Hi Patty, what cabin is Anke staying in?"

Patty's expression told me I'd better tone it down. I lowered my voice. "I just wanted to ask her a quick question."

"Anke's in Birch." She pointed to a cabin but I was already moving. Patty called out, "She's probably not awake yet."

I banged on the door until the woman opened it. Her eyes opened wide when she saw me, the first actual expression I'd seen on her face.

Now that we were standing together, I realized she was taller and bigger than me. I said, "You smoke Marlboros in front of Little's, right?"

She pushed the hair back from her face. "I have the right to smoke outside the restaurant."

I stuck my face inches from hers. "But not outside my cabin. What were you doing there?"

She lifted a shoulder. "I wanted to see where you live."

Wary, I stepped back. "Because?"

"I like your photography. I learned from the Internet you have won Pulitzers." Still unruffled, she said, "I take photos too."

The woman was a fan of my work? I wasn't buying it, not with everything that had been happening. I snarled. "Did you take my dogs?"

Her eyebrows shot up. "Why would I want your dogs?" She tilted her chin toward the camera hanging from my neck. "Is that your favorite kind of camera?"

The quick change of subject momentarily derailed me. Tires braked on gravel and Anke and I both turned as the deputy's car pulled up next to mine.

I backed down the steps with a parting shot to Anke. "Stay away from my cabin."

Before getting into my SUV, I leaned into the deputy's window. "Would you consider not telling Wilcox about this?"

His ears were pink and I doubted it was reflection from the rising sun. "What do you think? This time I'll follow you."

On the drive to Branson I was too numb and sad to think clearly about Anke. If she was interested in my photography, why not ask me? Why the skulking around?

I pulled into the hospital lot, squinting from the sun. Little would be awake and worried. The deputy behind me shot me a sour look and pulled away. Little hadn't texted me last night. He'd probably fallen asleep in the chair next to Lars.

But Little wasn't with Lars. He sat in the waiting room staring unseeing at a magazine. I hurried to him. "Is he okay?"

He spoke in a monotone. "The doctor's with him now. They attempted to bring him out of the coma, but he's not waking up." His eyes squeezed shut. "I really thought I would get Lars back today."

"What did Fromm say?"

"They need to give him more time."

"He'll come out of it when he's ready. You can't lose faith now, Little."

He focused on me. "I know you didn't go to Edgar's. Where were you?"

"Let's go to the cafeteria and get breakfast and I'll fill you in."

We ate our pancakes and syrup. Fork to mouth, chew, swallow. Sip of coffee. Repeat. When we'd finished, I told him about the wooden RIP headstone. He wouldn't have been able to eat if I'd done it sooner.

He took the news with less of an outburst than I expected, already too full of grief to consume any more. His voice sounded far away. "Rock is really gone?"

My cell rang and I motioned to him. "I need to take the call."

I went over to stand by the window. Ben's voice sounded weary as he said, "I'm sorry I couldn't get back to you earlier. We've been tracking this guy all night, but he slipped away again. Is everything okay?"

It was no easier to get the words out this morning.

His voice rough, he said, "What kind of sick shit is this guy into?"

"I'm so sorry, Ben. Gert left Rock for me to protect. He was my responsibility and my friend. Knute didn't deserve to go like that either."

He said, "Don't think like that. And be careful. I'm coming as soon as I can, but it might be a couple of days."

I nodded at the phone.

His voice gentle, he said, "I need to talk to Wilcox. I'll call you later."

Little and I stayed with Lars until Sarah returned midafternoon to take over. She tried to smile at us. "I'll let you know if there's any change."

We would come back for the night shift after a nap in Spirit Lake. Little would not allow Lars to be alone at the hospital. He believed Lars knew we were there, and I did too.

We went to Spirit Lake but only stayed in the restaurant for a few minutes before heading to their apartment at the back. Chloe stopped us to ask if there had been any word on Rock and Knute. "Not yet," I said.

Little's breathing changed almost the minute his head hit the pillow. I stretched out on the sofa, the SIG Sauer next to me under a cushion, and closed my eyes trying not to imagine what it would be like never to ruffle Rock's fur again. No black and white blur keeping me company on my hikes. My eyes closed and with Little's gentle snoring in the background, I drifted into an uneasy sleep.

My phone rang. Disoriented, I checked the time, two p.m. Only two hours had passed. Wilcox barked into the phone. He wanted Little and me to meet him in thirty minutes at an attorney's office in Cooper. "What's going on, Sheriff?"

"Just get here." The line went dead.

Chapter 17

The Law Office of Martin A. Anderson, a converted cottage, was on a side street off the main drag near the First National Bank of Cooper. Little and I walked up the steps, shooting puzzled looks at each other.

Wilcox met us at the door, led us to a small room and indicated two chairs. Wordless, he set his recorder on a table and sat down across from us. I would have said something sarcastic but he was already in a foul mood.

He waggled a finger in our faces. "I don't know what you two are playing at, but withholding information from an investigation will land your asses in jail."

I stood up, ready to tear into him.

He pointed at the chair. "Sit down."

I did as ordered, not sure I wanted to tangle with him after all.

Little cleared his throat. "We don't know what you're talking about, Sheriff."

"If that's the way you want to do this." Wilcox turned on the recorder and reeled off the preliminary date, time, location and who was present info into it. Steely eyes trained on us, he said, "Tell me what your connection is to the person calling himself Charles Patterson."

Little and I talked at the same time, insisting we weren't withholding anything. He grilled us on specific details about every comment we'd made to him about Charley, and when he was satisfied, he turned off the recorder and stood up. "Follow me."

We stepped back into the lobby. He tapped on an office door, opened it and ushered us in. A man in his early fifties with hair curling over his shirt collar came forward. "I'm Martin Anderson."

Wilcox said, "Marty is handling Rob Jenkins' clients."

Switching from being hammered by Wilcox to talking about Rob threw me. I scratched my head.

The attorney shook our hands. "Rob and I were good friends. He was getting ready to retire and we'd already arranged for me to take over his clients."

Little darted a dazed look at me, and I shrugged. Little said, "We're so sorry about Rob's death."

My confusion turned to impatience. "Why are we here, Mr. Anderson?"

"Please, it's Marty." He indicated three chairs across from his desk. Little and I took two next to each other and Wilcox sat on the end, his cowboy hat in his lap.

Marty faced us from across the desk and opened a packet of papers. After several minutes of lawyer-speak, he said something I understood.

"Charles Patterson left his home, land and savings to both of you." He pointed to a sheet of paper with numbers totaling close to a million dollars. "His plant business prospered over the years and he invested well."

We said, "Why us?"

Marty clasped his hands on his desk. "Charley originally left all his worldly possessions to your grandfather, Rolf Johansson, and when Rolf died, Charley changed the will and named your father as beneficiary. When your father died eighteen years ago, Charley changed the will once again, naming you two as beneficiaries."

Our mouths hung open.

Marty said, "Rob added notations that he'd spoken to Charley on the phone a few times over the years, but their last documented meeting was when Charley went to Rob's office to change the will, with you two as beneficiaries."

Wilcox cleared his throat, his eyes boring into Little first, then me. "You have no idea why he would leave everything to your family?"

I said, "We told you, he was our dad's friend, kind of a loner. He didn't join us for holiday dinners or anything."

Little said, "I made sure he had healthy meals in the winter. He was getting pretty old to be staying alone. I do that for a few old-timers."

Wondering why Wilcox wanted to hash over all this again, I leaned back and crossed my arms. "Our grandfather died from a stroke before I was born. Maybe they were friends and Charley got to know our dad through him. People leave their possessions to their pets, all kinds of strange things. Why do you think we're lying, Sheriff?"

Marty glanced at Wilcox and turned back to us. "Rob's notes said additional information was contained in a safe deposit box at the First National Bank here in Cooper."

I jumped up, ready to race across the street to the bank when it hit me. I faced the sheriff. "You went to the bank and opened the box, didn't you? What did you find?"

Wilcox shook his head. "It was empty."

Marty lifted his hand. "If you'll allow me to continue."

We returned our attention to the attorney.

"As a courtesy, because I'd soon be taking over Rob's clients, he digitized all his files and saved them on an external drive that I kept at my place. After Rob died, I went through the files to familiarize myself with the people who were now my clients." He leaned back in his chair. "When I read Charles Patterson's file this morning, I contacted the sheriff."

Wilcox pointed toward a pile of papers on the attorney's desk. "Marty found the information about the safe deposit box. We got a warrant and had the bank open it earlier today."

My eyebrow shot up. "Sheriff, shouldn't we have been included since it technically belongs to us now?"

He snapped. "It's a murder investigation." He spoke to Little. "The bank checked their records. An old gentleman using Charley's identification had a key and took whatever was in it."

Little asked, "When?"

"Two days before Britt found Charley."

Marty scrolled through a file on his computer. "It's probable Charley hadn't been to the bank in years. He hadn't checked the safe deposit box since he opened his account forty years ago. No one would know him there."

I stood at the window and watched two women cross the street, deep in conversation. "Sheriff, you're saying Rob's and Charley's murders were connected? Was Charley killed for the key to the safe deposit box? Thor had told me she found evidence of torture.

Wilcox joined me and we watched the street activity as if that's where we'd find answers. He said, "That's what we're thinking. Then someone posed as Charley and took the contents."

Little grimaced. "That's revolting. You're saying Rob's office was burned down and he was killed so no one could find the will and information about the safe deposit box."

I faced the sheriff. "How exactly did Rob die? You must have the forensics report by now."

"He was dead before the fire started. Someone bashed in his skull, most likely while Rob was still working that evening, left and came back to set the fire before dawn."

We all looked away from each other. Rob Jenkins was collateral damage.

I stood up. "This has been a lot to digest. My brother and I have to talk."

Little checked his watch. "Right now, I need to get back to Lars."

Marty gave me the keys to Charley's house, we signed papers and left. Little and I were too bewildered to talk about Charley and his will on the drive back to the hospital other than to agree that one of us should call our mother.

Wilcox followed us to Branson and came into the hospital with us. I overheard him at the desk asking the nursing staff to report any unusual activity to Seth. They nodded and went on about their work.

I overtook him as he walked toward the door. "Did you honestly think we murdered Charley so we could get his inheritance? He was past ninety. Why would we do it now? Why would anybody have done it now?"

152

He slapped his hat against his thigh. "I didn't think you murdered him but I had to find out for sure you weren't keeping information from us." He walked away, then turned back. "For what it's worth, I didn't enjoy being rough on you after last night, even after that stunt you pulled ditching my deputy."

"Have you talked to Anke? She said she's interested in my photography but she's never asked to meet me."

"We brought her in for questioning. I'm going over there now." He left with another warning not to go anywhere alone.

Little and Sarah were together in the waiting room when I came in. He said, "Sarah's got to go back to Chicago for a while."

She tugged at her scarf, agitated. "I hate to leave but my boss wants me to attend a big client presentation. It's my client." She bit her lip. "I don't want to lose my job and Dr. Fromm said it's impossible to tell how long Lars will be in the coma."

Little put his hand on her arm. "It's okay, Sarah. Do what you have to do."

She tapped at a screen on her phone. "My plane leaves in an hour. If I don't hurry, I'll miss my connecting flight in Minneapolis."

I said, "I'll take you to the airport."

Little hugged her and hurried to Lars. His entire life was in the hospital room down the hall from the waiting area. Talking to him about Charley's will was not a priority for him.

I parked outside the hotel while Sarah ran in to get her suitcase and check out. At the tiny Branson airport, I said, "Don't stress, Sarah. You'll be the first to know if there are any changes."

"I'll come back as soon as possible." She kissed my cheek and hurried inside.

Instead of returning to the hospital, I drove back to Spirit Lake. Guilt sat on my shoulders but I shrugged it off. When I'd said I wouldn't go anywhere alone, I hadn't had any place to go. Charley's will changed that.

***

The stake was gone from his garden but the mess of rotting flowers took me back to the morning I'd found him. I'd never again be able to be in the same room with a rhododendron.

Before losing my nerve, I used the key Marty gave me and opened the front door. I touched the SIG Sauer in my pocket to reassure myself even though I hadn't practiced with it in six months.

The other time I'd been inside Charley's home, I'd been looking for clues to his murderer—this time I'd look for his connection to our family.

They'd had a crew in to clear out the debris. A round table and three chairs separated the kitchen from the living room. The hate message on the wall had been removed. A sofa and one upholstered brown recliner faced an old television. There were no pictures on the walls or end tables. Gardening catalogs were stacked on the floor. The smashed coffee table was gone.

A double bed was centered against the west wall in one bedroom with a worn comforter and two pillows on it. One bedside table held a lamp, clock and nothing else. No family photos in this room either. Flannel shirts, jeans, one suit and a heavy coat with gloves tucked in the pockets hung in the closet. My hand trailed down a red and blue plaid scarf on a hook. On the floor were winter boots, gym shoes and one pair of dress shoes. No suitcase. I pulled out all the dresser drawers and ran my hands along the undersides to see if anything was hidden behind them. I riffled through a few handkerchiefs, socks, underwear and t-shirts that half-filled the drawers. Another time I'd bag the clothes and other items for the church rummage sale. The other bedroom was empty.

The only mirror was in the bathroom. On the vanity, brush, comb and toiletries were lined up on a tidy tray. Charley lived a Spartan life. He'd been here forty years and it might as well have been a hotel for all the personal touches.

I sat at the kitchen table, surveying the room again. The sheriff's people had gone over the place with much more professional equipment and experience than I had. I'd hoped something might speak to me, but what wasn't there spoke loud and clear. My brother and I had inherited a cottage and a chunk of lakeshore from an old bachelor who grew flowers, kept to himself and had no family. We'd also inherited his murderer, who'd said, "You Will All Die." Did that mean us? Should we alert our mother in Palm Desert? I didn't want to think about that, but she might be able to shed some light on my dad's connection.

I stepped around the side of the house to Charley's destroyed garden, feeling eyes watching me from behind every tree, but reminding myself that this killer hadn't harmed me before when he'd had the opportunity. A shed at the south corner was partly obscured by a lilac bush. An unlocked padlock dangled from it.

Charley's mud-caked garden shoes were beside the door. Bags of high-quality organic fertilizers were stacked in one corner. I picked through a coffee can full of nuts and bolts and old keys, searched through containers of plant food and open bags of fertilizer, coming up with nothing.

A fairly new rototiller sat in one corner. Sadness settled over me. Charley's garden was all he'd had in life.

We hadn't been able to have a funeral for him yet. His body was still in Minneapolis. In the meantime, burying his trampled flowers seemed like a decent way to say goodbye to him. I pushed the rototiller into the garden. It shouldn't take more than an hour.

I made my way down one row and up another, attempting to keep the unruly machine from zigzagging all over the place, and eventually found a rhythm. Charley must have hired someone to do the job; this would have rattled his old bones. Wilcox would have interviewed everyone who had contact with Charley, but I'd mention it.

The blades chewed at the stalks and decayed blossoms, dragging them under until there was nothing but furrows of soil where once a vibrant and magnificent garden had been. His plants would no longer reach to the sun, drink in the rainwater or bring joy to people.

After an hour of monotonous teeth-jarring effort, sweating in the humidity and heat, I stopped the jiggling machine and went to the house for a drink of water. Charley's glasses must have been broken along with the dishes. I held my damp hair back with one hand and tilted my head to drink from the tap.

Several big gulps refreshed me enough to resume. Rototilling was one more activity to add to the list of things I'd never do again. My shoulders ached but the trampled plants would soon be plowed under and we wouldn't have to look at the distressing sight again.

I wiped my eyes with my shirt and stripped to my tank top, also soaked with sweat as I neared the end of the last row. With one last burst of energy, I rammed the thing forward. The blades struck something hard, the machine shrieked and bounced back at me. It lunged again, jangling my entire body with its crazy dance. I got it under control, backed it away and shut it down, gasping from the effort. The rototiller would just have to sit there. I wasn't going to wrestle a rock out of the garden.

My hair hung heavy on my back and the cool lake water beckoned. At Charley's dock, I scanned the blue expanse, populated with sailboats on one of the few sunny days so far. I kicked off my gym shoes, peeled off my sweat-soaked jeans and dived in.

I rolled and floated under the cool water until my lungs ached. The silent and wavering lake world was a favorite hangout of mine, until I remembered that Rock and Knute might be somewhere down there—the wood gravestone hanging from my dock with their collars attached was the killer's message. My mouth opened in a silent sob.

A yellow perch slithered against my leg, startling me into realizing how vulnerable I was. I'd left the gun on a bench in the shed and my phone in my jeans pocket.

Feeling sad and stupid, I surfaced and pulled myself up on the dock. My breath caught. Someone watched me from a boat several yards out.

Peder waved and the boat moved in my direction.

My hand shot out to stop him. "Don't come any closer for a minute. I'll be right back." My wet tank top and underwear clung to me. I'd feel more comfortable chatting with clothes on. I hurried to the house, knowing he was watching.

I rooted through the closet and put on a worn white shirt, then walked back to Peder, buttoning as I went.

He'd tied up his boat. "If you don't mind my asking, why were you swimming here when your cabin is around that bend?"

"Little and I just found out we inherited this place. My dad and Charley were friends, and the old guy had no family."

His eyebrows lifted above his aviators. "You had no idea you'd inherited?"

"None at all. And do you always spy on women swimming alone?" My tone was light, but a spark of paranoia flared.

He pointed toward town. "I'm just on my way back from Little's. I could tell it was you from your hair streaming behind you under the water."

Peder's high forehead and the tip of his nose were slightly sunburned. His voice quiet, he said, "I didn't know if you'd still speak to me after I let you down."

"I'm sorry I was so hard on you. You warned me about the gas, but I wouldn't let you stop to refuel."

"How is Lars doing? You hear all kinds of things around town."

"We're hopeful he'll be able to identify his attacker when they bring him out of the coma."

"That's great news." He ducked his head with the shy smile I liked. "We should take advantage of this rare sunny day. Feel like going for a boat ride?" He held out his hand.

The wind in my face would feel wonderful under normal circumstances, but right now I doubted if I'd ever feel carefree again. "I need to get back to the hospital. Little worries."

We both turned as a green Forest Service truck pulled into the drive. "That's Ben!" I ran to him, wanting him to wrap his arms around me and hold me there until everything was better. "Why didn't you tell me you were coming?"

He got out of the truck, took in Peder, my half-dressed body and wet hair. "I see I should have."

Chapter 18

I hugged him and pointed toward the garden. "I was rototilling and got so hot I jumped in the lake."

"Rototilling?"

I took his hand and tugged him forward. "Come and meet Peder."

He stepped over my crumpled jeans on the dock. Peder waited by his boat, inscrutable behind his aviators.

"Ben, this is Peder."

Peder put out his hand. "I've heard a lot about you."

At six-two, Ben towered over him. He shook Peder's outstretched hand. "Little tells me you've been helping to keep an eye on Britt."

I darted a look at Peder, confused. What was Ben talking about? "Ben, how did you know to find me here?"

His gaze shifted back to me. "I stopped at the hospital and Little said you hadn't come back from the airport and weren't answering your phone. He told me about the will. I figured you'd be here."

"I must have been in the water when you called." My cell phone rang. "That's probably Little now." I fumbled for it in my jeans pocket.

Wilcox was on the line. I had to hold it away from my ear. "I'm with Little. Where are you?"

"At Charley's. I'm standing here with Ben and Peder."

Wilcox said, "The guy from the writers' retreat. We interviewed him when we canvassed the houses around there."

"He's a friend. I was just leaving, Sheriff."

He didn't sound mad anymore, just tired. "I can't protect you if you don't do what I ask. What would Little do without Lars *and* you? Think of that before you go off on another tangent."

I'd just had an idea and went with it as usual. "I'm sorry. Tell Little I'm fine."

"You said Ben's with you? I need to talk to him. Tell him I'm calling his cell now."

Peder started his motor. "It sounds like you need to get back to Branson."

I waved as Peder's boat pulled away, distracted that Wilcox wanted to talk to Ben. I hoped that's all he wanted.

Ben's brows were drawn together. I asked, "Are you mad about something?"

He pulled me to him. "Just worried about you running around by yourself."

My legs did that wobbly thing and I kissed him. "I'm sorry you were worried but glad you came."

He held me close. "We're still in the middle of my investigation, but I had to see you."

My head rested on his chest, my arms were still circling his waist. "Why don't we go to my cabin after you talk to Wilcox?" He bent to kiss me again but his phone rang.

The call from Wilcox was short and one-sided. Ben said, "Okay, Sheriff. I'll be there." His eyes rolled as he hung up.

"What about the cabin?" I was too old to pout but that's what was going on internally.

"This shouldn't take long. Let's meet at my place in Branson after I see Wilcox."

My mood instantly improved. "That works, and I can check on Little." I pulled on my sticky jeans and dirt-caked shoes and headed to my car. He waved as his truck rolled out of the driveway.

I remembered the rototiller and trudged over to the garden. Charley wouldn't want it left out in the damp night air to rust. I inspected the blade, hoping it wasn't damaged. Up close, what I mistook for a rock through my sweat-blinded eyes was a sharp corner that didn't appear rock-like. I dug the dirt away with my fingers, but that was taking too long.

With a trowel from the shed, I dug up a shallow rectangular box. It was padlocked. Wilcox had scared me so I tucked the box under my arm and rolled the rototiller back to the shed. A coffee can full of old keys and bolts sat on a shelf. One of the keys might open the box, so I stuck the gun in my waistband and grabbed the can, hurrying back to the safety of my car.

Miserably uncomfortable in my clothes and dying for a shower, I took a quick detour to my cabin.

I bent to pick up a small, white rectangle lying on the mat in front of the door. It said 'Morris Bolger, Developer.' I swallowed hard, remembering Charley stooping to pick up this man's business card. I hurried inside.

This time I showered fast, with the bathroom door propped open and my gun and phone at arm's reach.

Ten minutes later, I grabbed my laptop and a hammer and hurried back to the SUV. The hammer might come in handy if none of the keys worked.

On the way to the hospital, I debated calling Ben, but he'd let me know when he and Wilcox were finished. I intended to find out what Morris Bolger wanted from me, but first I called my mother to ask her about our family's connection with Charley. After putting up with my father for so many years, she was enjoying her retirement in Palm Desert, loving the year-round warm climate and doing all the things she'd missed out on early in life.

Little had already told her about Charley and Lars. Little and our petite mother had the same delicate features and sensitive nature. Neither of them stood a chance against my dad. A towering inferno of repressed anger most often expressed in verbal abuse and in Little's case, physical.

Mom and I caught up since our last chat, and I assured her she didn't need to come to Spirit Lake right now. I asked her about Charley.

"Your father never talked about his visits with Charley. Not a surprise since he didn't talk to me about anything."

"It sounds like you still hate him."

"I don't, but it wasn't right that he was so mean to Little, especially since his father did the same thing to him. You'd think he would have been more understanding."

"What are you talking about?"

"Your grandfather, Rolf, was hard on your dad. He never thought your dad was tough enough."

"The only thing I know about my grandfather is that he died before I was born."

"I don't know much either. After Rolf died, we inherited his house and moved to Minnesota. Your grandmother passed away years before that."

She changed the subject and told me she'd been thinking of taking a cruise with her boyfriend, and I encouraged her to do it sooner rather than later. Her parting comment rang in my ears. "You're watching over your brother, aren't you?"

The new information about my father's childhood collided with my own memories and instead of going back to the hospital, I detoured to the town cemetery.

Driving through the arched vine-covered gates, I felt the weight of all those souls but was looking for one in particular. I hadn't visited him since the funeral. I'd been sixteen and the reason why we were burying him.

A dead rhododendron plant sat in front of his headstone. Not even Charley would be visiting him now. With my heart as hard as the granite oblong anchoring him to the next world, I nudged the stone with my toe. "What was Charley's secret?"

I listened for an answer, but the only sound was a distant buzz of the groundskeeper riding his mower in drowsy circles among the graves. My heart softened a fraction. "What Mom said about your childhood doesn't alter the fact that you abused her and Little, but I'm sorry for kicking you out of the car that night." I bit my lip, holding back the flood of remorse. "If I'd been more mature, I like to think I would have handled it differently."

A breeze lifted the blades of grass next to his grave. I picked up the dead plant and dropped it in a bin before hurrying to my SUV.

***

Little's brows drew together when he saw me walking toward him. "You said you were taking Sarah to the airport. Wilcox was furious."

I'd done it again, following whichever way the wind blew, forgetting people were worried about me. I'd counted on Little sticking close to Lars since Sarah wasn't there and hoped he wouldn't notice how long I'd been gone. "I'm sorry and I'll explain, but first tell me how Lars is doing."

His voice was strained. "The same. The doctor's with him now." He pointed to the heavy bag dragging on my shoulder. "What's that?"

"A clue maybe." I set the bag between us on the waiting room couch and pulled out the box. "I'm dying to see inside, but wanted you to be with me when I opened it." I told him where I found it and reached for the coffee can. "Maybe the key's in here." A few people shot curious looks at us, but most were lost in their own worries.

Sorting through the nuts and bolts for keys and methodically trying them took Little's mind off Lars. I was willing to live with my impatience until he'd tried every key if that would give him a few moments of peace.

When he ran out of keys, I took the metal box outside where the noise wouldn't scare anyone and whacked it with my hammer. The lock broke, and I hurried back inside so we could open it together.

I set it on his lap. "You're the anthropologist, you unwrap it."

He carefully removed the airtight wrapping, revealing a five-by-eight-inch gold frame with a white mat, yellowed with age. In the photo, a fair-haired man in a gray suit stood next to a woman—a foot shorter, even in her pumps. She wore a dressy blue suit with wide shoulders. A matching hat with a feather and netting perched at an angle on her upswept hairdo. A few dark tendrils framed her smiling face. A white blouse with a loose bow at the neck and a string of pearls around her throat peeked out from her suit. She held a bouquet of yellow and white rhododendron. His hand covered hers; both wore gold wedding bands. The couple smiled radiantly at the camera.

I breathed, "It's a wedding photo."

Little pointed. "This has been colorized, and look at the lower right corner. Here's where it was taken. Gundersen Photography, Trondheim, Norway, 1940."

"Do you think it's Charley and that he had a wife?"

Little peered closer. "They look young. It's hard to tell if there's a resemblance, but this guy is tall and thin like Charley."

Not liking where this was leading, I paced in front of the couch. "If it was Charley's wedding photo, why not display it in his house?"

Little said, "Dad's family came from Trondheim."

I stopped pacing. "Let's not make assumptions." I sounded like Wilcox. "Coming from the same place could be the reason they became friends."

"I'll see if something's written on the back of the photo." He concentrated on the picture, turning the frame over and using his fingernail to bend tiny nails holding the backing in place.

I watched from behind his shoulder, a spark of excitement fluttering in my stomach. He pried it off and we both leaned in for a closer look.

His shoulders slumped. "It's blank."

I threw myself into a chair.

"Wait, there's more." He reached into the metal box and brought out another object. I would have ripped off the plastic, but Little took his time.

He squinted at a man's gold wedding ring. "Something's inscribed, but I can't read it. It needs to be cleaned."

I held it between my thumb and forefinger bringing it close to my eyes, but couldn't read it either. "I'll take it to Gray's Jewelers in the morning."

Little brought out the final object, a white lace handkerchief, now yellowed, with the initials, RS, embroidered in one corner.

We pondered the handkerchief, picture and ring until Nurse Connie stopped to tell us the doctor had finished examining Lars. "I'm afraid there's still no change."

Little went to Lars and I opened my laptop and Googled Trondheim, Norway, 1940. A section about Trondheim and Hitler's occupation of Norway during that time period caught my attention but my cell phone rang, interrupting further research. It was Marta.

Her words were more clipped than usual. "You don't return my calls, now?"

"I'm sorry. A lot is going on here and I'm in the middle of it."

"I know what you're in the middle of. That sexy forest ranger you couldn't wait to get back to see."

Ben was taking a long time with Wilcox. "He's been away on a case."

"We need you on this." Her voice turned urgent. "You're a hunter, Britt, but what you hunt for is not only the pain and suffering—your pictures catch those moments when people rise above. You're the best for South Sudan."

Marta was an expert at stroking my ego and appealing to my sense of duty. I grimaced at the ceiling. "I can't leave right now."

"You have the skills and experience we need for this, but I can find someone else. Shall I do that?"

"No! But Lars was beaten nearly to death and is in a coma. The guy has killed two people and threatened Little and me, and we have no idea why."

"I'm sorry, I didn't realize. What are the local authorities doing about this?"

"The guy leaves no evidence."

"Hold on." Marta carried on a muffled conversation with someone in the newsroom and came back on. "How long do you need?" I could practically hear the wheels turning in her head, strategizing how long she could stall and who else was available, just in case.

"There's more. Marta, he took Rock." My throat caught. "We think he's dead."

"Oh, sweetie, I'm so sorry. Do you want me to come out there?" Hardboiled Marta had a soft spot for pets. Humans in peril weren't that big of a deal to her.

"Thanks, but you don't need to. I'm worried about Little now. I have to make sure he stays safe. We don't know what motivates this guy but something connects all of us."

She sighed. "I'll check with you in a few days, since you seem to have lost my number." I winced. She hung up with a loud "Be careful!"

Another issue was whether I'd end up losing my job for the second time if I didn't grab this. It wasn't a choice though. Much as I wanted the work, Little came first. Mom's words rang in my ears.

I dug Bolger's card from my jeans and tapped in his number. He picked up on the first ring. "Mr. Bolger, this is Britt Johansson. You left a business card at my cabin?"

"Yes, thanks for calling. I have a proposition for you and I hope we can get together."

"What's this about, Mr. Bolger?"

"Please call me Mo. If you don't mind, I'd rather we discuss it in person."

I arranged to meet him at Little's the next morning, more than a little curious about what he had to say.

***

Ben followed as I drove down his winding tree-lined road and pulled into the driveway. The structure in front of me surprised me once again. He'd grown up in a cabin much like Gert's, at his father's resort, and only recently built this lovely cedar home overlooking the lake. I hesitated before leaving my car, nervous that I'd mess up again. The only other time I'd been here, I'd barged in when he was angry with me for going back to my now ex-husband, even though the reconciliation was short-lived. I had been too pushy, insisting that Ben still loved me. He'd said he didn't.

I straightened my shoulders. This time would be better. He did love me.

He got out of his truck and grabbed a grocery bag from the passenger side. "Sorry it took me so long with Wilcox."

"What's in the bag?"

"Steaks. I'm starving. How about you?"

165

I nodded. My stomach growled, reminding me I hadn't eaten since breakfast. So much had happened today.

He set the bag on his kitchen counter and I waited in the living room, taking in the high ceilings and clean lines, a contrast to the messy bachelor's existence he and his dad had lived at their resort.

He opened windows. "Been a while since I was home." Within moments, a cool breeze off the lake moved through the space.

He'd also brought a baguette and things to make a salad. I put the greens and veggies together while he grilled steaks, and we had dinner on the deck, watching the sunset. We didn't say much, letting go of the chaos from the past week and enjoying the soft swish of a breeze rustling the birches. His home sat on a rise, farther from the lake than my cabin, but close enough to hear the rhythmic waves against the shoreline.

After dinner I made tea and we sat together on the soft leather sofa, my head on his shoulder, his hand stroking my hair. He talked a little about the BW project, but I didn't mention what was happening in Spirit Lake. I wanted to shut that out and make this perfect evening last, and Ben understood without saying it.

His phone rang. He hesitated, as if debating whether to answer before picking it up. He listened, then jumped to his feet. "Yeah, I can be there in the morning. Alert Woz. I'll meet him in Ely and we'll head up together." He hit end. "They finally spotted the guy we're been looking for. At least they think it's him."

I was still leaning back on the sofa, my feet tucked under me. He dropped down beside me. "I'm sorry. I wanted to stay longer."

"I know you did." I unfolded from the sofa, took his hand and tugged him toward the loft. "Want to give me a tour?"

He held me in his arms and we stayed like that for a moment, then walked up the spiral stairs.

A king-sized bed, extra-long, faced a roomy deck overlooking Lake Branson. I pictured having morning coffee as the sun peeked through the pines.

He stood behind me, moved my hair aside and kissed my neck. I turned and reached for him, thinking we had to hurry, grab every second as if there'd never be another, but he held me away, his eyes on mine.

"For me, this is a dream, Britt. Coming home to you after a tough week." His arm waved in an arc. "I built this with you in mind. When you were away, I pictured you sitting across from me in your chair facing the fireplace. Waiting for the day we'd wake up together in this bed."

"It's my dream too. There's nowhere else I want to be and no one else I want to be with."

We'd been such good friends as kids, spending hours in the woods or on the lake. We'd built forts, camped, kayaked and fished. I admired his easy grace, how he could name the trees and bushes and wildlife and their cycles. I photographed everything.

And so it was an easy transition when a few months ago our bodies touched for the first time. I loved it all, giving each other comfort and pleasure, the sweaty ecstasy we shared together.

We undressed and slid under the covers but I couldn't shake off a sinking feeling.

"What are you thinking?" He raised up on one elbow, and traced the outline of my body with one finger.

"Here I am next to you and I'm already sad about being away from you again."

He kissed me. "How about saving that for when we're actually apart?"

"Good point." I pounced on him and that initiated a tussle that neither of us tried too hard to win.

***

In the morning, I woke before he did and watched him, one arm flung over the pillow, his usually close-cropped hair a little shaggy. His hawk nose was sharp against the pillow, the fan of laugh lines smoothed in sleep. I breathed in his male, woodsy scent and slipped out of bed.

Downstairs, I found the coffee makings, and wandered into the living room as it brewed, wondering what it would be like to share this home with him—the leather sofa, soft as butter, the blue-green plaid chair he'd picked out for me. I'd been instantly drawn to it when I saw it last year. I ran my hand over the soft fabric, dreaming. The coffee maker beeped and I poured coffee into a carafe, set two mugs with loon designs on a tray, found a *StarTrib* and *Branson Telegraph* outside the front door and carried it all upstairs.

The cups clinked against each other when I set the tray on a dresser. His eyes opened and he grinned, a sight that always caused a small seismic event in my stomach. I sat next to him on the bed and smoothed a chunk of his hair. "We could have coffee on the deck and watch the sunrise."

He pulled me close. "The coffee will stay warm for a while."

Chapter 19

Ben headed back to the BW. I could tell he wanted to go and wanted to stay, a conflict familiar to me. I drove to the hospital, dreading another day of uncertainty, wondering if Marta was still on my side.

Little stopped me in the corridor. "Good, you're here. I'm going to Spirit Lake. One of the ovens stopped working and Chum's in a panic. Wilcox said a deputy can pick me up in a few minutes." His head tilted toward Lars' room. "Promise to sit with him until I get back?"

"Of course."

"Call me if…, you know." He went to meet the deputy.

I said hello to Seth sitting in a chair outside Lars' room and went in. When he'd first arrived seven days ago, flowers and balloon bouquets covered nearly every surface. There were fewer now. His chest moved up and down rhythmically. The cuts and bruises on his face were beginning to heal and he looked familiar again. The only way I'd recognized Lars when I'd first found him was his fringe of reddish hair. I shuddered at the remembered image of his battered body. He looked peaceful sleeping, but I missed Lars and Little mocking me with their inside jokes, usually with affection, sometimes frustration. Lars belonged at the restaurant teasing and chatting with the customers, fishing with the guys in the summer, zipping around on his snowmobile in the winter.

Whispering close to his ear, I said, "You need to wake up now so we can catch the sadistic monster who did this to you. He's after Little too, and if you have any information that will help us, we need it now. No more lazing around in bed, my friend." I squeezed his hand.

Someone gasped and I straightened up, caught in the act. Nurse Cranky had come up behind me. "You can't talk to the patient like that. It might traumatize him."

"He's not the patient, Connie. His name is Lars."

"I know his name and you need to step out right now." She stood at the door, a sentinel.

My hand was still gripped around his slack fingers. I squeezed one last time, but before we lost contact I sensed a twitch. I squeezed back gently and his fingers tightened around mine.

I squeaked. "Connie, he moved his hand."

"His muscles twitch. It doesn't mean anything. You have to leave now."

I refused to move and squeezed again, but this time I felt no returning pressure. I let go. Maybe I wanted it to happen so badly I imagined it.

She cleared her throat. "Do I have to get an orderly?"

"I'm leaving." Keep your shorts on, Cranky.

I tucked his blanket around him, kissed his broad forehead and whispered. "I'll be back to continue our conversation."

She ushered me toward the door so she could begin her ministrations. I *was* grateful for her. She was the best nurse at the hospital, conscientious, timely, smart, but a tight-ass.

"Thank you, Connie. I know you're taking good care of Lars."

Her eyes widened at my unexpected compliment. It was no secret that I called her Nurse Cranky behind her back. I'd had several personal experiences with her over the past year. She'd helped me heal, but I could have done without all the tsk-tsking and frowning at my reckless behavior.

I went to the cafeteria for a cup of coffee and brownie, and then headed back to Lars' room, my hand still imprinted with his touch. Seth yawned. He'd been sitting there for hours. I handed him the coffee and brownie. "Hey, Seth, how's it going?"

He took a sip, peeked in the bag and brightened.

170

"Is Connie still in there?"

"She just left and said to keep everyone out."

"She didn't mean me. I'm sitting in for Little."

He nodded and reached in the bag. "Thanks, just what I needed." I slipped into the room.

Lars looked the same as before. I took a deep breath, held his hand in mine and squeezed. "It's Britt, can you hear me?" A movement. I tried again. "Open your eyes. You can do it." I detected slight agitation beneath his eyelids. "C'mon."

His fingers closed around mine. The cords in his neck and jaw tightened, and then everything slackened. My voice rose. "Lars, do it for Little. Open them."

His face turned red, and a groan came from deep in his chest. I prayed I wasn't making him worse but if he could, now was when he would do it.

His eyes opened to a slit and quickly closed. The light was too bright. I leaped to the light switch and turned it off. My face close to his, I said. "Try again."

More blinking and the slits opened and widened, trying to focus. And then the eyes on mine cleared. His mouth trembled and he croaked. "Little?"

With clumsy fingers, I tapped in Little's cell number. "Little, someone wants to say hello. Listen." I picked up a damp cloth from the side table and pressed it against Lars' parched mouth, then put the phone to his lips. He whispered, "Hi, babe."

Little's joyful noises brought a smile to Lars' bruised face.

I took the phone. "Little, I need to get the nurse and doctor in the room. I'll put my phone on speaker and you can keep talking to Lars."

He said, "Lars, I'm ten minutes away!"

I pressed the red button. In a moment, Connie burst in. She wanted to tear into me for disobeying her orders, but took one look at Lars and forgot me. The doctor came next and I was ushered out with my phone. Little hung up and I called Ben with the good news. We were still talking when Little flew past me. I said to Ben, "Hold on a second, I need to see this."

I stood in the doorway and used my phone to video Lars looking at Little. An energy field of love between them so large

171

it filled the room pushed Cranky and the doctor out the door. As if it was his idea, Dr. Fromm said, "We'll give them a moment."

Fromm and Connie had their heads together, talking. They saw me leaning against a wall in the hallway and converged on me. The doctor said, "Describe exactly what happened."

"Ben, I have to go. I have more explaining to do." All I did lately was account for my behavior.

Two sets of rimless round glasses focused on me. "I gently squeezed his hand and his eyes opened." No need for them to know I badgered a comatose man into waking up. They didn't look satisfied, but left me alone. I took a deep breath. Things were looking up. Lars was awake and Ben and I just had a wonderful night and morning together.

I peeked in the room. My brother turned to me with a radiant, teary smile. Lars had fallen asleep again, but Little wouldn't leave until he and Lars left together.

Wilcox arrived and told Seth he was rotating guards every four hours. He saw me eavesdropping and motioned me over. "If it gets out that Lars is awake, this guy could try something again. We'll have someone with you and Little too."

"Little's with Lars and I'll be fine on my own. I know how to take care of myself." I might have flexed an arm muscle, which was total bravado. The sheriff's intensity scared me.

Wilcox pulled his hat over his brow. "Remember, this guy wrote 'You Will All Die' on Charley's wall. It's an order. You go nowhere alone. No slipping off to rototill a goddamn garden."

"I found a photo and wedding band in the garden."

His eyebrows lifted. "Let's see it."

I pulled the box out of my camera bag and showed him the photo, ring and handkerchief.

"That's withholding evidence from the scene of a crime. When were you going to show me?"

I tipped my head toward the hospital room. "A lot happened today." I handed him the box and he headed toward the exit.

Head lowered, I walked down the corridor to the waiting room wondering about Charley, scared that Lars was even more vulnerable now that he might be able to name his attacker, heartsick over losing Rock and Knute and unsure whether the World Church was behind this. I'd been optimistic a few moments ago, but now my energy and confidence were at a low ebb thanks to the reality check from Wilcox.

I needed to talk to a friend. I punched in Henry's number at the casino and he answered on the second ring. "Hey, Britt, how you doing?"

Hearing his voice cheered me. "I was hoping we could talk. You busy?" Henry and I had become friends when I covered the casino theft last year. Managing the casino finances was a big responsibility, but the good-hearted man always made time for me.

He said, "Why don't you come out and have coffee with me?"

My teeth clenched. "I'm not allowed to go anywhere by myself."

Henry chuckled. "I never thought I would hear that from you."

"Me either, but I don't want the sheriff to have to stop his investigation to babysit me."

"That sounds like real growth." He got serious. "How about if I pick you up and we visit Edgar?"

I agreed. Since I wasn't leaving on my own, Wilcox would have no reason to jump down my throat.

An hour later Henry's heavy-duty Chevy pickup pulled into the hospital lot. I jumped in and we headed to Spirit Lake.

"Thanks for picking me up. I wanted to tell you that Lars came out of his coma and seems to be okay."

"That's great news, but you could have told me over the phone."

"Wilcox wants to keep it quiet until he's figured out a plan. He thinks the killer might come after him again."

Henry nodded. "I won't say anything."

I said, "Wilcox gave me a bad time over the visit to the island but I didn't mention you."

He chuckled. "You didn't have to. Ray told him I was there. The sheriff wasn't happy with me either."

"I'm sorry." Causing other people grief was another problem with being me. Guilt and regret were my constant companions.

Edgar's wasn't far from Spirit Lake, so we made a detour to Little's Café. I'd called ahead and Chum had chicken-wild rice hotdish ready for us to take to Edgar. Chloe stopped me as we were leaving. "A man came in earlier and said to give you this." She handed me a business card. Morris Bolger. I'd forgotten our appointment.

Henry navigated the winding reservation road circling the north side of Spirit Lake, and turned at the fork where a sign pointed to the right—Edgar Turner 1 mi. We bounced down the rutted road, crested the hill and slid down the other side. Henry had more skill than most at avoiding the lake at the bottom of the hill. In the winter the hill was icy and in the summer the gravel acted like a slide.

Henry parked close to the door, grabbed the rifle from its rack behind our heads and we joined Edgar, waiting in the doorway.

The compact cedar home's high curved windows faced Spirit Lake. Even though Edgar couldn't see details, they let in a dazzling light on sunny days. Today wasn't one of them, though; a thick blanket of moist air hung over the lake.

For most of his life, Edgar lived in a shack near where they'd built the new cedar home two years ago. He'd hated to leave the shack but his age and diabetes required central heating, and the Jacuzzi helped his circulation. His nose twitched.

"I brought hotdish, Edgar."

We followed him to the kitchen. Edgar sniffed the still steaming dish. "This isn't Little's."

"It's his recipe, but Chum made it for you this time. Little's not at the restaurant these days."

Edgar nodded. "Thank you. Let's sit and talk for a while." The old guy led us to his family room and took his usual seat on the sofa. I perched on the edge of an overstuffed chair next to the fireplace, jiggling my feet. "That's a new basket, isn't it? It's beautiful."

He took the basket from his coffee table and ran his gnarled fingers over it. "My great-niece Cecelia made it for me."

Henry brought us iced tea in tall glasses, and I told Edgar the good news about Lars, with the sheriff's warning not to share it just yet.

Edgar said he was relieved to hear it. He cocked his head toward me as if listening, and said, "You're not yourself. I see that fear has you in its grip."

I hadn't confessed my terror to Henry—it embarrassed me—but Edgar nailed it. I whined like a petulant child. "I can't even begin to guess what's going on here. Usually, I figure something out pretty quickly. It's not always right, but it leads me in the right direction. This time I went after an offshoot of the World Church of the Creator group in Iona that targets gays. They might not have anything to do with us but now I've stirred them up and they could retaliate."

Edgar sipped his tea. Henry stood at the window still as a slab of concrete, rifle in the crook of his arm, his almost black eyes tracking every movement outside.

My voice rose, an undertone of panic in it. "Wilcox is doing all he can but why hasn't he found the killer?" Tears gathered in my eyes and found their way to my voice. "Edgar, this guy drowned Rock and Charley's dog, Knute."

Edgar set his tea on the table. "Rock's a good companion. He's been here many times with Gert and you."

I sniffed, the tears still trickling. "You mean *was* a good companion."

"The ancestors haven't seen him."

I rolled my eyes—he couldn't see me so it wasn't really disrespectful. "You mean on the other side."

"It's all one side, but most people only see their own reflections."

"Please don't go there today, Edgar. You know it gives me the creeps when you talk like that." He grinned and a zillion more wrinkles surfaced. A geologist could map his face like a tree trunk.

He nodded. "Someone's stalking you like a cat after a bird."

I used the bottom of my tank top to wipe my eyes. "Not helping, Edgar. With all due respect, what am I supposed to do, fly away and leave my brother and Lars unprotected?"

He tried to suppress a chuckle. "You don't have to fly away, just hop out of his reach."

The more frustrated I became, the more it tickled Edgar, but this wasn't funny. I jumped up from the sofa. Legs planted wide, hands on my hips, I stood over him. "I'm no sparrow who needs to keep away from the pouncing cat, Edgar. I'm a bird of prey, and the killer had better watch out. I'm about to swoop down and make him my lunch."

Edgar clapped his hands together once. "Good. That fear you were wearing decided to go somewhere else."

I did feel more like myself when Henry and I left shortly after. Did that old fart manipulate me?

Henry dropped me off at the hospital, and I thanked him for being my bodyguard. He laid a heavy hand on my shoulder. "You need anything, let me know."

I headed inside. Grim reality returned as I walked down the too-familiar hospital corridors. Edgar hinted that Rock and Knute might still be alive, but the murderer had no problem killing a ninety-year-old man, attempting to kill a strong guy in his mid-thirties with arms bigger than my thighs, burning a man to char to keep anyone from finding out details about Charley and decapitating helpless animals just to scare us. Why wouldn't he kill the dogs? I shivered. Why didn't he kill me?

I peeked in Lars' room, pleased to see that his skin looked brighter. He was on the phone with Sarah, telling her it wasn't necessary for her to come back right away. I took Little aside and told him what Edgar said about Rock.

He said, "I've told you before, Edgar's so old he doesn't really see the difference in the two worlds."

I nodded. "By the way, what was Chum's problem with the stove earlier?"

"Not a big deal. I had to order another part and they'll have to make do until it arrives." His eyes rested on Lars. "I wanted to be there when he opened his eyes."

Linda Townsdin

"He didn't come completely awake until you were there, Little."

Midafternoon, Wilcox arrived to ask Lars a few questions. Little hovered, watchful and protective. I was across the room with instructions from Wilcox not to say anything. The sheriff pulled a chair close and began gentle questioning. "Do you remember where you were found?"

Lars looked down. "Little said Britt found me on the island but I don't remember it."

"Were you fishing over there?"

"Maybe. I have a lucky spot on the south side, an inlet. I usually check it to see if the walleye are biting."

Wilcox set his cowboy hat on his lap. "How about telling us as much as you can remember that day."

Lars closed his eyes. "I remember being mad at that guy, Neil. Then feeling bad for sneaking off to fish." He looked at Little. "But it was great to do something normal for a change."

Little patted his shoulder and Lars continued. "I put my gear in the boat and headed south to shallow water. I didn't want to get caught in high waves if the wind picked up. Fishing's no good and not fun in that stuff. But it can be decent over in those inlets. That's all I remember." Lars lifted bleak eyes to the sheriff.

Wilcox smiled. "That's fine. We made a good start."

I stepped forward. "Did you see any other fishermen? Maybe Neil?" Wilcox shot me a warning look and I retreated to my corner.

Lars scrunched his brows together trying to remember. "I'm sure there were a few." He let out an anguished cry. "I don't know."

I paced until Little and Wilcox spoke in unison. "Stop it."

An idea started to form. "Sheriff," I said, "What would you think about making a statement to the paper that Lars came out of his coma and is expected to identify his assailant?"

Wilcox rubbed his chin. "To get the guy to make a move."

Little grabbed my arm. "Are you insane?"

Wilcox pushed his hat back from his forehead. "Little, no one's doing anything without you and Lars on board."

177

I said, "We have to do something."

Lars focused on the sheriff. "How would that work?"

The sheriff pinched the bridge of his nose. "We had a situation like this in Denver. We moved the victim to a different room, but kept the guard outside the empty one as a decoy. The killer was dressed like medical staff and came for him, and we nailed him."

Little's eyes shot daggers at us. "I won't let you do this. Lars has been through too much already."

Lars said, "I think we should try it, Little. We need to get this guy."

Little's mouth turned down. "It's not foolproof."

Wilcox said, "I don't like it either, but it's a controlled environment, something we won't have once Lars is back in Spirit Lake."

That statement settled around us. Little swallowed and nodded. "I know."

Nurse Cranky came in and said Lars needed rest. We shuffled out to the waiting area. The sheriff said he'd let us know when he'd arranged all the details. I walked toward the exit with him.

"Anything on the stuff in that box, Sheriff?"

He kept walking. "The ring inscription read, To My Darling Gunnar. The only fingerprints Thor found on the metal box and the items inside were yours and Little's."

I sat with my fingers in my mouth, chomping my nails like they were corn on the cob. Now that it was going to happen, I had second thoughts about the sheriff attempting a bait and switch. I'd seen too many botched operations like this on television cop shows.

Chapter 20

The sheriff's office had called for an afternoon press conference outside the hospital. We needed local coverage for this plan to work and I'd contacted the *Branson Daily*, the *Cooper Weekly* and a TV news affiliate. The *StarTrib* wouldn't run a story on the press conference, but might use a photo from today's event when they caught the guy.

I moved through the crowd shooting and looking for anyone suspicious. Anke stood across the street, always easy to spot because of her height. The woman showed up everywhere. Wilcox hadn't shared what he learned from questioning her about hanging around my cabin.

Reporters shoved their mics close to the sheriff's face. Wilcox was brief. "Jacob Lars Weinstein, co-owner of Little's Café in Spirit Lake, who was brutally beaten on July ninth, has awakened from his coma and is able to talk. We're meeting with him this evening and hope to obtain information leading to the identity of his assailant."

A reporter asked, "Sheriff, did the same person who beheaded Charles Patterson and kill the lawyer here in Cooper do this thing to Lars Weinstein? We've also learned there's been an increase in vandalism in Spirit Lake. Is that true?"

Wilcox glared at him. "We're looking into all possibilities."

Anke pushed forward until she stood a few feet from Wilcox and leaned in, listening hard. I took her photo.

Several reporters swarmed closer and hit him with questions, but the sheriff was an old pro. He kept his cool and wrapped it up in ten minutes.

He had a harder time keeping cool with me. He jabbed a finger at me. "It's a bad idea for you to be here. You're one of the killer's targets."

I crossed my arms. "I'm hoping my camera caught someone in the crowd who didn't belong." I looked around to point out Anke but she'd melted away. "Want me to send my photos to you?"

A reporter bore down on him and he made a quick escape into the building, barking over his shoulder. "Send them."

Back at the bureau, I loaded my photos onto the computer. Cynthia's voice rose loud enough to penetrate her closed door. I cocked an ear. "Britt's freelancing for me and I need her, Sheriff."

Hearing her stand up to the sheriff brought a smile to my lips. *Good going, Cynthia.* She'd had a rough time last year with her husband so ill. She'd needed to keep her job so she'd have insurance to pay for his medical treatment, and was afraid to speak up to the corporate office or sheriff. I caused her a lot of trouble over that before learning about her husband. Sadly, he died from the illness. Marta had told me Cynthia was a tough old bird and I didn't see it at the time. Now, the old Cynthia was back.

Their next exchange wiped off my smile. "No, Sheriff, I can't keep her safe. Can you?"

I hurried to the hospital to join Little and begin our vigil. Little was allowed to be with Lars, but we had to be careful not to give away his location. I sat in my usual place in the waiting room watching the constant commotion of nursing staff, doctors, orderlies and volunteers performing their jobs. Wilcox said he had an undercover deputy stationed inside the area. I couldn't tell for sure but it could be the woman sitting across from me with a magazine on her lap. Her head was down as if reading, but she looked up a lot, scanning the waiting area, corridors and desk activity.

The usual visitors came and went but I didn't notice anyone skulking around. A kid delivered flowers and candy to the nurses' station to be taken by the nurses or orderlies to patients, or the hospital staff as a thank-you for their good care of a loved one. I should have sent something to Connie.

Moments later, she walked over to me, holding out a box. "These chocolates were just delivered for Lars. I'm afraid he's not allowed to have them yet."

"Thanks, Connie." The tag, "To Lars from the Little's Café staff," came from a familiar gift and candy shop in Cooper.

It was a nice gesture and I'd tell Lars about the gift, but I needed dinner and Little wouldn't want to eat it in front of Lars. I handed it back to her. "Why don't you have it, Connie? You've been so helpful."

"Thank you. I'll share it with the others." She took it back to the desk, lifted the lid and offered it to the staff. She pointed to me as a nurse picked out a piece. Even if it was a re-gift, she smiled.

Nothing happened in the next hour. My screaming stomach led me to the cafeteria, where I wolfed down a bland dinner, then headed back for another session of waiting. Maybe this guy wasn't as stupid as we'd hoped.

An hour later, my attention again flagging, I went to a vending machine for a cup of coffee. On my way back, the intercom called for doctors and nurses to come immediately to the nurses' station outside our waiting room. Sloshing coffee, I ran through the corridor and into the middle of a commotion. Connie and a group of medical personnel swarmed around a nurse lying on the floor retching.

I darted a look at the woman who'd been sitting across from me in the waiting area. She spoke into a phone but didn't leave her station. Hospital staff lifted the nurse onto a gurney and whisked her away. Connie took off down the hallway. I followed and squeezed through the throng. "Connie, what's happening?"

"Two nurses and an orderly are down. Get out of the way." I hurried toward Lars, trying not to draw attention to myself, and punched in the sheriff's number on my cell. It went to voice mail. My heart beat in triple time as I banged on the locked door. "It's me, Britt." Seth, on his cell, let me in. Little jumped up from a chair. "Quiet. Lars is sleeping."

It took a moment for my heartbeat to return to normal. "I thought the killer created a diversion so he could get to Lars. Has anyone tried to get in here?"

Seth ended his call. "No one's been here but you. The deputy just told me what's happening. Wilcox is on his way." Seth kept his hand on his weapon and stood at attention by the door.

The sheriff arrived in minutes, ordered us to stay in the room with Lars and took off again. After half an hour of pacing, I left the room against Seth's advice and found Wilcox and Thor at the nurses' station. The sick ones had been taken to critical care. Thor bagged the partially eaten box of chocolates that had been sitting on the counter. "We think this was poisoned."

I recognized the tag on the box and the blood drained from my face. "Sheriff, it was meant for Lars. I re-gifted it as a thank you to the staff. It came from Trudy's Flowers and Gifts."

He said, "Connie told us."

I whirled around and intercepted Connie leaving a patient's room. She tried to hurry past me but I put out my hand. "I'm sorry you had to deal with this."

She stuttered. "Things like that are not supposed to happen on my watch." Arms rigid at her sides, she hurried away.

I'd have preferred it if she'd blamed me. I called after her. "It was an accident." I walked back to Wilcox and Thor, feeling responsible and wondering if the three people who were poisoned would have died if they weren't in a hospital. In his weakened condition, Lars might have died anyway, and he would have shared the candy with Little and me.

Thor finished her work and left. I tried to follow Wilcox out the door but he commanded me to stay in the waiting room. The woman with a magazine checked me out and went back to her reading, or perhaps surveillance. The staff darted looks my way as they resumed taking care of patients.

Two more hours dragged by. I couldn't stand it any longer and called the sheriff. He gave me a quick summary of what he'd learned. "We located the kid who delivered the candy. He also delivered several bouquets of flowers to the hospital. He delivers for several businesses. Deputies canvassed the flower and candy shops in town with the picture of Matthew but no one recognized the photo. And there were no reports of suspicious-looking customers."

Not a surprise. The shops would be overflowing with tourists.

Wilcox said the chocolate was not made at Trudy's, and many such boxes of dark chocolates had been bought that day. He told me most were cash transactions and trying to track the credit card purchases hadn't panned out. A family bought one and ate it immediately and so on. No incidents of anyone else getting sick had been reported at the hospital.

I asked. "What kind of poison?"

"We don't know yet. It looks like he bought the chocolates, injected poison into the bottom of each piece, rewrapped the box and waited for an opportunity to slip it into the delivery kid's truck. We'll know more after Thor's finished."

I leaned back in my hard waiting room chair, drained of ideas. "I guess our plan backfired, Sheriff." Lars had gotten lots of flowers, plants and balloons from friends. They hadn't sent candy until now because he'd been in a coma.

Barely containing his frustration, Wilcox said, "Frankly, a cube of chocolate was not on our list of possible threats. Seems a stretch the same guy who chain-sawed Charles Patterson's head off could finesse this."

A light dawned. "Sheriff, this means the guy must have revealed himself to Lars."

"That's right, now we know something we weren't sure about before."

Little sat on the sofa facing away from the nurses' station. I dropped down next to him. He spoke barely above a whisper. "I just want our lives back again." He looked up at me, his eyes dull. "This won't be over until we're all dead, will it?"

I put my arm around his shoulder. "Hey, brother, the last time I looked, we were all alive. You, Lars and me. And we're staying that way for a long time. You will become a cranky old white-haired chef terrorizing the staff and cooking delicious food. Oh wait, that already describes you."

He half-smiled. "You think I'm being a drama queen."

I shook my head. "I don't think that and I don't blame you for being discouraged. If we could figure out why this guy's after us, Wilcox could catch him."

Little said he needed to get back to Lars. "You'll stay here tonight, won't you, Britt?"

"If you want me to, I'll stay."

He nodded. "Please."

I wanted to go home and check whether Sebastian had replied to my email but this time I stayed.

In the morning, after I'd spent another uncomfortable night at the hospital, Ben called to say he'd be in Spirit Lake that afternoon. A load of tension melted from my cramped body. "That's great, Ben. I can't wait to see you again."

"It's only overnight. I've been called to testify at a trial in Minneapolis tomorrow. From that meth bust six months ago."

It would have to do. "I'll be at the restaurant."

I called the sheriff and said I was going to Spirit Lake to meet Ben.

"Good. He can take over keeping track of you. Jerry will stay with you until Ben gets there."

"Thanks, Sheriff." I was grateful to have Jerry with me and more than ready for Ben to keep track of me.

At the cabin, Jerry pulled up alongside my SUV and opened his car door. I said, "No need for you to come in. I'll only be a second."

Jerry followed me anyway. "Wilcox's orders. I can't let you out of my sight."

I stomped into the cabin with Jerry on my heels. "I'm showering, you intend to watch that?"

He squirmed. "I'll wait outside your bedroom after I check it."

There was no way I could get to the computer with Jerry joined at my hip. I swallowed the disappointment, showered and changed clothes. One look at my face in the bathroom mirror told me I needed to add another stop to my itinerary. Violet might be able to do something.

Still frustrated that I couldn't get to my secret office, we headed to Bella's.

She was snoozing in her rocker when the bell tinkled and did a fake alert look. Violet was bent forward over her manicure table, adding the final touches to a woman's fingertips. The woman held up one hand. Pursed lips and raised chin said grumpy tourist. "I wanted it brighter. Don't you have any of the new colors?"

Violet prided herself on keeping up with all the latest trends and products. She stammered, her cheeks flaming. "Tangy Tangerine is one of the new summer colors."

Drawing myself up to my Wonder Woman height, I looked down at the woman. "You're probably still wearing those deadly dark polishes, right?"

I turned to Bella. "Violet is such a find. I don't know how you persuaded her to come to Spirit Lake. You must have literally blackmailed her."

Bella went to the register. "I live in fear one of those fancy outfits in the Cities will lure her away."

Violet's lower lip trembled. "I'd be happy to change the color to anything you'd like."

The woman frowned at her nails. "It will do." She paid and hurried out. Bella slammed the cash drawer.

I watched from the window as the woman tried to open her car door without messing up her tacky finger tips. Dyed henna hair, tights and a glitzy top said she wasn't a regular. "Who's the nice lady?"

Bella plunked back down in her rocker. "That was Ginger Bolger, married to Morris 'Big Mo' Bolger from East St. Louis—a shady developer with a good lawyer."

I wiped my hands across my eyes. I had forgotten to meet him yesterday and then forgot to reschedule.

Violet cleaned up her nail station. "They spend a lot of time up here in the summer—at that big new home south of Charley's—but they don't like to mingle with the locals unless it's an emergency, like today with the chipped nail."

I hadn't expected sarcasm from Violet.

Bella said, "Mo Bolger was after Charley to sell to him, but Charley wouldn't do it. Bolger *said* he wanted that whole southern tip of shoreline for a family compound."

That explained the business card Wilcox found on Charley, but how could he know we'd inherited Charley's land? "You don't often see big homes like that on the south shore."

Violet waved her hands as if shooing the Bolgers out of her mind, and focused on my face, always a challenge. "Shall we finish the facial we started last time you were here?"

I flopped into the chair. "Make me pretty, Violet. Ben's coming today." That was the only thing on my mind at the moment.

Violet's round, pink face came close to mine, her eyes like magnifying glasses taking in the dark circles, worry lines and tell-tale puffy skin that revealed my poor eating habits and lack of sleep. "You need to hydrate. Not so much caffeine and lots of water." She set to work, a true professional with a healing touch. What I'd said to that haughty woman about Violet was true in spirit if not in fact.

"What's happening in town, Bella?" My life had been focused on the hospital and keeping Little safe.

Bella pulled out her knitting and worked the needles. "Things are a mess over at the restaurant. Chum's been drinking on the job, the waitresses are fighting with the kitchen staff and the customers are leaving in droves to Fisherman's Café up in Cooper."

There went my moment of relaxation. "What exactly am I supposed to do about that right now?" I couldn't help the frustration in my voice.

"Wilcox doesn't seem to have made much progress," she said. "Not his fault though. Investigators from the BCA field office have been in the BW working on that trafficking deal with Ben."

"I didn't know that, Bella." The Minnesota Bureau of Criminal Apprehension was headquartered in Minneapolis and assisted county law enforcement all over the state with the big cases. The BCA might have been helping Wilcox if their staff hadn't been stretched thin as well.

Violet massaged something cooling into my face so my end of the conversation stopped. The sound of Bella's needles clicking and CNN in the background soothed me until Violet finished.

Bella's head wobbled slightly as she swiped my credit card. Some days her palsy was worse than others. She handed the card back but held my eyes. "Take care of yourself."

Jerry waited outside. "Lookin' good, Britt." He winked, "Ben should come to town more often."

"Thanks, Jerry. Want to join me for lunch?" I wasn't looking forward to going to the restaurant after what Bella had said.

Jerry opened the restaurant door for me, but I had to step back. One of the waitresses flew past me, crying. "I quit!"

Chum yelled from the kitchen. "Good!"

We walked in. A smaller crowd than usual craned their necks to see the ruckus. Jerry picked up a menu and seated himself at the counter and I headed for the kitchen. "I'd better sort this out."

Chum's face was scrunched up. "This is bullshit. Everyone hates me and my cooking."

Lars was much better at dealing with overwrought emotions, but I gave it a shot. "I know it's been tough on you, Chum. You've been great, taking on all this responsibility. I promise it won't be much longer. The guys really need you now."

He turned to the stove and flipped a few burgers with more power than necessary. "It's not fair."

"We know how hard you've been working."

He moved to the counter and picked up a knife. I stepped back, but he'd let go of the anger. Hunched over, dicing onions, he said, "What am I supposed to do now that Emily left right in the middle of her shift?"

"I'll see if I can get her back. But you need to lighten up on her, okay? She's just a kid."

He nodded. "You want a burger?"

"Sure, thanks." I gave him a thumbs up. It was all I could think to do in the motivation department.

Jerry had coffee in front of him when I came back into the dining room. The customers had returned to talking and eating. From the café windows facing the lake, I saw Emily sitting at a picnic table near the city dock. "I'll just be a minute, Jerry. I need to talk to that waitress who just left."

He looked longingly at his cup of coffee and stood. Before we reached Emily, I asked him to stand back so I could have a private chat with her. He nodded and leaned against the side of the Chamber of Commerce a few paces away.

Usually a cheerful person, Emily looked glum. I straddled the bench across from her. "Rough day?"

Her eyes rolled. "Try rough week. Chum's acting like a big baby. It's not my fault people miss Little's cooking."

"Chum's upset about that, and I know he's been taking it out on you guys. He says he's sorry. He wants you back. We all do."

She jammed her hands in her apron pockets. "I was coming back anyway. I don't want to let down Little and Lars. They've been great to me and I need the money for college."

We walked to the restaurant, Jerry trailing behind.

Inside, a mother with three restless children waved at Emily. She pulled out her pad and went to the table.

My bodyguard and I sat down just as our hamburgers arrived. "I don't know how long we can keep this up, Jerry. It's all falling apart."

He swallowed a sip of coffee, made a face at it. "Cold." He nodded. "Wilcox is a bear to be around on good days but nothing like this. The whole office wants this solved."

My phone rang, Ben's ID came up and my heart blipped. I jumped up to look out the window. "Are you almost here?"

He hesitated before speaking. "I'm sorry. They settled, so I won't be needed in court after all. I'd better stay up here and wrap this up so we can really be together."

I barely responded to his explanation. After he hung up, I propped my chin on my fist and looked at a couple holding hands at a corner table.

Jerry nudged me. "You going to finish those fries, Britt?"

I pushed the plate across the counter to him.

Chapter 21

Lars was going home. Dr. Fromm released him at noon with a physical therapy schedule and meds. Fromm peered over his glasses. "He's got a long way to go yet. It's going to take time."

Fromm's voice of reason couldn't dim our joy. Little, Lars and I kept up a constant patter on the way home about how everything would be all right now. We didn't talk about the killer still being on the loose. We felt like celebrating.

I parked my SUV at the restaurant's front entrance and opened the passenger side door for Lars. Little helped position his crutches under his arms. Lars took a deep breath and made his way up the side ramp and into the restaurant. His face was flushed with exertion, but a smile broke out when a group of friends waiting inside cheered and gathered around him.

One of his snowmobiling buddies clapped him on the shoulder. "About time you got back to work, Lars. You been taking it easy too long."

Lars grinned. "Jaysus, Tim, I already miss not having to put up with your BS."

The crowd would have kept him all afternoon but after a short while, Little hustled him off to their apartment. I explained that Dr. Fromm said Lars needed a lot of rest and followed in their wake.

Lars looked around at the apartment and sighed. "It feels good to be home again, only I'm a little shaky." Little helped him to lie down and made him as comfortable as possible. When he came out of their bedroom, Little said, "He fell asleep instantly."

"You look like you could use a nap, too."

"I'm just happy he's home. I'm going to take a shower."

I double-checked all the windows, noting Jerry stationed at the back, and tested the doors with their new locks. My gaze went to Rock and Knute's food dishes on a mat by the back door. Caught off-guard by the stab at my heart, I put their dishes in the dishwasher, then sat on the sofa. The euphoria over Lars coming home hadn't lasted long.

Hair still damp and not looking that refreshed, Little flopped into his recliner. "What's the matter, Britt?"

I twisted a strand of hair. "Thinking about Rock and Knute."

Blue crescents dark as bruises underscored his eyes. "I used to make Rock special biscuits on Wednesdays."

Rock had spent more time with Little and Lars than me the past few months. Lars took him fishing sometimes. If I'd asked him to take Rock, maybe Lars wouldn't have gotten hurt, but I'd thought Knute needed Rock.

That kind of thinking wasn't helping. I pulled my brother to his feet. "Let's see if you remember how to cook. I'm starving."

A grin spread across his face and he took off for the kitchen. "I'm pretty sure I can come up with something."

I sat at a small table facing the tables and booths. Back on duty now that the guys were home, Gene lifted his scruffy chin in greeting and went back to reading the paper.

A short, wide man sitting in a booth watched me, appraising. His chair scraped back and he came toward my table, a friendly smile barely hiding the determination behind it. Gene half rose from his seat. Mid-fifties, a bit jowly, the man held out a manicured hand. His Rolex and ruby ring glinted in the overhead light.

"I hope you don't mind my interrupting, but I've been waiting for you to show up, Ms. Johansson. My name is Mo Bolger."

"I apologize for missing our meeting, Mr. Bolger. A lot's been going on lately." I gestured toward the chair across from me. "Please have a seat."

Gene settled back down.

Bolger reminded me of politicians I'd known. Pressed designer jeans, polo and new deck shoes showing he was just like everyone else, but not really. Politicians were usually smiling, ingratiating, always wanting something from you, typically votes, and confident they were going to get it. Those guys loved to have their pictures taken with their acquisitions: a boat, trophy wife, or cutting a ribbon in front of something they'd built or bought.

"What can I do for you, Mr. Bolger?"

A big smile. "Please call me Mo."

"Okay, Mo."

He looked around. "Is your brother available to chat with us?"

"I'll check." I went to get him, curious about Bolger's request to see us.

Little wasn't happy to leave his kitchen but he followed me back to the table. I introduced Mo. He shook Little's hand. "I know you're busy so I'll just state my business and let you get back to your work."

I hadn't mentioned the business card to Little. A lot was slipping my mind lately.

"Here's the deal. I'd been trying to get Charley to sell me his property for years, but he wasn't interested. Now, my daughter is getting married and I want to build a place for her next to mine and Ginger's as a wedding gift. I already built one for my son on the southern end of my property."

His face turned sappy, he even put his hand over his heart. "I want both my children next to me, one on either side—the whole family together in the summer. It's my dream."

I said, "You're a developer, right? East St. Louis."

A flash of irritation crossed his face. "This is more to me than an investment in lakeshore property. It's about family."

Little's eyes narrowed. "How did you find out we'd inherited? I mean, we only just learned of it."

The smug smile. "My attorney's job is to see that I get what I want. He'd fly up here tomorrow to handle the paperwork. I'm willing to take it off your hands immediately."

Little and I shook our heads slightly at each other. Little got up. "Thanks for the offer, but we can't think about that right now."

I said, "My brother's right. We're not ready to make any deals." I put out my hand. "But thank you for your interest."

Bolger's face turned a ruddy red. "Charley wouldn't even consider it, the old fool. I don't think you understand. I'm prepared to offer much more than the property is worth."

We stared at him, not commenting.

He took a breath to calm himself and turned another full-wattage smile on us. "Sorry I came on strong there." He aimed a compassionate smile at Little. "I know you've had a rough time since your partner was hurt." He stood up, knowing he'd lost this round. "Please think about it and maybe we can talk again. I really want this for my daughter's wedding present." He shook hands with us. "I'll be in touch."

When he was out of earshot, Little said, "That guy gave me the creeps."

"That bit about Lars almost sounded like a threat, but then everything sounds suspicious to me lately."

He shuddered and headed for the kitchen. "I'm going to make us something special for dinner."

I'd gotten what I wanted from the meeting—to see what Bolger looked like, get a sense of what kind of person he was and what he wanted. I called Wilcox and told him about the visit.

"Stay away from him. He's a suspect and could be dangerous."

I wanted to know more but he ignored my questions, warned me again and hung up.

If Bolger was responsible for all the things that had happened to us because of a chunk of lakeshore property for his family, the man wasn't just shady, he was insane. Charley's property was worth about five hundred thousand dollars. Enough to kill for?

The next morning Little was back in the kitchen. Chum worked at his side, his shoulders no longer hunched up under his ears.

Lars stayed in the apartment, using his crutches to pace from room to room, mumbling; a grim reminder of Dr. Fromm's warning about the long road ahead.

I switched from watching Little to checking in with Lars on a varied schedule. With one deputy outside and one inside, I couldn't imagine how the killer could get to them now. But we were taking no chances.

Midafternoon, Lars dozed in his recliner and I sat across from him on the sofa half-watching the news. Images of explosions in the Mideast switched to bobble-headed pundits and back to more explosions. It reminded me that Marta wanted my answer yesterday, or was it the day before?

My neck tight with tension from this forced inactivity, I looked at Lars, now awake. "Have you been able to remember anything at all about that day on the lake? Did you see a big guy?"

His hand hit the chair arm. "Don't you think I'm trying? It's on my mind all the time, but my memory of that is wiped out. The therapist said it might never come back."

I jumped at his outburst. Lars was the mediator, the compromiser. "I'm sorry, Lars. I shouldn't pressure you."

He stared at Wolf Blitzer pointing to images on a big map and sighed. "I'm the one who's sorry. I don't know what just happened. I didn't mean to yell at you."

"I know you want to remember more than anything. I'm too impatient."

"Wait a minute. I just got a flash of something." He looked up at me, eyes wide. "Someone standing over me, a rain slicker with the hood pulled up, the face is in shadow."

I held my breath as he struggled for more and then slumped back against the chair. "Jaysus. It's gone."

"But it was something. That's great, Lars."

He frowned. "Not much."

Everyone on the lake that day wore rain gear and had their hoods up. But maybe more would come to him now that the door to his memory was ajar.

Lars needed to lie down again. I tried to make him comfortable and went into the restaurant. Word must have traveled fast that Little was back in the kitchen. The booths were full. I sat at a small table with a cup of coffee in front of me, itching to do something. None of the writers' group were at their usual table. Had they stopped coming in for afternoon coffee?

I was still sitting there, my coffee untouched when Wilcox stopped by. He slid in across from me and barked orders. "Make sure you keep those alarms armed on the residence and restaurant after hours. With the three of you staying close and my deputies watching, it makes no sense for the killer to go after any of you." He rubbed the back of his neck. "I doubt if he's given up, though."

Lars' mood had infected me. "This is no way to live. Eventually, something will happen like when Lars got fed up and went out alone in his boat. The killer will wait us out."

Wilcox's jaw worked. "He has to wait too, and that must be hard for someone with vengeance on his mind. He wants to finish it. He'll get sloppy." He pointed a finger at me. "That's why you'll remain focused and stay put."

I rocked my coffee cup so hard it spun out of my hands and crashed to the floor. Conversations in the crowded restaurant stopped for a second. Chloe had the broom and dust pan out before I could get out of the booth. "Sorry," I stammered.

"You need to chill." Wilcox left the restaurant, wiping his wet pant leg.

I peeked in the kitchen. Little pulled fresh rolls out of the oven, dashed to the giant refrigerator for a covered dish and whirled around to answer a question from his helper. He didn't even see me.

Staying busy like my brother was the answer. I put on an apron and cleared tables while keeping a watchful eye on people coming and going. Every customer who entered the restaurant looked like a psychopath killer to me. I glanced out the bank of windows above the booths. A hint of sun tried to break through, but it wouldn't have a chance—a dark cloud hovered behind it, waiting to make its move.

After an hour, I checked the booths and tables to make sure all the dishes were cleared and waters and coffees filled before taking a break to see how Lars was doing. He dozed in front of the television, but snapped awake when I came in. "Why are you always spying on me?"

"Sorry, I wanted to see if you needed anything."

"I need to walk to the bathroom without feeling like I'm going to collapse. I need my memory. Have you got any of that for me?"

I edged away apologizing again and stood by the back window looking out over the garage and street. A familiar pickup turned the corner by the garage. Matthew Willard drove. He turned left at the intersection and pulled into the northbound traffic. I punched in the sheriff's number.

Wilcox said, "We'll find out what business he had in Spirit Lake today."

I grabbed my keys and camera. "It's the second time I've seen him hanging around Little's, Sheriff."

"What are you doing right now, Britt?"

My hand was on the back door. "I'm going to follow him."

"Don't. I'll ask the highway patrol to check him out."

"Jerry's out there. Tell him to go after the truck."

"Jerry stays where he is."

Wilcox reminded me again not to leave, then hung up. Lars came into the nook, his crutches propelling him forward. He lowered himself into a chair, arranged his cast as comfortably as he could in the small space and raised an eyebrow. "The look on your face just now. You're planning something, aren't you?"

I set my keys and camera on the counter. "This place is Fort Knox. He can't get to us in here. I know he's not giving up, so what's his next move?"

"You want me to go fishing again or maybe try to get poisoned?"

I'd missed his deadpan humor but this time it wasn't funny. "Don't joke about that."

Little came in, his eyes darting from me to Lars. "Joke about what?"

Lars looked like he wanted to choke us. "I don't need two mother hens." He pushed himself up, positioned his crutches and lurched to the bedroom. The door slammed.

Little said, "Lars never used to snap at me. I understand given what happened but it scares me." He looked at the closed bedroom door, his shoulders drooping. "I might as well go back to the kitchen."

I followed and urged him into a corner where no one could hear us. "Have you talked to Dr. Fromm about the change in Lars' personality? Sarah gave the doc permission to share any information about Lars with you. Ask him if this is normal, under the circumstances."

He lifted worried eyes to mine. "What if he's always going to be like this now? Lately I've been thinking coming to Spirit Lake was a huge mistake. Maybe we should go back to Minneapolis."

My body sagged against the wall. I didn't know what to say. Chloe spotted us and held up a food order. "Little, do you want to make this or should I ask Chum?"

He sighed. "Take it to Chum. I have a call to make."

Peder came in shortly after and invited me to have tea with him. "It seems like a long time since I've seen you, Britt."

"Tea sounds good." I was more than ready for the diversion and walked back toward the bistro with him. "Where's the rest of your group?"

We sat at a table for two. He said, "The workshop is officially over. Vik and the two students leave tomorrow. I haven't seen Neil or Anke. It's time for me to go back home as well."

"We'll miss you at Little's." I didn't blame any of them for clearing out. They'd all been questioned by the sheriff. Wilcox didn't fill me in on the details, so I didn't know if he was letting them leave town.

"Thank you. I've enjoyed spending time here and getting to know all of you. By the way, that's a nice blue kayak on your dock. I assume a gift from Ben?" He raised an eyebrow.

"What blue kayak?"

He looked alarmed. "Did I give something away?"

I took off at a run. "It wasn't Ben. I'll have to have that tea another time."

Little stopped me mid-sprint for the door. "You're not supposed to go anywhere alone."

"Peder said someone left a kayak on my dock. I want to check it out."

Little called out. "Peder, do you mind running Britt to her cabin?"

He came up behind me. "Not at all." He trotted to keep up with me on the way to his boat and we were on the lake in minutes.

The kayak had a big red bow wrapped around it. I jumped out of Peder's boat and onto my dock. An envelope was taped to the seat. I tore it open and read an invitation for Little and me to come to dinner that night at Ginger and Mo's at eight p.m. Please rsvp.

I waved the invitation in the air. "This guy thinks he can buy me off with a kayak?" I told Peder the story.

He said, "You must be careful. He sounds aggressive."

I started to thank Peder for always being there when I needed him, when something Ben said came back to me. "This isn't the first time Little has asked you to keep an eye on me, is it?"

He did the deer-in-the-headlights blink. "It's been my pleasure, believe me."

I was irritated at my brother for going behind my back, and slightly insulted that Peder was doing a favor for my brother when I'd assumed we were friends. "Thanks for the taxi service. Do you mind if we have tea another time? It's getting late."

He nodded. "I really only stopped by to see how Lars is doing."

"They've started him on physical therapy already. His first session is tomorrow. It seems soon to me, but that's the way they do it."

Peder dropped me off at the city dock and turned his boat toward his cottage. "Please tell him hello for me."

Little was in the kitchen. I didn't mention that I was aware of his subterfuge. He wanted to protect me and I might have done the same thing if our roles were reversed. I showed him the Bolgers' invitation.

"You can go if you want, but I'm not. Charley wanted us to have his place and we should honor his wishes, don't you think?"

I called Bolger and told him I couldn't accept the kayak and declined the dinner invitation. He wouldn't take no for an answer on the dinner, even when I told him again we still weren't interested in selling.

"Please come. We've already begun preparations. Ginger's really looking forward to the evening. She gets lonely up here."

His smooth voice reminded me of my ex, an expert at using charm to get what he wanted. I agreed because I still hadn't quite figured him out.

Before heading to dinner, I called a friend at Lakeshore Realty, the company that owned the building where the *StarTrib* bureau was located. After I hung up, I wished I'd called him sooner.

That evening, with special dispensation from Wilcox to drive myself, I loaded the kayak into my SUV and headed for the Bolgers' summer home. Wilcox told me Eddy would be parked outside with instructions to call Jerry if anything suspicious occurred. I set the kayak beside the house and rang the bell.

Ginger and Mo offered champagne and were disappointed when I declined, but I made up for it by tasting and complimenting every appetizer the server presented. We sat down to dinner and I devoured each course under their watchful eyes. When we'd finished, I suppressed a burp and pushed my plate away, feeling like a fatted calf. "That was the best meal I've had in weeks. Thank you."

Whitened teeth gleaming in the chandelier's light, the Bolgers smiled at my appreciation and we moved outside. I sank into a cushy deck sofa. Conveniently placed on the coffee table, Ginger opened an album of their daughter's engagement photos. She described in detail the fabulous wedding they were planning. After I'd admired the daughter's beauty and congratulated them, Mo beckoned for me to join him on the deck overlooking the lake.

He talked about his plans for Charley's land. I reminded them we weren't selling but Mo wasn't hearing me. "We'd tear it down and build a smaller version of this house, similar to the one we built for our son." He pointed at the woods toward Charley's. "We'd create a pathway between the homes but leave most of the trees." He winked. "Newlyweds need their privacy."

Surprised I'd kept my temper this long, knowing that everything he'd said all night was a lie, I left the couch and stood facing him. "Mo, we both know the reason you want Charley's property has nothing to do with your family. You want to build a mega-resort on the southern tip of Spirit Lake and have been buying up as much land as possible for several years now." I crossed my arms. "Selling to you so you can destroy the eco-system of this lake just to make more money is the last thing I'll ever do."

Mo's jugular jumped and he started for me. I put up a hand. "Not a good idea, Mo. A sheriff's deputy is sitting outside right now. Take a look." He didn't need to know it was Eddy, probably snoozing.

Ginger's head swiveled from Mo to me, as if she wasn't quite sure how to handle the situation. I backed toward the door. "I can find my own way out. Thank you for the dinner."

His angry growl followed me out the door. "Not going to sell to me? We'll see about that."

Eddy followed me back to Little's and I was thankful for the company. The reason I'd accepted the Bolgers' invitation had been to watch them squirm when I exposed their lie but I couldn't deny that Bolger frightened me.

Chapter 22

In a food-stupor from stuffing myself at the Bolgers' dinner table and tired after the long day, I wanted to sleep but still had work to do. I dozed for a few hours and woke when my alarm beeped at three a.m.

Wearing a long-sleeved black turtleneck, pants and ski mask I'd packed the last time I went to my cabin, I was ready to sneak back to see if Sebastian had answered my email. I peeked out the kitchen window.

Jerry's Branson County Sheriff's vehicle was parked across from the back door. He would move his car to the front parking lot off and on during the long night. A car passed, its lights illuminating the street. Eddy doing his rounds. Likely bored with the routine, he pulled up next to Jerry and chatted for a few minutes.

Transformed into a shadow, I took that opportunity to slip out the back door, reset the alarm and step behind a lilac bush. The sliver of moon was in my favor as I faded into the trees behind the bistro.

Eddy drove away. They hadn't seen me—not real comforting. My face itched under the ski mask but I didn't dare lift it. I intended to take the Paul Bunyan Trail, the quickest route to my cabin and I'd be less visible than on the road, but a light flickering in a back window of the garage stopped me. I waited, and it flickered again.

Had the Willards been casing the garage earlier with a plan to come back tonight and do damage? The fire at Rob's flashed across my mind. Or maybe Mo Bolger intended to demonstrate one of his strong-arm techniques. If I went in alone to look, I could get hurt. If I called Jerry, whoever was in there might hear me and get away.

Leaving the cover of trees, I inched around the back to the garage. Jerry's car faced the other direction, toward the restaurant. Lars always left the garage door open. Whoever was inside would have to come out eventually and this was the only way in or out other than the electronic garage doors facing the street.

I peered into the ink-black space. A workshop area was separated by a door next to where the guys' cars were parked. A couple of grease-stained easy chairs on an oval braided rug were across from a workbench. Nothing moved. I slipped inside and crept to the door into the garage and peeked inside. I didn't smell smoke. Little's Jeep hood was up. Muffled noises came from behind it and a pinpoint of light flashed. I reached in my back pocket for my SIG Sauer and came up empty-handed. Not the best time to forget it. Who was I kidding anyway? Could I see myself telling someone to come out with his hands up?

I crept back outside and texted Jerry. He might shoot me if I loomed up at his car window dressed all in black.

–It's Britt. There's someone messing with Little's Jeep in the garage.

–Where are you?

–I'm over by the workshop door in case he tries to get away.

–Get away from there! I'm coming now.

Jerry's car door opened. I turned to move farther away when someone flew out the garage door, slammed into me and knocked us both to the ground. Before I could recover, he scrambled over me and took off into the woods behind the bistro.

Jerry ran up with his gun drawn. "Are you hurt?"

The breath was knocked out of me for a second but I jumped to my feet. "Go after him."

He raced to the edge of the woods, then turned back. "That's as far as I can go. My orders are to stay with the residence." He called Wilcox, listened and hung up.

"Jerry, he'll get away." I wanted to make him chase the guy but it was already too late.

He said, "Wilcox is on his way."

"Get Eddy then, tell him to keep his eyes open."

"Eddy's better off nowhere near that guy."

When Wilcox arrived, I explained, but with a slight factual error. "I couldn't sleep and happened to look out the kitchen window. A light flickered in the garage and I went out to tell Jerry. The guy came flying out of the garage and knocked me down. I don't think he saw me." It embarrassed me that he'd caught me off guard. "He hit low at my knees and didn't seem to be muscular, fast though."

"What was he wearing?"

"Black ski mask, dark clothing. I couldn't tell his height, but average weight." It occurred to me that it wasn't necessarily a man.

It didn't take long for them to discover what the masked person was doing in the garage. The brake lines had been cut on the Jeep and Lars' SUV next to it.

When Wilcox finished with the garage and coordinating with Thor, he pulled his cowboy hat low over his forehead, a sign he was agitated. "I scheduled Seth to follow Little and Lars to therapy tomorrow, but no telling what could have happened." He turned to Jerry, thunder in his voice. "How did you miss this?"

I stepped up. "There's no garage window where Jerry was parked. It's only a fluke that I happened to be looking toward the back and saw the light flicker."

Wilcox shifted his gaze to me, took in the ski mask sticking out of my pocket, my black hoodie and jeans. "What the hell were you are doing wearing that get up at three in the morning?" He took off his hat and worked the brim like he was squeezing my neck.

I was grateful he went for the hat instead, but I was done with back-peddling. "It's time for the hunted to be the hunter, Sheriff. That's what I'm doing. My understanding is that you need all the help you can get since the BCA isn't available. I guess we're not important enough for them."

He stalked off. "I can't protect someone who has a death wish."

I followed. "I know you haven't found evidence connecting the Willards to Charley's or Rob's murders, but I told you I saw their truck this morning. And it's not the first time they've been hanging around here. Did you check them out when I told you he was in town?"

"HP stopped him. He said he came to Spirit Lake to pick up a load of junk from one of the resorts. It turned out to be true."

"Maybe he was multi-tasking, Sheriff. And what about Bolger? He didn't like it when I turned down his offer to buy Charley's." My phone vibrated. Little was calling. "What's going on out there?"

"Someone broke into the garage. Stay inside. It will calm down in a while."

I turned back to Wilcox. "You have an entire county to protect, but my brother is my *only* issue. If I hadn't been watching, when Little took Lars to his therapy in the morning, they could both have ended up dead."

Thor caught up to me as I stalked away, her face bunched up in a frown. "The sheriff hasn't slept since Charley's murder. He's grilled everyone in that writers' group, the Bolgers, the Willards and other known crazies in the area and he's looking at everyone who fits the profile and lots who don't."

I waved her off. "He's letting this killer slip through his fingers. He doesn't even have a motive."

She flared up. "He's close, but every time he gets distracted by you going off on your own it sets him back. He's using every resource he can on it and that has an impact on the rest of the county."

That stopped me. I'd been badgering him nonstop and my seeing the light in the garage was pure luck. I nodded. "Point taken."

***

I'd fallen asleep on the couch still wearing my clothes. Lars's voice woke me at nine a.m. He stood at the bedroom doorway in his underwear, already appearing worn out. "The deputy is on his way to pick me up for therapy. I could use help with my jeans."

One pant leg was cut off to fit over the cast, but still tricky for him to maneuver. Little jumped up from a chair to help, and we made our way into the restaurant. Little shot me his owl scowl on his way to the kitchen to make our breakfast. I hadn't had a chance to ask what he found out about the mood swings from Dr. Fromm, but it must not have been good.

Lars lowered himself into the booth and propped the crutches against it.

I tried for upbeat. "Ready for your physical therapy?"

He shrugged, his face haggard. "Has Little told you we're talking about moving back to Minneapolis? Going back to teaching."

"Whatever you need to do." They'd been through so much and maybe they would be safer away from here. What had happened to Lars would haunt him forever. I couldn't blame him for wanting to be far away from the horror of the past weeks. But the idea of there being no Little's Café in Spirit Lake and no Little and Lars left a big empty place inside me.

In a few minutes Little brought platters of blueberry wild rice pancakes. We thanked him but neither of us had much of an appetite.

Gene read the paper at his usual table in the corner. Today, his camouflage was a Twins baseball cap and a t-shirt with a moose on it. Little talked to him for a minute, frowned, and then bee-lined to our booth. He leaned toward me and whispered. "Gene gave me more details about last night. You could have been hurt."

I was ready to defend my actions but Lars put a hand on Little's arm. "We're just glad you saw the guy, Britt."

Little mumbled something that sounded vaguely grateful. He always got cranky when he was worried about my safety. I let it go and poured more maple syrup on my pancakes.

Jerry came into the restaurant, saw us and walked over. "Britt, Wilcox wants you in Iona. I'm supposed to follow you."

I hopped up. "He must have some evidence on the Willards."

"I honestly don't know. He didn't tell me."

I glanced over at Little and Lars. "We can't both leave."

He pointed to the parking lot. "Seth's out there, Gene's in here and Wilcox sent someone to pick up Lars for his therapy."

I grabbed my camera bag and headed for the door with Jerry following. "You worked all night and now you guys are doing another shift?"

Jerry stifled a yawn. "Resources. A homicide up in the eastern part of the county last night. Several deputies are headed over there."

***

Matthew and his father sat slightly forward, hands cuffed behind them in the back seat of a deputy's car. I zoomed in on their sullen faces. That shot was worth the trip.

Feeling vindicated, I swaggered toward Wilcox. "Thanks for inviting me, Sheriff. Did they confess?"

Wilcox leaned back against the side of his vehicle. Cowboy hat pushed back, arms folded across his chest, he was barely able to contain the smile twitching at his mouth. Had I ever seen him smile?

Something moved behind him. He stepped away from the window and pulled open the door. A barking flash of black and white leapt out. "Rock!" I ran the last few yards, aware of Wilcox reaching into the back seat to lift Knute to the ground but my arms were already full of barking, licking, squirming dog. Knute got into the hug fest too. After a few more minutes of bliss, I ran my hands over every inch of them to make sure they weren't hurt.

Wilcox coughed. I stood up and brushed myself off, embarrassed at the unleashed abandon of our joyful reunion. I wiped my eyes with my shirt tail. "How did you find them?"

"We came over here to check on the family's whereabouts last night, and to question them about what they were doing in Spirit Lake earlier in the day. Plus, we got an anonymous tip this morning to check the property. I'll show you where the dogs were hidden."

I looked back at the deputy's car with the Willards in it, wanting to grab them by the throats, but followed Wilcox down the lane to the building where they'd held their meetings.

He pushed open the door. "They were in here."

I took pictures of the interior but there wasn't much to see. No dog food or dishes, no scratch marks on the door.

"Rock would have tried to get out unless they caged him."

Wilcox said, "They took decent care of the dogs. They were muzzled and on short ropes, but they didn't seem to be thirsty or hungry."

"Stealing them and locking them up was decent care?"

He tugged at his hat. "I'm saying they weren't starved or abused."

Rock dug at the junk pile but came when I whistled and we walked back. The Willards were still waiting in the sheriff's car.

The window was open a couple of inches. I yelled. "Why did you steal my dogs?"

Matthew opened his mouth to speak but his dad told him to shut up. "We didn't have anything to do with that. Those dogs were not there yesterday."

"You're lying." I hit the window with the palm of my hand and Matthew flinched.

Mr. Willard said, "Someone all along has been trying to get my boy in trouble." His mean eyes peered at me. "I bet it was you."

"That's ridiculous."

"I want a lawyer for me and my boy."

I shot more pictures of father and son. They protested and I kept shooting just for the fun of making them mad.

Wilcox told the deputy to take them to Branson.

I stepped back. "Where's Mrs. Willard?"

"Grocery shopping. We sent a car to pick her up, but thanks for helping me do my job."

It was easier when he was being his usual sarcastic self but still hard to talk past the lump in my throat. "Sheriff, thank you so much for finding my dogs."

He cocked his head toward the Willards. "If you press charges I can hold them long enough to question them about this other stuff, but stealing dogs is a misdemeanor. I can't put them in jail."

"I'll press charges."

They pulled away and I called Little to tell him the news. He shouted it out to the staff, and I heard cheering in the background.

Rock tried to climb into my lap in the SUV. Knute stretched out on the back seat, a spot familiar to him. I buried my face in Rock's neck, glad the sheriff couldn't see my sloppy tears. "I'm not taking my eyes off you guys ever again."

Jerry materialized at my window and I jumped a foot. "Are you okay, Britt?"

He was parked behind me, waiting to follow me back to Little's. I coughed. "Just getting the dogs settled." My red-rimmed eyes stared back at me in the rearview mirror. My nose looked like I worked for the circus.

Jerry said, "Finally some good things are happening on this freaking case." He got in his car and waved for me to go.

***

My call to Ben went to voice mail. He was likely out of cell range. I gave him the message, knowing how happy he'd be when he listened to it.

Little laughed and cried and ended up with so much dog slobber on him, he'd have to shower before going back to the kitchen. He ruffled Rock's fur. "They're getting steak after what they've been through."

No doubt grateful to be back home, Rock and Knute ate and went right to their beds. As they slept under my watchful eye, I tried to figure out why the Willards took them but I needed more information.

Jason had said he'd look at statistics for me. Maybe that would lead to something. I called him. "Remember when I asked you to check on hate crimes in Iona Township?"

Jason said, "Right, the statistics showed that hate crimes were down in the county from previous years."

A thought began to take shape. "Did you check on other types of crime?"

"Just the anti-gay stuff. You didn't ask about anything else." He sounded defensive.

"I wasn't accusing, but I'm curious. Could you check stats on other crimes in the area?" It couldn't hurt to throw out a wider net.

"Sure. If I get anything interesting, I'll send it to you."

Leaning back on the sofa with my feet on the coffee table listening to Knute's rhythmic snoring soothed me, but doing nothing was unacceptable. I'd been looking at this like a victim and not like a photojournalist. What would Britt the photographer do if this were someone else's problem and I wanted the story?

A surge of energy shot through me and I shot to my feet. I'd go after it. I'd been trying to wear too many hats. It was time to do what I did best. From now on the sheriff could do the job of protecting and I would investigate and shoot what I saw. I needed to act now, while the Willards were locked up, in case they were connected with Charley. Unsure of what action to take, I set out to talk to the one person who might point me in the right direction.

Chapter 23

Edgar and I faced the lake in his red Adirondack chairs, with tall glasses of iced tea perched on the wide arms. He patted Rock's head. "It's good to see you again, friend." Rock took off after a squirrel and Edgar turned to me. "You say the Willards had them locked in a shed?"

I nodded, then realized he couldn't see my nod. "Yes, Wilcox is questioning them now but he's never been able to connect them to Charley."

I told him about the interaction with Mo Bolger.

He nodded. "That explains a few things."

Rock ran to the lake and I tossed a branch into the water. He dove in after it and brought it back. We did that about ten times and I finally quit. I grumped. "I can't even swim. I have to be watchful all the time now."

"Go ahead. You have nothing to worry about here."

"I've told you what this guy's done, Edgar. What if he comes after you to get to me? You think your ghost ancestors will protect us?" I looked around. "I don't see them."

"You're too distracted to see them. Go for your swim. When you said you were coming, I asked a couple of neighbors to watch the road."

The lake beckoned me. My limbs wanted the stretch and pull, the cold water washing the tension away. I stripped off my shirt and jeans. "I'm going in."

Edgar perked up.

"I'm in my tank top, Edgar."

He cackled. "I may be old and blind but I still have a memory."

I waded out and dove in the water. The day was clear and the sun warm on my shoulders. Rock swam alongside me until he tired and went back to sit with Edgar. The past weeks dropped away until I was part of the water, all motion.

I'd gone about a mile and reluctantly turned back. When I was close to shore, Rock jumped in and swam the last few yards with me. I stepped out of the water quietly, not wanting to wake the snoozing Edgar, grabbed my camera from the bag and shot photos of the old man from the side—the long gray braid resting on his faded blue shirt, gnarled hands folded in his lap, his form shaded by three birches, their branches swaying.

Rock ran up and shook himself all over me. I took his picture for the nine thousandth time, catching the drops of water flying in all directions, and his paw prints in the sandy soil. The scarred indentations on Rock's prints reminded me of how they'd gotten that way. He'd scratched at the cabin door until they were bloody, trying to get outside to Gert as she was being murdered. I sighed, thankful I hadn't lost him, too.

Edgar's eyes opened. "Did you have a good swim? I see the weather is turning again. Rain is coming."

"I feel much better." I plunked down in the chair and waited to dry before putting my jeans and shirt back on, shivering a bit. Edgar was right, the air had turned cooler, the sky dim.

"Thank you for visiting an old man, but you have more important things to do today. We haven't talked about the purpose of your visit."

I'd learned from Little not to jump right into quizzing Edgar, to wait until he invited the conversation. When I didn't wait, he'd ignore my questions and talk about his Jacuzzi and how it helped his circulation. Or he'd talk about Little's chicken-wild rice hotdish. I was glad I'd waited for him this time.

"Time's running out and I don't know which way to focus. That buried box I found at Charley's isn't enough."

His fingers steepled. "Do you keep all your treasures in one place?"

For a second I wondered if his mind wandered, and then understood where he was going with the question. I had lots of hiding places for my treasures—buried under the rose bushes, my secret office in the garage and a few more. I jumped up and grabbed my jeans. "Thanks, Edgar!" I might have stopped digging too soon. Charley could have left more clues hidden in his house or garden.

Edgar stood on wobbly legs. I slung the camera bag over my shoulder and helped him up the hill to his house, his frame fragile as paper.

He stood in his doorway waving goodbye. "Be wary. This killer is trying to impress you, prove he's a great hunter. But he'll go after you wanting to kill when the game bores him."

None of Edgar's neighbors were visible as I drove over the hill. That was the idea, I guess. I waved anyway and turned onto the main road back to town.

Edgar's warning chilled my bones. The killer had passed up several opportunities to harm me, and I had taken chances thinking I wasn't a target. The word "yet" hadn't occurred to me.

***

Lars was back from therapy. He sat in the apartment's kitchen nook looking out the window. I'd left Knute behind, but Lars hadn't seen Rock yet and Rock seemed to know not to jump on him. Lars scratched Rock's ears and his gaze turned to me. "Your hair is soaked."

"I took Rock for a swim at Edgar's. How was your therapy?"

He looked out the window again. "Loads of fun."

"Are you okay, Lars?"

He shook his head. "Not really. I'd rather be like you, out risking my neck instead of sitting here waiting to heal." He rubbed his hand over his almost hairless head. "Not that I'm not grateful to be alive." His cheeks puffed out in a resigned sigh as he tilted his chin toward the restaurant. "At least Little is so busy he can't worry constantly. I'm happy for that."

Lars didn't look happy at all. "At least now I have Rock and Knute to keep me company."

Eager to follow up on Edgar's hint, I left the dogs with Lars and planned my getaway. Gene was on duty in the restaurant and Jerry outside in his unmarked car. I put on an apron, picked up the pot and filled coffees along the booths. At Gene's table, I leaned in and told him I had to meet with my editor at the bureau and would be back in a couple of hours.

He reached into his pocket. "I'll have to ask Wilcox."

"Go ahead but I'm leaving now." He tapped in the sheriff's number. I pretended not to see him gesture for me to wait, tossed my apron on the kitchen peg, snagged my camera bag from under the counter and headed out the door. Thor's rebuke about distracting the sheriff by going off on my own caused a twinge of guilt but hadn't I discovered something he'd missed every time I followed my instincts?

I turned south instead of north toward Branson, my eye on the rearview mirror. No one followed me as I passed my cabin and kept going to Charley's turnoff.

The sheriff's people did a thorough search of his house the day I found him and hadn't discovered any helpful evidence, at least none they'd shared with me. My own search of the house and shed hadn't produced anything either. But maybe I hadn't uncovered everything in that corner of the garden where I'd found his box of memories.

At Charley's, I craned my neck to see if all was clear, and then left the safety of the car, camera strap around my neck, gun in hand. Edgar's warning reminded me what was at stake. To keep Little safe, I first had to keep myself from harm.

I grabbed a shovel from the shed and trudged across the garden to the hole where the first box had surfaced. The shovel only hit soil and small rocks. My neck prickled and turning slowly in a circle, I willed my eyes to penetrate the woods. When nothing out of the ordinary caught my attention, I turned back to the job at hand determined not to let fear or discouragement stop me. Maybe he'd hidden boxes at each corner.

Nothing happened when I jabbed the shovel into the dirt at the northeast point, and my next effort yielded the same result at the southeast corner. Something crackled in the woods behind me. I whirled and peered into the trees. Another twig snapped. I focused the camera into the woods. Two sets of eyes looked at me, too low to the ground to be human or deer. The hair stood up on my arms. Ears forward, a pair of grey wolves watched me, unmoving.

I took a deep breath and clicked. They turned and blended into the brush. Only then did it occur to me that I should have reached for the gun. If it had been the killer, my camera wouldn't have stopped him. Adrenalin pumping, I almost wished it had been the killer so we could get this over with one way or another.

The wolves visit unsettled me. I reached into my jeans pocket and brought out the agate Edgar gave me last year with a wolf's paw etched into it. He'd said the gift was to remind me that even lone wolves needed their pack. I slid it back into my pocket, squinted one more time at the woods and hurried to the northwest corner of Charley's garden.

I found more rocks. Not quite willing to give up, I set my boot on the shovel and gave it one last push, frustration driving the spade deeper into the earth. It hit something hard, jarring my shoulders.

My heart beat a little faster. I reminded myself it was likely a rock. After another quick look around, I leaned into the shovel and dug around the hard surface until a rectangular shape emerged. I slid the spade under it and strained to lift it out of the ground.

A small, brown suitcase with straps, the kind found in antiques stores, came out with a pop and I nearly fell over backward. I used the spade to break the lock, then dropped to my knees to undo the straps.

A leather-bound journal wrapped in plastic and held with a rubber band sat on top. Next to it was a jeweler's box, also in plastic. I lifted out both items but didn't want to take them from their wrapping with my dirty hands. A bag full of silver dollars filled the bottom. Emergency getaway money? I'd count it later.

I stepped back and photographed the scene—the spade stuck in the ground, suitcase with silver dollars spilling out of it, plastic-wrapped journal and jewelry box.

213

Shoving the bag of coins back in the suitcase, I closed it and dashed to the house with the journal and jewelry box. Fumbling for the key, I hurried inside and locked the door. Leaning back against it and breathing hard, more from tension than exertion, I looked around.

The interior smelled musty and hadn't been disturbed since the last time I'd been there. When my heart rate returned to normal, I set the gun and items on the table, opened the kitchen window a couple of inches, washed my hands and angled my chair to face the door.

Now would be a good time to call Wilcox. I reached in my pocket for my phone when it rang. Marta's name came up on the display. I debated answering but picked up on the third ring. "Hey, Marta."

Her voice came through loud and clear amid the newsroom din. "How long are you going to stall? South Sudan is in the middle of a civil war, the *Times* needs to be there and I can't keep them from giving it to someone who really wants it."

I jerked to attention. "Who really wants it?"

"Randy Gonzales is lobbying hard and he's ready to leave today."

I yelled. "Don't give it to Gonzales. I need a couple more days." He was my arch nemesis at the *Times*. We were in constant competition and being available was crucial.

"The sheriff and your Ben Winter can handle one murder. Your job is here and you know what's at stake."

She meant my job was at stake. I couldn't lose it again. "I told you Ben's working a different case in the BW." She would throw him in my face. I'd be leaving again and we'd hardly been together. The memory of those two spectacular nights made my heart hurt.

A theatrical groan on the other end of the line. "It's not totally up to me, you know that."

"Please, Marta. I'm the one to do it. It's what I'm best at."

"I know, but we have a small window on this. Gonzales could take a different assignment and my judgment would be questioned for stalling him."

214

Linda Townsdin

It wasn't the first time Marta had put her reputation on the line for me. "Seriously, I'm packed, ready to go as soon as I nail down one remaining detail on this guy."

"I'll do what I can." She hung up with a grunt.

The detail was that I didn't know who the killer was. I aspired to total honesty in our friendship, but wasn't quite there yet. Gonzales had been the one who told management my drinking affected my work, and he'd argued against hiring me back. Marta had likely dangled him in my face just to get me moving faster. She was not above coercing when she wanted something, and I'd been known to weasel around a subject. I rolled my eyes—another relationship that needed work.

I put Marta and South Sudan out of my mind and slid the jewelry box from its plastic casing. Inside the box was a tarnished silver locket. A lock of blond hair fell into my palm when I opened it. It held a picture of the man in the wedding photo and a baby. I replaced the hair and zipped into the bathroom. Charley's hairbrush sat on the sink counter where he'd left it. A flutter of hope lifted my spirits. The DNA door had just opened to finding out if the man in the photo was Charley.

Next, I concentrated on the journal—four by six inches, the cover cracked with age, pages yellowed. With extreme care, I opened it. Inside the front cover, in neat script was the name, Gunnar Johansson.

I didn't remember hearing about a family member with that name but he must be related to us. I turned the page, holding my breath in anticipation of getting some answers.

It was written in Norwegian. I wanted to bang my head against the table. I should have expected that. A yellowed newspaper clipping fell out as I thumbed through the pages. I unfolded the thin newsprint. The headline and copy were in Norwegian. Under that, a picture of a man in uniform posed with a woman and two boys, a teenager and younger child. Below it, a photo showed the distorted face of the same man— his head cut off and staked in front of a house. My stomach lurched and I peered closer. Two mounds of similar size with white coverings lay nearby. I couldn't read the writing, but the

215

next photo showed a head shot of the man in the wedding picture, the name Gunnar Johansson in bold above it. Were we related to a murderer?

I looked closely at the rest of the photos. There were two children in one photo, one teenager and one much younger, but the two mounds on the ground were similar in size. If the small child escaped, he would be in his seventies now, at least. I re-wrapped the journal and locket. I needed someone quick who could read Norwegian. Peder.

Holding the gun in front of me, I slid into my car and reached for the ignition. The journal and jewelry box were on the seat next to me, my camera around my neck. A shadow flitted across my driver-side mirror. I went for the gun, but a shout stopped me from aiming, and then I recognized the figure outside.

I jumped out of the car and threw my arms around Ben. "What are you doing here?"

He unwrapped my arms and stepped back. "Trying to get myself killed, I guess."

"How long have you been here?"

"Not long. I looked in the kitchen window and saw your gun and decided not to risk my life by making any noise."

My chest heaved as if I'd run a marathon. I might have shot him. "Wise choice."

"Besides, I wanted to keep watch in case someone was out there."

I nodded. "A couple of wolves came too close for comfort earlier, but that's all. Ben, I found a journal. It's in Norwegian so I haven't read it yet." I stopped. "How did you know where to find me?"

"Process of elimination. You weren't at the cabin or at the bureau." His eyes showed their disapproval.

"You still didn't answer my question about why you're back in Spirit Lake. I suppose my brother had something to do with it." I leaned back against my car.

"I got three calls this morning." He ticked them off on his fingers. "Bella, Wilcox and Little, all telling me you were running around alone and about to get yourself killed."

Itching to learn what was written in the journal, I snapped. "Heartwarming to know my friends and family have such faith in my ability to take care of myself."

His look stopped me and I offered a weak smile. "But I'm glad you're here."

He faced me in the classic Ben fighting stance, his legs apart, arms crossed, head lowered. Something else upset him. My chin came up. "What have I done now?"

His voice sharp, he said, "Were you just going to leave? Could you have picked a more dangerous time to go to Sudan?"

I pushed myself off the car. "It's my project and I need to get there before Marta gives it away." The look on his face told me that was the wrong thing to say. I tried again. "This is important, women and children are dying."

His jaw clamped. "I feel like an idiot racing to get my case wrapped up. No wonder you were in such a hurry for me to go back to the BW. You were already planning to leave. You never intended to stay through August."

I reached out to him. "That's not true. All I wanted was to be with you this summer, but Marta moved up the timeline."

He didn't move and my hand dropped to my side. I should have told him about the change in plans sooner. It wasn't that I didn't care. My head snapped up. "Wait a minute. How did you find out?" I hadn't told anyone about Marta changing the timeline on Sudan. I hadn't even had time to think about it.

He pointed toward the house. "I was outside the kitchen window watching you. You always yell into your phone."

He walked away. "My car's on the road. I'll wait for you."

I called out. "I found out who the guy in the wedding photo is."

He turned his head toward me, still walking. "Meet me at Little's. You can tell us all at the same time. I'll call Wilcox." He turned to face me. "You haven't called him yet, right?"

"I was just going to." I opened the door to my SUV and watched him—long stride and broad shoulders, now slightly bowed—until he rounded the bend to his car. I leaned back against the seat. I'd ruined it again. Maybe if I could get him to stay until tomorrow, I could make it up to him. We'd been doing so well.

I put the SUV in gear, then remembered the bag of coins in the garden. I'd rebury it and tell Wilcox. I could have asked Ben to help bring it to the car, but he'd gone. I didn't want to ask him anyway. My feelings were hurt too. Nobody ever saw my side of things.

I nudged the suitcase back into its hole and kicked dirt over it. On the way to my car, I flipped back through the photos to see if I'd gotten good shots of the scene where I'd dug up the suitcase. I went one too far to the photo of wolf eyes and did a double-take. Several yards forward and to the left, a hooded human shape crouched behind a tree, blurry as if ducking from the camera. I forwarded to the next photo when the wolves turned away, but the human had disappeared.

With the gun in front of me, I stalked toward the tree. I'd had enough of being watched.

No one was there, no surprise. There were footprints but the familiar cigarette butt was evidence enough. Scooping up the Marlboro cigarette butt in a leaf so oil from my skin wouldn't contaminate it, I sprinted back to the car and fishtailed out of the driveway.

Ben was still waiting at Charley's turnoff. He said, "You were supposed to be right behind me. I was about to go back for you."

"Anke was out there watching me. It's not the first time." I jumped out of the SUV and showed him the photo and cigarette butt.

He dug a bag from his glove box and put the butt in it. "I'll get Wilcox. Send me the photo and go to Little's. Wilcox will want to pick up Anke, and he'll have Thor meet us at Charley's. It will be a while."

I pointed back toward Charley's. "There's a suitcase in the garden with coins in it. Northwest corner."

He barreled down the road.

Chapter 24

The sheriff and Ben would round up Anke, and then go back to Charley's. I had time to make a quick stop at Peder's before turning Gunnar's journal over to Wilcox. The sheriff wouldn't tell me what the journal said until he was ready. I drove along the lake's south loop toward Peder's cottage, hoping to find him home. Others in town could read Norwegian but tracking them down would take precious time.

Keeping an eye on the rearview mirror, I tried a couple of driveways before finding the right one. I pulled farther into the yard until the lake was visible and saw Peder's speedboat tied up at the dock.

The cottage looked like other modest summer home on the lake, although I wouldn't have chosen a location so shaded. A haze of fog had set up camp in the trees surrounding it. The land sloped down, lower than Charley's or my place and dense trees blocked any effort the sun might make to penetrate the gloom. No wonder Peder spent so much time at Little's.

The secluded road reminded me that no one lived close enough to hear a cry for help. Anke could have followed me. My gaze darted to the bag on the passenger seat with my camera and gun. A voice in my head said, "Do not leave your car."

I'd almost talked myself into turning around when the door opened and Peder came toward me waving. I waved back, relieved.

He said, "I'm so pleased you came by. It will save me a trip to the restaurant to say goodbye." His mouth turned down. "My poor Sasha is sick and I must hurry back home."

"I'm sorry about Sasha and sorry you have to leave." I hesitated, then asked anyway. "I stopped by to ask your help again, only this time I don't need a boat ride."

"Of course, please come in. My flight leaves Minneapolis tonight, so I don't have much time."

"This won't take long." I grabbed the journal and we walked up the slight rise to his porch. He ushered me inside. "Please tell me what I can do for you."

The living room opened to a small kitchen; a round table with four chairs separated the spaces. I unwrapped the journal at the table. "This was at Charley's. It's written in Norwegian and I wonder if you could translate it for me. It's just a few entries."

He reached for it. "Yes, of course. Let's sit down, shall we?"

I pulled a chair close to Peder's. He turned to the first page, cleared his throat and began reading Gunnar Johansson's journal.

March 23, 1941—I never expected to be this happy. I thought falling in love with Ruthie and getting married to her was the best day of my life. And today, Ruthie told me I am going to be a father. I had always dreamed of having a family of my own and now I am. I love her so much. She looks like a tiny beautiful bird, but she is strong and so smart. I hope our baby is just like her. I don't care if it is a boy or girl. We want to have many children.

Her father did not want us to marry because of our different faiths, especially now. They are Jewish and Hitler is occupying our country. My parents were against the marriage as well, but both families relented when they saw how much we love each other, and they are pleased about the baby. I am the luckiest man alive. I'm writing this journal so one day my son or daughter will read it and know how much this day meant to me. And to renew my vow to do everything I can to protect my family and our citizens from the Nazis.

I've been working with the resistance for more than a year now. It's true, the Germans overcame our resistance forces in the April 9, 1940 invasion because we weren't prepared for the attack. The Norwegian army and Allied Forces put up a good fight, but were outnumbered and had to retreat within two months. But the Nazis will never stop us. We are armed, and those who aren't support us in our activities in many other ways. We sabotage the Nazi operations, go out at night on raids and gather intelligence. We have destroyed their ships and supplies. Some prefer passive resistance and civil disobedience but they are not successful with these thugs.

Peder licked his lips, swallowed and looked up at me. I leaned in. "Please, keep reading." Gunnar sounded like a good guy. Maybe I'd gotten the wrong idea from the photos. He nodded and read quickly through the next entries.

April 24, 1941—Ruthie wants me to stop my work with the resistance. She is afraid for my life and now that I have the responsibility of becoming a father, she said I have to think of family first. But what kind of man am I, and what kind of father will I be, if I don't try to stop the Nazis from taking over our country? They have already removed our government. It is up to the resistance to stand up to them. She cried when we argued over this. It was the first time that has happened since we met. It made me so ashamed to have made my beloved wife sad, but I must continue.

May 11, 1941— Ruthie's father believed he was safe as a math professor at the Norwegian Institute of Technology, but the Nazis have taken him to a concentration camp along with about fifty other men who were members of their Synagogue. The Germans are using Norwegian police to do their dirty work. How can they turn on their own countrymen?

September 19, 1941—I had to tell Ruthie her father was killed at Auschwitz. She is inconsolable. He was her only family. I begged her to leave the country but she won't go. She doesn't believe they will find her because her last name is Johansson now. A border guard I know has said he will help her get to Sweden, but she continues to say no. She grows bigger with our baby every day, and I am afraid for both of them.

I hadn't known much about the Nazi occupation of Norway and must have made a sound because Peder stopped. I said, "I'm sorry to make you read such a horrible story, but please go on."

He continued reading.

November 26, 1942—On this day of hell police officers arrested and detained Jewish women and children throughout the country. They sent them by cars and train to the pier in Oslo where a cargo ship waited to transport them to Auschwitz. Ruthie and our sweet baby girl, Anna, were among them. To my shame, I was not at home but working with the resistance.

The crooked Norwegian Police Chief Helmuth Krogstad and several of his officers, who were working for the Nazis, took her. Krogstad knew I was in the resistance and when they found out Ruthie was Jewish and my wife, they used her as an example for others. On his orders, they raped and beat her to death and then they killed our Anna. I know this because he bragged about it.

All known Jews in Norway have been deported, imprisoned and murdered. Some were able to flee to Sweden. A few may still be in hiding in Norway. I have nothing to live for now but revenge for what was done to my family and so many others. First, I will kill the chief of police's family while he watches. He will feel my wrath come down upon him in a reign of terror even those inhuman creatures of evil who follow him will be horrified to witness.

Peder's voice lowered to a whisper as he read the final entry.

July 1946—The war is over. I'm leaving for the United States to be near my brother, Rolf. There's nothing for me here but terrible reminders of what I have lost and what I have done.

My hand went to my heart. The newspaper photos made sense now. The beheaded man was the police chief who tortured and killed Gunnar's wife and daughter. Gunnar had done this, even killing Krogstad's wife and son. Gunnar was my great-uncle, and Charley was Gunnar. I sat in stunned silence.

Peder set the journal on the table and the newspaper clipping slipped out. He looked at it,   blinked and hurried down a hallway, talking over his shoulder. "Excuse me, I need to use the bathroom."

He probably wanted a moment to collect himself. I had to call Wilcox. They must be finishing up at Charley's or maybe they were questioning Anke. She was German. Maybe she had a connection. There were two boys in the family picture but only one son and the mother had been killed. The child would have to be in his seventies. Vik popped into my mind. He was Norwegian and the right age. He'd been keeping a low profile in Spirit Lake during the timeframe that everything had happened. Maybe the captions would reveal more information. I'd ask Peder to read them unless he was too upset.

I'd left my phone in my bag. I walked out the front door calling to Peder, "I'll be right back. I'm getting my phone."

My gaze was on the ground as I hopped off the porch and started toward the SUV. A set of animal prints caught my attention. The spongy ground sucking at my boots, I squatted for a better look. Those ragged paw prints shouldn't have been there. Cold terror washed over me.

The door flew open behind me and Peder leaped from the porch and shoved me to the ground. I jumped into a crouch, ready to spring at him. "You took my dogs."

I hadn't noticed the gun aimed at my head until he came forward and knocked me on my side with a ferocious kick. I grunted and crab-walked backward. "What I can't figure out is why you didn't hurt them."

His head snapped back, eyes wide. "I would never hurt a dog. I love dogs." His foot came toward me again. I shrank away but this time it was a nudge. "Get up."

Tongue-tied with too many questions fighting to be asked, I scrambled to my feet. He waved for me to enter the house first.

He pulled a chair away from the table. "Sit." He saw my eyes on the journal and whisked it away. "You won't be needing this."

Keeping the gun pointed at me, he reached into a drawer and showed me a length of clothesline and a zip tie. "Planning. I'd hoped to get you here much sooner."

He pushed me forward. "Hands behind your back." One hand held the gun as he slipped the tie over my hands and pulled tight.

"How did you get them to go with you?"

"The dogs? Easy, I have a way with animals. Rock already knew me so I told him if he came with me, we'd go see Britt. Knute followed. When Rock figured out we weren't going to see you, I already had the muzzle on him."

"How did you get in?"

He waved a hand. "Also easy. The restaurant has been in chaos since Lars' accident."

I spat. "We both know it was no accident."

"Okay, happy coincidence."

I stared at him as if seeing him for the first time.

"They keep their keys on a peg just inside the kitchen. I slipped in and grabbed the key ring. If they'd asked, which they didn't, I would have said I was on my way to the bathroom. I went back to the bistro for a few minutes, then slipped around back and unlocked the door. Back in the bistro, I gathered my things and returned the key ring to the peg before leaving. I'd driven to town and parked on the street. No one would recognize the car; I always came to town by boat."

"Why take them and then let us find them?"

His lips stretched, but it wasn't a smile. "Wilcox had a deputy here asking questions. I needed to do something to point them back at the Willards." He came closer and stroked a strand of my hair. I jerked away. His face darkened. "But now I need to get back to Sasha."

"I get it that you must be connected to what Gunnar did in the '40s, but we had nothing to do with that."

He stuck his face close to mine, perspiration beading along his upper lip. "My mother and father had nothing to do with it

224

either, and yet I never knew any of my real family because of what your kindly old flower-growing great-uncle did to my grandparents."

I scrambled to make sense of what he said. "The people in the news clipping?"

He seemed lost in his thoughts.

I said, "There's no need to go after Little, now, right? You have to get out of here fast or you'll be caught." I tried to keep my voice neutral, but the reedy warble gave away my terror. "They know I'm here."

His lip curled. "You didn't tell them because they wouldn't have let you leave by yourself."

He stood over me, his finger tapping his chin. "True, Little's not going to propagate the Johansson family line." He caught his lower lip between his teeth. "I have to get moving and he's being guarded as if he's the President. I'm out of time."

He looked like a little kid who wanted to show his mommy the picture he drew in school that day. He needed to get killing me over with so he could go to his sick dog, but desire to brag about what he'd done must be even stronger.

"Why Lars? He's not related." I worked at the tie biting into my wrists but couldn't loosen it.

He raked the hair away from his face. "Lars was a spur of the moment opportunity."

"But you were in the restaurant when he was on the lake."

He shrugged. "I had plenty of time to make my usual appearance."

I hadn't even considered that. "How did you get to him?"

"I happened to be looking out my window at the incessant rain when Lars passed by in his boat. I followed him into that cove at the island. I called out, but he wore earbuds. He drifted close to shore, I cut my engine and used the oars to get closer."

"Lars is bigger than you. What if he'd seen you?"

That open, friendly smile I'd found so engaging spread across his face. "I'd say hello and go on my way, but he still faced away from me when I pulled up alongside, so I bashed him in the head with my oar. He fell out of his boat and hit his head on a rock. I thought he'd drowned."

I wanted to cover my ears. I'd tried to get him to talk and now I wished he would shut up. His voice rose and he paced back and forth. "I dragged him into that clearing, but he started to wake up. You'd told me he was half-Jewish and it infuriated me that if it wasn't for the Jews I would still have a family. I beat him until I thought I'd killed him."

I lunged at him. "If it wasn't for your monster of a grandfather you'd still have a family." He stuck the gun in my face and pushed me back down. Why had I never noticed how cold his eyes were? But he'd looked so unthreatening. He didn't even appear strong enough to drag Lars into the woods.

His voice flat, he said, "I'd never been a violent man before, but torturing Charley to get the information about his lawyer and the safe deposit box and then killing him was such a release, I needed to do it again." He turned predatory eyes on me. "And I need to do it again now."

Nervous sweat trickled down my back. "What was in the safe deposit box?"

"Gunnar's Norwegian identification papers, proof that I had the right man. Keys to the boxes you found, but no information about where they were hidden." He came closer, a menacing smile played at the corners of his mouth.

I leaned away, frantically tugging at the tie around my wrists. "We have a piece of the oar. They'll trace it to you."

That stopped him. "Impossible, I dropped them in the middle of the lake."

"I guess you missed a chunk that flew off when you attacked Lars. That explains why you didn't have oars when you ran out of gas."

"I wasn't out of gas when we found him. I was trying to get you away from there." He shot another gloating smile at me. "I dumped the gas when you sent me for help so I had a good excuse." He checked his watch, stuck the clothesline in a pocket and pulled me up by my elbow.

He shoved me out the back door and pushed me up against a tall pine. Then he wound the clothesline around my chest and waist, anchoring me to the tree.

A limb from a birch lay on the ground next to an axe. He sat on the back step, pulled a knife from his jeans pocket and whittled the top into a sharp point. I tried not to visualize what he intended to do with it.

I said, "I've never met anyone like you before." It wasn't true. I'd met worse scumbags than him who did their murdering on massive levels but better to keep him talking.

He tossed his hair back, pleased with himself. "I needed to find the most important thing to each of you. For you, you said it yourself, it was your brother's safety."

He continued pushing the knife in an upward motion through the birch, honing the point, using his thumb to test it, and watching the effect his words had on me.

Chills shook my body. When he saw my reaction, his eyes glittered.

"What did I miss? How could you have tricked me so thoroughly?" I didn't realize I'd spoken out loud.

"You're not the brightest. I did my research and discovered you have a big blind spot. You're a crusader. Some articles even use that term to describe you. You have to stop bullies, so I gave you the gay hate thing and you came up with the Willards. Bolger, another bully, came along on his own. That's why you didn't suspect me." He pointed the stake at my throat. "I'm a different kind of animal."

I shrunk away. "You're a weasel."

He tossed his hair. "I'd have had you sooner but Wilcox must not have anything better to do than watch over you." His head jerked toward the road as if wondering if the sheriff was there.

I looked too, mouthing a silent prayer. *Sheriff, I promise to always do everything you ask if you get me out of this.* Thor's admonishment about how my actions had distracted the sheriff from doing his job came back to me. And I'd done it again by sending them after Anke.

Peder leaned the sharpened stake against the house and paced in front of me, lost in thought.

When I'd gotten my voice under control, I said, "You're alive so it's not true your entire family line has been ended."

"You don't know anything." He looked like he wanted to cry.

"Why don't you explain then, because I just think you're a madman."

"My father was four when Gunnar killed his parents, my grandparents. He even killed his older brother. A neighbor, Mrs. Jorgensen, saved my father. She was giving him a violin lesson when Gunnar attacked the others. The Jorgensens brought up my father as their own child. My father grew up, married and had me, an only child, but didn't tell me the true story until he was dying."

I listened hard, trying to figure out a way to stay alive.

"He showed me newspaper clippings and photos of my real grandfather's head on a stake, same as the one in that journal. My father had tried his entire life to find Gunnar. He'd researched Trondheim Johanssons who had family in other countries and it took him years of searching to find the connection to your grandfather, Rolf.

Near death, he asked me to finish his work, and I promised to destroy Gunnar if he was still alive, and all his living relatives. Charley was the only ninety-year-old man in this area who had a relationship with your father, so I tortured him and threatened that I'd kill all of you unless he confessed."

Poor Charley. "You did this for revenge because you have no family? Surely there must be relatives still living from your father's birth family."

"Don't you think I tried to find them? I was so happy when my research gave me names and addresses. I went to see them, expecting to be embraced as a family member. But they didn't want to have anything to do with me because of what my grandfather did to the Jews."

He picked up the stake and poked it at my throat. "Your great-uncle killed my family and ruined my life. Now I'm going to make sure your family line ends with you in the grave."

I tried to reason with him. "Why would you want to be part of a family that had a member who raped, tortured and killed innocent people?" I had to keep him talking. As soon as he stopped, he'd kill me. "You could start your own family line."

He shrieked. "I can't have children. My wife left me because she wanted a baby, the selfish bitch. I suggested we adopt, but she wouldn't do that. Our divorce was final three months ago, and she's already pregnant. I found out she was having an affair when we were still married." His lips opened in a snarl. "When I finish with you I'm going back to deal with her. She can't do this to me."

What would a psychologist make of this? His wife divorced him, his father died and he learned the horrific family history. His original family rebuffed him because they didn't want to be reminded of the past and he was all alone. Had that been enough to make a sane man lose all reason?

My brain scrambled for ways to keep him talking. "Peder, you don't want to do this."

His eyes were lifeless. "My name is Fredrik."

I blinked. "Who's Peder Halvorson?"

He threw back his head of silky blond hair dark with sweat, and laughed. "He's my ex-wife's fiancé."

His jugular bobbed with each swallow of air. "All I care about is my Sasha. I have to get back to her. To both of my beautiful dogs."

He dropped the stake and grabbed the axe lying next to a birch limb. He held it high in the air. My life could not end like this. I swallowed the voice inside me that wanted to beg for mercy. "That's not what you used on Charley."

"His chain saw is in the middle of the lake."

Desperate, I said, "I thought you liked me. We were friends."

He rested the axe on his shoulder and smiled at me with affection. "It's true. I liked the way you swam with such grace and power. And the way your hair blew back in the wind when we were on my boat, like one of those wooden figureheads on the prow of a ship facing fearlessly into the wind."

His hand caressed my forearm and my skin retracted. "You're so direct, not like my ex-wife with her subterfuges and betrayals. You were the reason I didn't end this sooner. I didn't want to stop seeing you."

If this was what he did to women he liked, what might he do to his ex? I wanted to spit in his face but forced myself to look into his eyes, my voice gentle. "Stop now, and get help. We can get you a good lawyer. I'll be there for you." I'd be there to see that he got the maximum penalty.

He wavered for a moment and then laughed again. "You are lying."

"You've made your point by killing Charley. Why don't you get away while you can? Leave me tied to the tree. I'll probably get eaten before they find me." The mosquitos alone would drain my blood by morning.

He hesitated, and I hoped he was considering it but he untied me from the tree, shoved me to the ground and raised the axe. I stared up at it, my pulse racing. "That's going to take a long time, especially for someone who doesn't know what he's doing."

The axe stopped midair. I said, "Ben and Wilcox are probably on their way now, tracking me through my SUV's GPS. They expected me at the restaurant an hour ago. Even if I'm dead, they'll track you anywhere you go."

His eyes widened. "I've got to get out of here." He brought the axe down. I screamed and rolled away. The blade came down and the blunt end caught me at the back of my head mid-turn.

Half-conscious, I was dimly aware of my head banging on the steps, back scraping against the threshold as he dragged me into the house. He said, "As you Americans say, Plan B. They'll never prove anything or find me."

Peder grabbed a gas can from the back porch, emptied it on the kitchen table and chairs, then lit a match and tossed it. I blacked out.

I woke to fire licking at my hair and the back of my shirt and I flattened myself against the rug to extinguish the flame. The room was filled with smoke so I squat-walked, keeping low to the floor and made my way to the door. I used my shoulder to push through, lost my balance and fell down the steps.

A car engine roared and I opened my eyes. Had I blacked out again? Peder backed out of the garage, saw me and came running. I tried to roll out of the way but he jumped on top of me, his hand grabbed for my throat. My martial arts trainer's voice came to me. "When things get meaningful, unleash the beast."

I bucked up and snapped my legs around Peder's neck, trapping the arm that had reached for my throat tight against a pressure point in his neck. Adrenalin pumped through me and I squeezed harder. His head slumped forward. I hoped I'd killed him.

Chapter 25

Windows exploded and flames climbed the walls, devouring the cottage. Using every ounce of my strength to keep Peder locked between my thighs, I watched the sparks shooting up like a fireworks display, disappearing into the trees and dark sky.

Screaming fire engines snapped me out of a daze. The driveway filled with vehicles. Fire fighters raced toward the house with hoses and equipment. Someone yelled, "Get those flames out before we have a forest fire." More lights and sirens filled the night. Someone half-lifted, half-dragged us away, and still I squeezed.

Ben's face came into view. He knelt next to me. "You can let go now. We'll take him." Wilcox pried Peder from my death grip and checked his pulse. "Still breathing."

Ben lifted me to a sitting position, then moved behind me to cut the tie on my wrists. I heard a sharp intake of breath. He yelled at the medic. "Get a gurney here now!"

Adrenalin zapped through my system like an electric current and I yelled out a victory whoop. "We caught this psycho! Ben, get my camera!"

They lifted me onto the gurney and rolled me toward the ambulance. Ben tried to gently press me down. "You can't take any photos right now."

I popped back up to a sitting position. "My hands are a little numb from being tied. It's not a problem. C'mon!"

Ben turned to the medic, his voice urgent. "Do something."

I tried to get off the gurney, but the medic stuck me in the hip with a needle. Ben said, "How about if I take the photos?"

"Fine, hurry!" I raised my hands for a high five.

But they weren't my hands. They were something else.

***

Nurse Cranky adjusted the blinds and morning sunshine poured in. "You're awake." Her tone was oddly gentle.

"Connie, I feel great. I'm out of here." Unfortunately, my words came out slurred and my limbs didn't get the message that I wanted to get out of bed.

She moved toward me. "Doctor will be here in a minute."

"Gotta go." I tried to pull the sheet off, but the fingers on my right hand were four times their normal size, each digit wrapped in layers of thick gauze. I lifted my left hand and it looked the same. My gaze swiveled from one to the other, not getting it. I whispered. "What's happened to them?"

She glanced toward the door, maybe sensing the situation was about to get out of control. "They were burned in the fire last night."

I blinked, trying to think through the haze in my head. I couldn't let anything be wrong with my hands. I tried to grip the bandages to pull them off but couldn't with the giant blobs. I yanked at the bandages with my teeth and pain shot through my fingers, electrifying my entire system. My voice was a shrill soprano. "Take this stuff off."

"Calm down, Britt." She spoke into the intercom. "I need an orderly in Room 112. Now." I climbed out of bed, trying to get away from the bandages, and the IV slipped out. I almost made it to the door where, a foot shorter, Connie stood firm in front of me. "You're not helping yourself."

I listed sideways but still fought to get past her. The orderly rushed in and caught me before I hit the floor. Dr. Fromm arrived and the three of them hauled me back into bed. Connie reconnected me and fastened another bag on the IV stand.

Dr. Fromm frowned down at me. "You shouldn't get excited with that concussion you have."

Breathing hard, I said, "I don't care about the concussion. My hands."

He emphasized each word. "You have severe burns on both hands and right now we're focusing on managing the pain." He studied the IV. "We've increased your sedative."

Maybe that's why he had three heads. I squeezed my eyes closed and tried again. The orderly and Connie stepped back and Fromm came into focus.

"This can't be happening." I tried to grab him to make him understand, but my hand could only bump his arm and pain zapped me again. I flopped back on the pillow. "Where's Ben? He'll get me out of here."

Dr. Fromm nodded at the orderly. He opened the door and Ben came in with a look in his eyes that scared me. Pity. He sat beside me on the bed and put his arm around my shoulder, gesturing toward the hovering trio. "You can all leave. Go on, now." Even Dr. Fromm backed off and left the room.

"Tell me, Ben." The words sounded like they came from a tunnel.

His voice soft, he said, "Your hands were scorched pretty badly, but the doc thinks you'll have complete use of them again."

"Thinks?" My heart quickened.

He smoothed my hair behind my ear the way he always did when I was upset. "Of course, they will."

"They have to fix this quick. I'm going to South Sudan, remember?"

"There's plenty of time to talk about that."

"I am going." My head lolled sideways and my eyes dropped to half-mast. Little and Lars swam into view and out again like a couple of walleye. When had they come in? Little whispered to Lars, "Don't even mention the Sudan thing for a while. If you tell her she can't do something, she gets obsessive."

Little was still there when I woke up. "How long have I been sleeping?"

"Not long." He came to the foot of my bed, looking as if he wanted to crawl under it and hide. "I have something to tell you and I'm so sorry."

"I'm still a little fuzzy-headed, Little. What are you sorry about?"

"It's my fault you trusted Peder. You kept taking off so I asked him to stick close to you, especially on the lake."

The confrontation with Peder washed over me. "You picked a great babysitter."

He cringed. "He acted like a good guy." His head hung low.

"He tricked us all." I couldn't stand to see Little upset. "I'd already figured it out, anyway. You weren't that subtle."

Little said, "Wilcox found that journal and newspaper clipping in Peder's car. Bella told us what it said. We should have guessed Charley was our great uncle. He and Dad were both more than six-feet-tall and had light hair and blue eyes."

"You realize that describes half the male population in Minnesota."

He shuddered. "Still, I'd rather not be related to someone who did what he did but I guess we can't choose what's in our family history."

I nodded, but picturing the sweet-tempered old gardener as a young assassin, even if he did go after a Nazi was difficult. "Yet another one of our dad's secrets. He must have known all along."

Little winced at my bandaged hands. "That looks really painful. I've been thinking maybe it's best if you *aren't* in Spirit Lake. Every time you come home, you get hurt and end up in here." His gaze took in the room.

It was on the tip of my tongue to deny it, but after a quick recall of the last year and a half, I closed my mouth.

His eyebrows were all knotted up. "That never happens when you're in the middle of a conflict thousands of miles from here, even working in places where photographers get kidnapped or killed."

"Things have happened, I've just never told you about them, Little."

His eyes rounded. "Why didn't you?"

"You worry too much already." He didn't need to know about the bomb detonating only yards from me in Iraq, blowing me forward, my back and legs covered with cuts, deaf for days.

I'd run for my life more than a few times and narrowly escaped. "Besides, I can take care of myself. Why do you think I work so hard at staying fit?"

"But why do you have to do it?"

"We've talked about this. It's not just me. Journalists who do what I do want to show the world what's happening, hoping things will improve. It's dangerous, but for us, worth the risk."

His mouth turned down. "I know you'll never stop." He reached into a cooler and pulled out a green smoothie. "You can drink this with your bandages."

I held them up. "Mickey Mouse hands." We both tried to smile. My stomach growled and I eyed the drink. I'd been hoping for a sandwich but he was right, I'd have no way to hold it.

He propped the smoothie between my bent knees and guided the straw to my mouth. "It's loaded with nutrients."

I slurped it down and nodded. "Surprisingly good."

Nurse Connie pushed through the door rolling a tray filled with gauze, ointment and instruments of torture. I turned away before looking any closer. She said, "Little, you'll have to leave while I clean and re-bandage."

He stowed the cup in his cooler and said he'd be back later.

Connie bit her lower lip. "I know how brave you are, but you might not want to look while I'm doing this."

"It's okay, Connie. That pain med is helping. We might as well get the healing going."

She unwound the gauze wrapped around my palm and wrist, and then moved to each finger, gently unwrapping them. My breath caught. They looked like cooked sausages. Tears clogged my throat. "No, Connie."

She let down her guard for a moment and I saw the compassion. "You're going to need some of that bravery I was talking about now, dear."

I leaned back against the pillow and looked at the ceiling while Connie cared for my hands. Even with her tender touch, it hurt so much tears streamed out the sides of my eyes. I clamped my jaw and fought the pain, knowing no medication could take it all away.

When she finished the long process of re-bandaging, she hesitated at the door. "You did great, Britt. The swelling will go down in a few days."

I drifted off again, thankful for the respite from pain.

When I opened my eyes, Lars sat in a chair under the window, his crutches resting on the arm. My first instinct was that he shouldn't be here alone, and then I remembered, the threat was gone.

I blinked away tears at the sight of my cotton candy-sized hands. "What time is it?"

"About three p.m."

I'd slept most of the day. I lifted my chin at him. "Aren't you supposed to be resting?"

"It's my day for therapy so I'm keeping you company until my appointment."

"How's it going?"

"Which one? After my physical therapy, I see a psychologist to help me deal with the memory and anger issues." His head drooped. "I'm messed up. The therapist 'suggests' that I'm angry at myself. I blame myself for what happened, and I need to let that go."

"You're going to get through all of it, Lars. Me too, for Little."

"Yeah."

Mapping the pain centers in my body sapped my energy— the dull throbbing at the back of my head, the pain in my hands a country of its own. It was difficult to find a comfortable position on my back, although apparently it wasn't badly burned. I leaned to one side. "Have you seen Ben?"

"He and Wilcox are wrapping up stuff about the case."

I drifted away again thinking about how I'd misjudged everything. Bolger, the Willards, Anke and Neil had nothing to do with any of it. I'd even suspected the workshop leader. Instead, the charming writer was a psychopath. I thought I could tell the bad guys from the good and now I'd always doubt myself. I'd very much like to know details about what Wilcox and Ben were wrapping up.

As if on cue, the two entered the room. Lars talked to them for a minute and moved slowly to the door. "Gotta go."

"Thanks, Lars," I said. He handled his crutches with more assurance today.

Wilcox removed his hat and pulled up a chair. Ben stood next to the bed. He didn't put his arm around me this time. This was official business, but I didn't want to talk, I wanted to bury my head in his shoulder and stay that way.

The sheriff cleared his throat and set a recorder on the stand between us. "Sorry for the intrusion, but I need your statement."

"Not a problem. I've been wondering how you found me last night. Was it the fire?"

Ben said, "We used your phone GPS."

Wilcox leaned back. "We would have gotten to you sooner but we were busy with Anke Schmidt. She confessed to being at Charley's, but said she was only watching. We already considered her a person of interest."

"Why?"

"Vik, the workshop leader, said she'd been writing her thriller using details from Charley's murder, Lars' beating, Rob's fire and all the other stuff that happened. It disturbed him so we were collecting evidence on her."

Ben nodded. "Peder/Fredrik Jorgensen was also on the sheriff's radar."

"I didn't kill him?"

Relief washed over me when Wilcox shook his head.

"But he had a hard time talking after what you did to him, and his feet were too close to the fire so he can't walk yet." Wilcox leaned forward. "Before we get going, I'd like to know where you learned that trick with your legs."

"It's all about pressure points on your opponent's neck. You basically use his own arm to disable him. I've had some training." The effect of the pain meds made me chatty. "Kajukenbo is all about doing what it takes." I was about to deliver a blow-by-blow of how the move is executed when Wilcox interrupted. "Don't know it." He turned to Ben, a question in his eyes.

Ben said, "It's not the martial arts you usually see in a tournament where everyone's following the same rules. The training she's talking about teaches self-defense and survival in the real world."

I'd have to call my trainer and thank him. Andre grew up on the streets of Compton. Muscular and lightning quick, he rarely needed to use his skills outside of training people. He could intimidate just by walking into a room.

Wilcox said, "Are we ready?" He turned on his recorder. For the next hour I answered questions and repeated what Peder, or Fredrik said. When we were finished, I asked, "Did he confess to messing with the cars?"

Wilcox nodded. "He said he knew his time was short, so after the poisoned candy didn't kill the three of you, disabling the brakes was a final effort to get Little and Lars, and also shift the investigation back to the Willards. He'd heard you talking about their truck hanging around the garage."

I winced at the rebuke. I couldn't look the sheriff or Ben in the eye. "I guess I did part of Peder's job for him, but Charley's murder wasn't about being gay, so who sent the original letter to Lars and Little calling them faggots?"

Wilcox said, "People in the restaurant were gossiping about Charley's murder being a gay hate crime. Peder-Fredrik thought building on that would add "character" to his campaign to kill all of you and throw us off his trail."

"And I took it and ran full tilt after the Willards." I would have slapped my own forehead if my hands worked.

Wilcox took off his hat and ran his hand across his head. His hair looked thinner, his eyes puffy. "The Willards are bad people, no doubt about it and they're up to something. We're still investigating them."

He rubbed at his eyes. "We learned from Fredrik's ex-wife that he'd had trouble keeping jobs. She said she divorced him because of his violent mood swings. Branson County is negotiating with Oslo authorities about how he'll be brought to justice."

Connie came in and held the door. "The doctor is doing rounds."

Wilcox rarely shared information with me but I still had a lot of questions, like why Matthew had been hanging around Spirit Lake.

Wilcox gathered his hat and recorder. "We'll finish this later."

Ben kissed my forehead and followed the sheriff out the door. Our last interaction, before Peder tried to kill me, hadn't been one of my stellar moments. That reminded me of Marta—I had to heal fast.

Dr. Fromm came in with his eyes focused on my chart. Connie unwound my hands for the second time that day. The pain jolted me wide awake. "Doctor, I leave on assignment in a few days."

His thin lips stretched in a quick grimace. "That's not possible." He examined my hands and checked my head wound and eyes. "You'll have to stay here until we're sure there's no infection in your hands, at least a week. Your back was burned, but your clothing kept you from the worst of it. No damage to your legs or feet. Good thing you were wearing jeans and boots." He wrote something on my chart.

Connie began the slow medicating and re-bandaging process. My fingers looked pathetically sad as she wound them into their white cocoons. I tried not to wince, and swallowed the lump in my throat. "Dr. Fromm, how much time until I can take these bandages off?"

"It's difficult to predict with burns. Infection is a danger. We have to change them frequently, and if you want full dexterity, you'll need occupational therapy every day for however long it takes."

Connie said, "The bandages won't be bulky like this for more than two weeks if all goes well. We'll change them to something that looks like netting, and you'll be able to do a few more things."

My heart pounded. I needed to be in South Sudan in a week or sooner. "Two weeks won't work. Get me someone who can fix this now. Can't you fly me to a burn center? I need my hands working right away." My fury over-rode the sedative. I was about to bolt again.

Fromm pushed his round glasses higher on his nose. "We're fortunate Nurse Connie has worked in burn centers. Be patient. Do what she says."

"I want another opinion. Your timeline isn't acceptable."

Connie and Dr. Fromm's mouths formed identical straight lines. He said, "Very well, if that's what you want."

Ben came in. "What's going on here?"

I turned on him. "You're no better. No one cares whether I'm getting shoddy care as long as I stay in your precious Spirit Lake."

Ben put a hand up. "That's not fair. Everyone's doing their best for you."

"When it's your own job you're the famous disappearing man, but when I'm the one who has to go, it's not important. You don't even care about anything but yourself."

Connie and Fromm looked at each other. She put her hand on Ben's elbow. "Maybe it's best if you leave." Shooting a furious look at me, he turned on his heels and left. I still had more to say and wanted to go after him, but Connie slid next to me and adjusted my blanket, effectively holding me in place.

Dr. Fromm said, "You can go wherever you choose, Britt. I'll see what I can arrange."

Connie stayed behind after Dr. Fromm left. More brusque than usual, she asked, "Can I do anything else for you?"

"Could you please scroll through my messages?" She picked up the phone and held it so I could see who'd tried to reach me. There were several from Marta. I didn't need to read them. "Do you mind calling Marta and putting it on speaker for me. I have to tell her I'm coming."

Her eyes widened. "That's not possible. Any doctor who looks at your hands will say the same."

I gritted my teeth. "Just please do it, Connie." She punched in the number, hit speaker and set the phone on the table.

Marta picked up immediately. "Britt, I'm so sorry about your hands."

"Don't worry about it, I'll be fine in a couple of days."

Connie's tsk was audible from across the room.

Marta said, "Just listen for a minute, Britt. I have to tell you something you won't want to hear. Gonzales is already on a flight to South Sudan. We couldn't wait, especially not knowing how long it would be before you healed."

"This is payback from before, isn't it? You'll never trust me again. I promise I'll be fine in a few days."

"I've talked to your doctor. You have weeks of therapy ahead to even get movement back in your fingers. Don't worry, there will be other projects. Take care of yourself."

"Dr. Fromm doesn't know what he's talking about. I never miss an assignment. You know I have to prove to management that I'm reliable. I can do it Marta. Please."

"I have to go, Britt. We'll talk when you're more rational."

I yelled at the phone. "You're supposed to be my best friend, and you're selling me out. Firing me last year wasn't enough? Now you're taking this away from me, making me look bad? You're a shit, Marta, a shit."

"I'm sorry. We'll talk next week."

"Don't hang up!" The line went dead.

Connie turned off the phone and set it back on the table next to me. Looking at me as if I were some pitiful mental case, she adjusted something in the IV, nodded at someone in the corner, and left.

Chapter 26

I followed Connie's gaze. Partially in shadow, Little's downcast eyes meant he was ashamed of me. He came over to the bed. "Ben said you were acting like a jerk. Do you want to talk about it?"

The IV sedative took the edge off. My head flopped back against the pillow, the anger disappearing as swiftly as it had taken me over. I'd wanted it all at the same time—to find the person trying to harm my brother and Lars, cover the Sudan story, and Ben too, and when I couldn't have it all, I lashed out like a two-year-old.

"I didn't mean what I said." I wanted to take back every insulting word I'd said to Ben, Marta, Dr. Fromm and Connie.

"I'd better get back to the restaurant." He pointed to an insulated bag. "Another smoothie for when you get hungry." He hesitated on his way out. "I do understand why you're acting this way. You've worked so hard to get your life back together after the drinking and now you think your job's being taken away again. But we're part of your life too, and we'll never abandon you." The door closed behind him.

I watched him leave with a heaviness inside that hurt worse than any of my injuries. Little had always looked up to me and I'd blown it last year with my drinking and unpredictable behavior. I'd tried to make it up to him and now I'd disappointed him again.

When I woke, Edgar was sitting in a chair under the window, eyes closed, mouth slightly open, snoring. I scooted into a seated position and the bed squeaked. His eyes opened.

"Hi, Edgar."

He sniffed. "They say you've been kicking butt and taking names."

My chin dropped to my chest and I mumbled. "More like making an ass of myself. Pushing away everyone who cares about me."

He nodded. "That too."

I leaned forward. "I photograph war and poverty—and the women and children who are forced to live in depraved conditions—working toward social justice, and in the meantime I hurt the people close to me. What's wrong with me?"

"Forces can be at work within you that you aren't aware of. One day you'll catch up to yourself."

I lifted my bandaged hands. "I won't be catching myself for a while."

"Good joke. Ha, ha. His arthritic hands felt for his cane, and he stood. "Henry's on his way."

"Thanks for stopping by."

He turned at the door. "They let those Willards go now that you caught the killer."

I nodded. "They should be locked up; they're bad people."

His head bobbed. "Now that you have all this time on your hands, you can figure out what they're up to."

Did he really just make a joke about my hands?

The door opened and Henry came in. "Hey, Britt, how're you doing?"

"I think my karma's caught up to me."

Henry crossed the room and put a hand on my shoulder. "You did a good thing. Sorry I can't stay and talk. The casino's really busy today." He took Edgar's elbow. "Ready to go, Grandfather?"

Thinking it must be that vision thing he did, I asked, "Edgar, how did you know Henry was here?"

He reached in his pocket and pulled out a cell phone. "It buzzed."

Henry's eyes disappeared behind his cheeks. "It's our signal when we don't have a fire and blanket."

I smiled but it didn't last. I'd insulted the people who were trying to heal me, probably lost Ben, my job and my dear friend.

I'd never again enter the *L.A. Times* building lobby, walk past the old telephone booth, the row of clocks or the hallway lined with *Times* Pulitzers, mine among them. If I kept this up, no one would ever love me, not even Little.

In the morning, Dr. Fromm introduced me to Dr. Hillary Oliver, a burn specialist from the Mayo Clinic. "I've asked her to examine your hands." His voice was chilly. "You can certainly be transferred to Dr. Oliver's care. Let me know and I'll make the arrangements."

Shame made it hard to speak. "Thank you, Doctor, but there's no need. I was out of my mind yesterday."

"I insist." Dr. Fromm signaled to Connie. She unwound the bandages and stepped back. Dr. Oliver's gray head bent forward and she began her examination. She nodded at Dr. Fromm. "I see you've done some nice repair where the plastic ties melted into the flesh."

My stomach flipped. That was new information. I looked at Connie but she turned away.

When Dr. Oliver finished, she said she wouldn't have done anything differently and named the same timeline for recovery. I thanked her and forced myself to look at Connie and Dr. Fromm. "I'm sorry for the way I acted yesterday. You're great at your jobs and if you'll still have me here, I'll do whatever you ask. I won't be any trouble."

They exchanged one of their telepathic glances and Dr. Fromm nodded. Professional and detached, Dr. Oliver said, "Well, then, Britt, if you don't have any questions, I'll be on my way."

I swallowed. "What about scars?"

She said, "You might not have much scarring, but there will likely be some discoloration of the skin in some areas."

If that was the worst, I'd take it. The doctors left and Connie finished re-bandaging.

"Thank you, Connie. I'm lucky you're taking care of me." I'd have to stop calling her Nurse Cranky behind her back. Her bedside manner wasn't the best, but that didn't seem to matter anymore.

The edges of her mouth tipped up. I slept again and woke up thinking about Edgar's comment yesterday about the Willards. In fact, I couldn't stop thinking about them. Evil wasn't a word I used often, but whenever I'd been near that family, a chill settled over me. The reason I couldn't see past them couldn't be all stubbornness on my part. We must have missed something. I needed to talk to Jason. Something he mentioned last week needed a follow-up.

I was spared asking one of the orderlies or nurses to help me call him when he and Thor came in mid-morning. I said, "Just the people I wanted to see."

Thor must have dressed in whatever was left on her apartment floor. "We wanted to see how you're doing."

Jason opened his laptop. "If you're up to it, Cynthia needs info for the *StarTrib.* She sends her best."

I pointed. "My camera's in the drawer."

Jason plugged the camera into his laptop and with a few deft strokes from his normal healthy fingers, sent my photos to the bureau. As I told him the details about Peder and our encounter, he tapped it out on the laptop. Thor twiddled with her multiple piercings until Jason finished and packed up to leave.

"Jason, I know you're itching to get back to the bureau to work on the article but can you wait a second?"

"Sure, what do you need?" He and Thor sat in chairs under the window.

"Before all this happened, I asked you to check on other crimes in Iona Township, not just hate crimes. Have you had a chance to do that?"

"Sorry, I forgot to tell you. I found out that even though hate crimes are down, they've had an upsurge of missing persons in the past three months."

"How much of an upsurge?"

"More in the past three months than in the past three years."

I bolted upright. "Were you able to find out any details about the missing people?"

"All I got from the data was that some were men and some women, all different families. One was a child, but that turned out to be a guy abducting his own kid from the ex-wife."

"Do you think you could contact the families of the missing people and try to find out if there's anything that connects them?"

He crossed one leg over the other, frowning at the new wrinkle in his khakis. "I'm kind of busy with this Nazi story."

Thor glared at him.

His head bobbed up and down. "But sure, I'll see what I can find out and call you."

I lifted my puffy hands. "I can't pick up the phone."

Thor narrowed her eyes at Jason. "We'll bring it over."

He nodded. "Ready to go, Thor?"

She said, "You go ahead. I want to talk to Britt a minute." He ducked his head like an awkward teenager and backed away.

When he'd gone, Thor leaned forward and lowered her voice. "The BCA is helping us now and they've already gotten the results on that hairbrush. There's a match with Charley and you, but information that can be obtained from a strand of hair without the follicles attached is limited. The hair in his brush had the follicles, but the baby's hair didn't. Sorry. Oh, and the oar was from Peder/Fredrik's boat."

"Did you find out what poison he used in the candy?"

She nodded. "He made a liquid out of rhododendron plants. The whole plant is poisonous. Then he injected the serum into the bottom of each piece. The bitter dark chocolate masked the taste." She made a face. "The sheriff said Peder was really pleased with his creative touch and hoped Wilcox would tell you it was rhododendron poisoning."

I involuntarily shuddered. Locking me in my bathroom, taking Rock and Knute, the raccoon head in my camera bag, the rhododendron poison, all conceived to tease and impress me, just as Edgar had said.

She stood up. "There's something else." The words rushed out. "I've enrolled at the University of Minnesota to finish my degree. I'm starting in the fall."

"That's great, Thor. I know you've wanted to." Not sure if I should be getting into the details but she brought it up, I said, "Jason must be taking it pretty hard."

She twisted an earring. "I haven't told him yet." Her shoulders slumped and she left shortly after.

Thor probably wouldn't come back to Branson. She was ambitious and the recent excitement had likely whetted her appetite for more challenges. For the most part, homicides here generally involved drunk driving. I ached for Jason, but nothing stayed the same. The bureau might not even be here in six months. I hoped they'd figure it out.

The time dragged. Waiting for Jason to get back to me was torture. I wanted to be working on the story, not lying in my hospital bed trying to ignore the throbbing where Peder whacked my skull. Every move aggravated the scrapes and muscle aches. But mostly, I tried not to think about my hands.

When Violet arrived mid-day with a satchel full of the tools of her trade, I almost jumped out of my bed to hug her.

"Mother said she heard you look a fright." Violet's cheeks turned a shade pinker than her blush. "I meant that some of your hair was singed off and with those burned hands you might need help freshening up."

Wearing her judgmental frown, Connie followed Violet into my room and let her have it through pursed lips. "Britt has a head injury. Come back another time."

Violet swooshed past Connie and plunked her bag at the foot of my bed. "I'll be careful. I'm a professional."

A voice came over the intercom. Dr. Fromm needed Connie in room 103. The doctor's summons trumped everything and she hurried out the door.

Violet pulled a spray can out of her bag. "It's instant shampoo. You spray it in and brush it out and your hair is magically clean and smells good again."

I slid out of bed and used my foot to push the IV rack next to a chair. Violet pulled a round mirror out of her bag and held it to my face. Some of my hair was plastered to my head and the rest stuck out in burnt and frizzy nests. I waved the mirror away.

She snapped open a cape and draped it around my neck. "I'm just going to even it out." She trimmed off three inches and when she was finished, a crispy mess littered the floor. I must have looked alarmed. Violet said, "You still have lots left and the layered style is great on you."

She sprayed her special shampoo, brushed and styled my hair, and then produced a whisk and dustpan from her tote bag. "You are so lucky. That could have...."

I held up a gauze-encased hand. "Thanks, I get the picture."

She grimaced, then reached into her bag again. "Want me to add a touch of makeup?" She winked. "In case Ben drops by."

I nodded, although Ben had been absent since my meltdown. First, I'd blindsided him with Sudan and then insulted him for not having my best interest in mind when the doctor said I couldn't leave. Ben always had my best interest at heart. I didn't deserve him. A stab of self-pity made me wince.

Violet finished and held the mirror to my face. My hair did look much better, my face less pale. I said, "You're Wonder Woman. Thank you." Last year when I'd been chasing a bad guy and ended up in Branson Hospital, Violet came that time, too. I choked up.

"Oh now, don't do that. You'll get all red and splotchy and undo all my work."

"This is getting to be a routine. I'll triple-pay you for the hospital visit."

"Don't be silly. After what you did to get that awful man who hurt Lars and killed Charley? It's our way of doing our part."

Violet packed her bag, checked me over one more time and left the room with a satisfied smile.

It wasn't easy getting back into the high bed while keeping my hospital gown from exposing too much and accidentally mooning someone coming into the room. It's crazy how many things we do with our hands. I'd have to ask Little to bring my pajamas.

I watched the door all day, but Ben didn't show up.

Jason bounced in before breakfast the following morning, eyes bugged out with a caffeinated buzz. "You're so right. Data doesn't always tell you everything. I had to track down the families of the missing and ask a lot of questions."

"And?"

"Three gay men and two middle-aged gay women who lived together vanished. Family members and police concluded they left town because their families didn't approve of their lifestyle. In fact, the Iona police didn't see any type of foul play so they didn't do more than a quick investigation."

"Great work, Jason. Now you need to talk to the sheriff and tell him I have an idea about where those missing people might be."

**

Wilcox stood in the door and cleared his throat, waking me from a drug doze. I blinked myself awake. Ben was there too. I wanted to apologize to him but not with an audience.

The sheriff stood at the foot of the bed. "Jason's been over at the office talking about missing people in Iona. This better be good. I'm wrapping up the Peder case."

My mouth was too dry to talk. "Sheriff, could you hand me that water?" He passed it to me and I pulled my knees up, glad Little had brought my pajamas. "Just prop it up there." With my knees clamped around the water jug, I sipped from the straw and told them my theory on the Willards.

Wilcox crossed his arms. "You're guessing. I already had to apologize over the dogs."

"Just get a warrant. I'll go out there and get them to admit what they're doing, and you can be ready with backup."

Ben stepped closer. "They'll probably shoot you this time." He leaned in and I got excited, but he took the water from my knees, set it on the stand and moved away.

I said, "They won't. They don't want anything to cause suspicion."

Wilcox said, "My understanding is that you're not leaving this hospital for a week."

I shot straight up in bed. "That's negotiable."

Ben and Wilcox exchanged looks.

We talked it over and in the end they both agreed and we came up with a plan. All I had to do was get Fromm to spring me. Wilcox had to have the last word. "You're assuming I can get a warrant with no evidence."

***

He got the warrant the next morning. Dr. Fromm released me on the condition that someone bring me in daily for bandage changes and visits to the occupational therapist, and that I continue with bed rest for another week. I would have promised anything to get out of the hospital.

Ben had picked up clothes for me and told Little I'd be in Spirit Lake by noon. My part of the plan should take less than half an hour. He set the bag on my bed.

I looked up at him. "I'm sorry for what I said, Ben. You know I didn't mean it."

He nodded, his jaw tight. "I know."

I held up my immobile hands. "Could you help me get dressed?"

He hesitated, then opened the bag and took out my jeans. I leaned on him for balance as he pulled on one pant leg and then the other, tugged them over my hips and zipped me up. He reached in the bag for my bra, bit his lip and put it on me, concentrating hard on the hooks. Then he pulled my tank top over my head and torso before stepping back. He'd managed all that as if no one was inside my skin dying for his touch to linger just a moment. My cheeks on fire, I whispered, "Ben."

His voice faltered. "We'd better head to Iona."

Chapter 27

Jerry drove my SUV to a location close to the Willards' drive. Ben had brought Rock as I'd requested. He sat in the back, tail wagging. The sheriff had made an appointment for a junk pick up at a fictitious address nearby.

Jerry's phone rang. He listened and hung up. "The sheriff said we're clear to go in now. Mr. Willard and Matthew left in their truck at nine-fifty. Mrs. Willard is still home."

Jerry hopped out of the SUV and I slid behind the wheel. He leaned in. "Wilcox told me to tell you not to be a wiseass with those people and get yourself killed."

I couldn't think of anything to say that wouldn't sound like I was being a wiseass, so I nodded. He hurried through the woods to join the sheriff behind the shed and junk pile within easy listening distance of me. Ben was stationed in the woods, his high-powered rifle trained on the Willards in case of sudden movements.

I put the car in gear and moved toward the Willards' driveway. Ben didn't think I could steer the SUV with my bandaged hands but I'd assured him I could handle it.

He was right. My hands wouldn't bend in the bandages, and they hurt. Even going slow, the rutted road jerked the steering wheel, so I used my elbows and knees to steer slowly past the Willards' house. The plan was for Mrs. Willard to see me and call her husband. He'd turn around and come back.

I parked by the junk pile and Rock ran to it. A minute later, Mrs. Willard's car bounced down the washboard road and pulled up next to the shed. She threw her car in park and jogged toward me, muffin top jiggling in her too-small tank top.

"I don't know what you think you're getting away with. My husband is on his way home and you'd better be gone before he gets here."

"Or what?"

I heard the truck before it rounded the corner. Dust flying, the Willards bore down on us. Brakes squealed, doors slammed and Mr. Willard came forward, rifle in hand. Matthew was a few steps behind, unarmed. Mrs. Willard scooted next to her men.

Rock growled but I told him to wait.

Mr. Willard's mean eyes bored into me. "I told you the next time you came on my property I'd shoot you for trespassing."

He hadn't pointed the rifle at me yet. I tilted my head toward the junk pile. "What are you hiding under there?"

His eyes widened. "Now wait a minute."

"I'm thinking bodies."

Matthew grinned, his mismatched teeth dominating the bottom half of his face. "They're right where they belong with the rest of the garbage no one wants."

Mr. Willard darted a nervous look at his son, clearly uncomfortable with the alpha dog role reversal.

I said, "That's the big project, right? Ridding the area of gay people."

Mr. Willard recovered his bluster. "Whoever's doing that down in Spirit Lake isn't with us but we thank him for taking on the cause."

Matthew spit a stream of tobacco at the ground and pointed at the junk pile. "This is what makes a difference and you and that dog will be joining them today." I said, "You're not worried about the sheriff?"

Mr. Willard said, "We've had to scale way back on our project because of you. But I doubt your sheriff is going to be bothering us anymore." He sniffed. "He was damn embarrassed when he found out we had nothing to do with those mutts or that old guy." He lifted his rifle.

I stepped back as Wilcox came out from behind the building. "Put the weapon down." Jerry walked toward us from his crouching position behind the junk pile, gun raised. Ben came out of the woods, his rifle trained on Mr. Willard's head.

Matthew's head swiveled. "She's trespassing." He sounded like a whiny kid tattling to his teacher.

Mrs. Willard stepped behind her husband. "You got a warrant?"

Wilcox held up an envelope. I said to Rock, "What did you find, buddy?" He ran to the back of the junk pile and started digging.

That's where they found the first body.

***

A three-ring circus arrived on the scene—Branson and Iona police, forensics, a BCA investigator. Someone came with an earth mover to get the big junk out of the way and a crew with shovels set to work.

A news van arrived. Jason was there, of course, and Thor. My camera bag was in the SUV. I asked Jason to take photos, explaining what to shoot and which lens to use.

Two hours later, they'd found a total of six bodies. One of them had been there longer than the others. Not feeling steady, I leaned against my car at the edge of the scene. Jerry and Wilcox had their heads together, then Jerry came over to me and asked if I was ready to go to Spirit Lake. I hated to leave but nodded. "Little doesn't know I'm out here."

Ben intercepted us. "Britt, are you sure you're okay?"

I said, "We're on our way to Spirit Lake."

His face had a stubborn set. "Let me take a look at that left hand."

I brought it out from behind my back. The gauze was red-stained in several places and coming loose. He said, "We're going back to the hospital. Jerry, you can assist Wilcox."

Too tired to resist, I let him boost me into his truck. He pulled the seatbelt across my body and his lips grazed my forehead. "You have a fever."

I wanted to ask him to keep doing that with his lips but remembered my brother was waiting for me. "Do you mind calling Little to tell him I'll be late?"

Ben tapped in the number. "It's Ben. Britt's having her bandage changed so we'll be delayed a while." When he hung up, he said, "You shouldn't have left the hospital."

I said, "Worth it to have the Willards behind bars, though, right?"

He whistled for Rock.

My hands and head were throbbing by the time we arrived at the hospital. I wanted pain meds and bed.

Dr. Fromm discovered an infection on my left hand, the more badly burned of the two. Instead of heading home, I'd be spending another night in the hospital with an IV drip of mega antibiotics.

Ben gave Little the message and then said he had to go.

"Thank you for looking out for me, Ben."

He nodded, moving toward the door. "I won't be in Spirit Lake for a while."

My head drooped from the meds. "You said the BW project was wrapped up."

"For now. I'll be at the forestry office clearing up all the work that didn't get done while I was up there."

"What you're really saying is that you don't want to be with me, even though I'll be here the rest of the summer."

His voice had an edge. "Or maybe Marta will call in a couple of weeks, and you *won't* be here."

My chin lifted. "You said you loved me and would always be there for me."

The squint lines at the sides of his eyes deepened. "Do you know how hard it was for me to do my job, worrying every minute about you? You almost got yourself killed. Again. Maybe my attitude is part of the problem, but I can't change that." He turned away. "Take care of those hands."

Late in the evening, Wilcox came into the room. His eyes were bloodshot but no longer haunted. I cradled yet another green smoothie between my knees. Utensils were still impossible to deal with. I wanted milkshakes, but Little said first I needed antioxidants. He'd left a strawberry milkshake for dessert.

Wilcox leaned against a wall. "Five of the bodies matched the missing persons in the county. Tell me again how you were so sure the bodies were under that junk pile."

"It was kind of free association. I remembered how Rock wouldn't leave it alone every time we were there."

His eyebrow went up. "I told you not to go back after that first time."

I studied my bandages. "I'd overheard them talking about a big project that would really make a difference, not like the small-time stuff they'd been doing. Plus, they were extra-protective of that junk pile. And when Jason's research showed a dramatic number of gay people had gone missing, I thought it was worth a look."

"That body that had been there longer than the rest has been identified as the Willards' oldest son."

"I figured."

"Good work, Britt." The sheriff sagged into a chair. "This has been one hell of a rough summer for all of us."

"Did you ask Matthew what he was doing in Spirit Lake all those times I saw him near the restaurant?"

He nodded. "They wanted to keep an eye on you, but made sure Matthew had alibis."

I snorted. "Mr. Willard likes to think of himself as "strategic." That worked out well for him."

Wilcox said he had to go, but I stopped him before he reached the door. "Sheriff, I wanted to tell you I'm sorry for not listening to you. I'll do better from now on."

He half-grimaced. "Let's hope the rest of the summer is quiet so we don't have to test that statement."

***

A warm breeze blew through the open windows and white dots of sailboats tacked back and forth across Spirit Lake. Customers were back in full force and the kitchen hummed under Little's direction, but he lacked his usual energy. Using a cane, Lars stood behind the counter telling customers where to catch the biggest fish. His voice wasn't as hearty, his laugh less engaging.

Maybe time would help but they'd been talking about going back to teaching.

Grateful for the ability to use utensils again, I awkwardly finished my pancakes and looked across the counter at Lars. "Are you going with me to therapy? The skin on my hands had dried and cracked and it hurt to bend them, but I went to the hospital every day. Occupational therapy was a matter of survival. If I couldn't take photos, I wouldn't exist.

"We're too busy for me to leave right now. I'll have to reschedule." A family of four came in, and with his cane in one hand and menus in the other, he led them to a table.

On the days he had therapy, Lars and I drove together. He wasn't angry anymore, although he still didn't remember what happened to him. We all thought that might be for the best.

The writers' group had dispersed, no doubt having gotten more ideas for their writing than they'd bargained for, especially Anke. She'd almost gotten arrested. Lars had told Neil he couldn't use the information Lars had given him about fishing on Spirit Lake. I'd finally checked messages on Gert's computer. Sebastian had sent information about Peder Halvorsen from Oslo, noting that he wasn't the same person in the photo I'd sent. That information would have helped if I'd gotten to my cabin earlier.

And I was in the same situation as at the beginning of the summer—no Ben. Two weeks had passed and Ben hadn't been seen anywhere near Spirit Lake.

Before heading to Branson, I stopped in at Bella's for a shampoo. I could shower with the plastic mitts the hospital gave me but had trouble doing my hair. I'd be lying if I said I didn't enjoy Violet's soothing scalp massages and citrusy shampoo.

Ginger Bolger was just leaving the salon. She waved a hand, heavy with diamonds. "Not selling us your little piece of property was no biggie. Mo's working on a deal on the other side of us. The place recently burned down and Mo says the owner is a motivated seller."

I winced at the memory of that fire and offered Ginger my best fake sweet smile. "Now your 'family' can all be together."

Bella, in her corner rocker, watched CNN on the wall-mounted TV. A reporter talked into the camera as scenes of civil war in South Sudan played out in the background. I turned away. No amount of Violet's ministrations would make this a better day.

Violet swooped in from the back of the duplex. "Ready for your shampoo?"

I slumped into the chair and stared at the TV again. Bella turned down the volume. "What's got you so mopey?"

"Everyone in town knows why, Bella."

"You and Ben have been obstinate since you were kids, but one of you has to make the first move and it might as well be you; you're the one who's always doing something foolish."

Violet tipped the chair against the sink and tucked a towel under my neck. Her cupid's bow lips turned up. "He might be ready now. It's been nearly two weeks." Warm water sluiced over my head as she sudsed and massaged with gentle fingers.

She was right, why not give it another shot? I had nothing to lose.

His green truck was parked in front of the forestry building. I pulled in, rehearsing what I'd say to make him trust me again.

I braced myself and walked in. The freckled volunteer looked up from a rack of brochures she was straightening. "Hey, Britt! I haven't seen you in ages. Ben's in his office."

"Thanks, Lisa." His door was slightly open so I tapped once, then went in. His desk faced the door, the blue expanse of Branson Lake visible in the window behind him. He smiled from behind his computer.

Stepping closer, I said. "I'm on my way to therapy and saw your truck."

He tilted his head toward my hands. "How's it going?"

I held them out. They were normal size now and covered with a thin gauze as if I wore fishnet gloves. "Fromm says they're right on track. I'm getting flexibility back. It's slower with the left because of that infection."

"Good." He moved some papers on his desk, a hint he wanted me to go, but he didn't look angry, just indifferent.

"Ben." I waited until his eyes met mine. "Can't we start this whole summer over?"

He sighed. "That's always your solution."

I spoke past the lump in my throat. "It's a way to keep from losing each other."

His dark eyes were fathomless, likely pondering how to say no to me again.

"I have to get to my therapy." I backed out the door.

On the way to the hospital I mentally ranted at Bella. Did I really need to humiliate myself with Ben again? He had it right. I never learned.

***

That afternoon, as the waves slapped at the soles of my feet dangling off the end of the dock, I decided things were okay. I couldn't swim, but I'd run for an hour and worked on reps of situps and squats. Marta hadn't fired me. Gonzales was in South Sudan and the important thing was that someone was covering it. My hands were healing and there would be other projects. I congratulated myself for thinking like a grownup.

Rock rolled in a dead fish that had washed up on shore a few yards away. Knute was flopped on his side next to me. He no longer walked in circles in the driveway or howled at the moon. Remembering Gert, as I often did, I said to him. "That feeling of loss never goes away, Knute, but there's still a sweetness in life and if you think about that person in one of those moments, they're with you and they know you're sharing it with them." The old dog's tail thumped a couple of times.

I raised my eyes to the sky at a buzzing sound off in the distance. A low-flying plane came into view. I held up my hand to block the glare. The plane veered toward my side of the lake. It flew closer, and I recognized Woz's blue Beaver heading straight for my dock. It circled and landed, bounced on the floats, skimmed for a few yards and stopped. I waved, wondering why Woz was making a personal visit. He wasn't the social type and not usually on the scene unless there was trouble.

In the next second, the door opened and Ben jumped out. He waded over, soaking his shorts and pulled himself up next to me. Rock raced to him, tail wagging. Ben reached over to pet him, wrinkled his nose and pulled back. "Rolling in fish again, buddy?"

I found my voice. "You and Woz tracking down bad guys on Spirit Lake?"

"We're heading to the BW but I wanted to see you first." He put his hands on my shoulders and turned me toward him. "I've been thinking about what you said this morning."

Hope quivered in my chest. "You want to start over?"

"No, I don't want to start over because then nothing changes."

A defiant heat rose to my cheekbones and I pointed toward the plane. "Then I guess that means you aren't carrying me off to the BW in your mighty blue steed."

"I'm sorry, not this time, but what you said is true. I do dangerous work and the cases take over my life and I expect you to be cool with it. But when you're in the middle of something like what happened here, I go crazy worrying about you even though you're as tough as they come."

He shook his head. "Maybe I'd handle it better if you were trained in law enforcement. You hardly even know how to use a weapon."

"I hate guns. My martial arts training and instincts have worked for me so far."

"It's not about guns, it's about training, learning how to protect yourself." His eyes searched mine as if asking for understanding. "I don't see how I can change my attitude but I'm going to work on it."

I threw my arms around his neck. "I could go to one of those citizens' academies and learn some law enforcement stuff."

We turned as Woz started the engine, a hint our time was running out.

Ben kissed me. "I'll be gone a week and when I get back we'll find a lake all to ourselves, no tourists, no fishermen, just us. How does that sound?"

I grinned. "You and me in a tent in the middle of the wilderness sounds good."

He put his hands under my arms and raised me to my feet. The right side of his mouth twitched. "You probably won't be able to keep your hands off me."

My newly dexterous index finger beckoned him closer. Our lips nearly touching, I said, "Worth it even if it sets my recovery back a bit."

I waved as the Beaver lifted off, then walked into the cabin feeling light as air. A week wasn't that long. Across the room, my landline message light blinked.

Marta's message was brief. "Pack your bags."

Acknowledgments

Special thanks to my dear friend and tireless reader, editor and supporter, Julie Williams; my talented and wonderful mystery critique group, Pam Giarrizzo, Michele Drier and June Gillam; early reader Rae James and Sisters in Crime for all your support. Jennifer Fisher, who helps make my manuscripts stronger. Doug Kelly, proofreader; Karen Phillips, cover artist; and Rob Preece, formatter. To Anthony Wade for his information on Kajukembo, and burn nurse Holly Olmsted—I hope I got it right. Finally, I'd like to thank my husband, Gary Delsohn, for his loving support, and my children, Joseph and Amanda, who inspire me every single day.

About the Author

Linda Townsdin worked for years in communications for nonprofit and corporate organizations, most recently as writer/editor for a national criminal justice consortium. Townsdin's work included editorial and marketing assistance in projects involving cybercrime, tribal justice and other public safety issues. Published in 2014, *Focused on Murder* is the first book in her Spirit Lake Mystery series, inspired by her wonderful childhood in Northern Minnesota. *Close Up on Murder* is the second in the series. She lives in California with her husband.

Connect with Linda Townsdin
http://lindatownsdin.com/
https://www.facebook.com/LindaTownsdinAuthor
http://twitter.com/ltownsdin

42696252R00158

Made in the USA
Charleston, SC
02 June 2015